TAKING OFF

ALSO BY JENNY MOSS

Winnie's War

TAKING OFF

Jenny Moss

Walker & Company ✸ New York

First published in the United States of America in January 2011 by
Walker Publishing Company, Inc., a division of Bloomsbury Publishing, Inc.
www.bloomsburyteens.com

For information about permission to reproduce selections from this book, write to
Permissions, Walker BFYR, 175 Fifth Avenue, New York, New York 10010

Poem on page 171 from "August 19, Pad 19" by May Swenson. Reprinted with permission of The Literary Estate of May Swenson. All rights reserved.

Poem on page 238 from "Funeral Blues" by W. H. Auden, from *Collected Poems of W. H. Auden,* published by Random House, Inc.

Poem on page 275: "News Item," copyright 1926, renewed © 1954 by Dorothy Parker, from *The Portable Dorothy Parker* by Dorothy Parker, edited by Marion Meade. Used by permission of Viking Penguin, a division of Penguin Group (USA) Inc.

Library of Congress Cataloging-in-Publication Data
Moss, Jenny.
Taking off / Jenny Moss.
p.   cm.
Summary: In 1985 in Clear Lake, Texas, home of the Johnson Space Center, high school senior Annie Porter struggles with her desire to become a poet, and when she meets Christa McAuliffe, the first teacher to go into space, just before her space shuttle flight, Annie's resolve to pursue her dream is strengthened.
ISBN 978-0-8027-2193-8
[1. Self-realization—Fiction.   2. Poetry—Fiction.   3. Interpersonal relations—Fiction.   4. High schools—Fiction.   5. Schools—Fiction.   6. McAuliffe, Christa, 1948–1986—Fiction.   7. Challenger (Spacecraft)—Accidents—Fiction.   8. Texas—History—1951—Fiction.]   I. Title.
PZ7.M8533Tak 2010   [Fic]—dc22   2010025492

Book design by Danielle Delaney
Typeset by Westchester Book Composition
Printed in the U.S.A. by Quad/Graphics, Fairfield, Pennsylvania
2 4 6 8 10 9 7 5 3 1

All papers used by Bloomsbury Publishing, Inc., are natural, recyclable products made from wood grown in well-managed forests. The manufacturing processes conform to the environmental regulations of the country of origin.

For Emily Easton,
who had this wonderful idea

"I have painted him a little like a poet, the head fine & nervous standing out against a background of a deep ultramarine night sky with the twinkling of stars."
—Vincent van Gogh, 1888

TAKING OFF

PROLOGUE

I have a secret, a quiet one. But I can't tell my friend Lea or my mom and certainly not my boyfriend. I don't think even my dad would understand. Or maybe I don't want to tell because they would look at me funny.

The other day, while browsing in a used bookstore, I found a book of the letters of the painter Vincent van Gogh. I felt like he was a friend talking to me. In one letter, he wrote that people see him as the lowest of the low: "I should one day like to show by my work what such an eccentric, such a nobody, has in his heart." His words were so beautiful and honest they made me cry.

No one labels me as an eccentric, but that's because they don't know what's in my heart. I keep it close.

I live in a town of engineers who worship math and science, and think solving for x gives insight into the soul.

- - - - -

I want to be a poet.

PART ONE

"Reach for the stars."
—Christa McAuliffe

CHAPTER 1

I skipped the bus because my friend Lea had promised me a ride after school. Then I found out she wasn't going to take me home right away because she had an appointment with the dentist my mom was dating.

"You are evil," I said, my hand out the window, palm forward, catching the breeze. I was enjoying the cool November day after a long, humid summer on the Gulf Coast.

"Yeah, sorry," Lea said. "Hey, can you spend the night Friday?"

"I can't. I have to work."

"What about Saturday?" Lea asked while twisting a lock of her short hair. She had an Audrey Hepburn pixie cut, which made her eyes look bluer and wider.

Her style was the opposite of the big hair on most of the girls in the senior class. I didn't have a real hairstyle—just long, wavy, and easy to take care of.

"I have stuff to do," I said.

"Bogus!" she said. "Come on, Annie. My parents are having company from work."

"I don't know, Lea," I said. "That means I'll have to talk to people I don't know."

Lea didn't have a shy bone in her body. It was nice having a friend who chattered through my awkward pauses when someone else was looking at me and waiting for me to reply and I couldn't seem to put words into sentences fast enough.

Lea had been rescuing me since we were thrown together to act out two half scenes from *Romeo and Juliet* in ninth-grade English. She made me play the role of Juliet, so she could be the nurse and get the funny lines.

I'd been so nervous, not able to eat much for days before. To my surprise, it wasn't so bad. I found I didn't mind standing up in front of the class when the words were already written:

Give me my Romeo; and, when he shall die,
Take him and cut him out in little stars,
And he will make the face of heaven so fine
That all the world will be in love with night.

Forget about Romeo; I'd had a crush on Will Shakespeare after that.

"A couple of astronauts will be there," Lea said, bringing me back to earth. "There's this one I want you to meet."

"Not another astronaut crush, Lea."

"You used to have them too," she said.

"Not like you. Anyway, remember how you want to get out of this town, where everything is space, space, space?"

We lived in Clear Lake, Texas, home of Johnson Space

Center—or, as the natives called it, JSC—and its astronauts. It was officially Houston, even though Clear Lake was thirty miles from the center of the city. But Clear Lake had been kidnapped by Houston and made a part of the larger city, so the phrase uttered by Neil Armstrong on Apollo 11, "Houston, the Eagle has landed," could be immortalized. Soon to be replaced by Apollo 13's "Houston, we've had a problem."

But that was years ago. It was now 1985, and the space shuttle had been flying for four years. The nation was excited about the new Teacher in Space program. High school teacher Christa McAuliffe had arrived in Clear Lake in September and was now in training at JSC.

"I haven't been *as* bored," said Lea, "with my parents' talk-talk-talk about NASA since I met Him. In fact, now it seems rather fascinating."

"Who's 'him'?" I asked.

"The Astronaut. I adore him."

"Adore him," I repeated. "You've met astronauts before."

"This one is different, Annie. He's so nice."

I laughed.

"What?" she asked, widening innocent eyes. She did that so well. Then she burst out laughing. "Okay, he's *wicked cute*. But he is nice too."

"I still don't know," I said. It'd be cool to meet astronauts, but I was still wishing for an evening alone, especially since Mom had a date with Donald. This was senior year. I should be excited. But the world was crowding too close lately. I wanted time to be alone—to knit, to write poetry, to be still.

"That teacher will be there," Lea said.

I looked at her.

"You know, Christa McAuliffe," she said.

"Yeah, I know."

"Come on, Annie. I never see you. You're always hanging out with Mark or working with Mark."

"*He* thinks I'm with you too much."

"Ga! I can't get you away from him."

"I thought you liked Mark."

"You kidding me? I love Mark. But I like you better, and he takes up way too much of your time. We only have a few months left together."

"Six months," I said, not wanting to think about graduation and the decisions between now and then. Lea was lucky. She knew what she wanted to do.

"So will you come?" she asked.

"No, I won't come. You must be punished for dragging me to see Donald. He's your dentist, not mine."

"I don't know why you don't like him," Lea said. "He's been making my teeth pretty since I was five. See." She flashed a smile in the rearview mirror and then to me. "He's like family, Annie. And he's a nice guy. Which is why my mom introduced him to your mom. Aren't you happy your mom is dating someone nice?"

"I like him fine," I said, pressing my lips together. Dry. I dug around in my purse for my ChapStick, which always managed to work its way down to the bottom corner. I pushed aside my empty wallet, all the crumpled-up tissues from my fall allergies, and the Scary White Envelope I'd been carrying all week.

I tuned back to what Lea was saying once I finally found the ChapStick and put it on.

"The Astronaut is beautiful," she said, as we waited at a stoplight in a tangle of traffic. "Hey, give me some of that."

I handed it over. "I would expect your future husband to be no less than beautiful."

"Okay, so he's not . . . really beautiful," she said, looking in the mirror to apply. "But he's hot."

"So you've said," I said, taking the ChapStick back. Lea tended to steal things.

I looked out the window and fidgeted, flicking the cap on and off, obsessing about the envelope. I should tear it up.

"You're doing that stare-in-the-distance thing you do. Don't get all think-y on me," she said. "Now, listen, it's important that you meet the Astronaut—"

"No."

"—so you must come to dinner."

"Nope."

"Why?" she asked, exasperated.

"I'm no good at these things. I can't ever think of what to say."

"You'd rather sit on your couch and watch TV?"

"I happen to like TV," I said.

"You're a coward, Annie Porter, afraid of life."

"I'm not a coward, I'm content."

"You'll like the Astronaut," she said, turning into the parking lot. "He was in the military."

"And that appeals to me how?" I asked.

"He's a jet jock."

"Okay," I deadpanned.

"He flies jets," she said. "Won't it be fun talking to someone who flies jets?" She hit me again. "Won't it?"

"I really wish you wouldn't do that," I said, rubbing my arm. "Really. And look, we're here. We're stopping. And we've parked. Can we go in now?"

"Fine." She opened her car door. "Well, aren't you coming in?"

"In a minute," I said, waving her on. I hoped to miss the awkwardness of talking to Donald.

When I got into the office, I was relieved to find Lea had already disappeared into the back. I settled down into the waiting room. Ah, peace and quiet. Except for one teenager in the corner immersed in reading, which is what I wanted to be doing.

I flipped through the stack of magazines beside me and found a *People* from August. Three months old. I looked for a more recent issue, but there wasn't one. Donald should update his magazines. I wasn't asking for the latest *Kenyon Review*. Just a brand-new, barely read *People*.

The cover was falling off this one, and a small square was cut in the bottom where the subscriber's address should be. *I should have brought a book of poems*, I thought, as I flipped through the limp, outdated pages. I usually didn't leave the house without one. All that was in my purse now was the scary white envelope.

I stopped on page 28. It was an article about the teacher in space: "Christa McAuliffe Gets NASA's Nod to Conduct America's First Classroom in Space."

I deliberately didn't follow the space program. But it was kind of cool that I'd just been invited to meet someone who was in *People* magazine.

The article covered the first day in the life of the new "teachernaut." I noticed the reporter was a little cynical about the Teacher in Space program. His tone made me defensive. After all, a high school teacher from Concord, New Hampshire, was actually going into space. *Space.*

I'd always thought space was for people with science degrees, and I hated science. But here was this teacher who was going to fly alongside people like Lea's jet-jock astronaut. And she seemed so, well, normal. She could be one of my teachers. Or could she? I wondered why NASA chose her.

I stared at her photos. In one, she was squatting down to kiss her young niece. In another, she was setting her dinner table with her husband and two kids. I could pass this woman in the mall and not think she was any different from any other mom I knew.

So weird to find this article on the day I was invited to meet Christa. Things like this made me think I was cosmically connected to something. Maybe I was just cosmically connected to *People* magazine. But I guess it wasn't too weird the magazine was here because this *was* a NASA community. It was understandable this particular issue would be kept.

Or maybe it was a sign.

So I stole it. I put it in my purse, right next to the scary white envelope, hoping some of Christa's daring would leap off the page and talk my envelope into mailing itself.

The door opened. Lea came out with clean teeth. Donald

was behind her. He had glasses and a nice dentist smile. "Hi, Annie." I *did* like that his bulky black glasses tilted on his face and that his smile was slightly nerdy. I liked different because I felt like I was different too.

"Hi, Donald," I said, pushing the magazine down farther in my purse.

Then we all stood there awkwardly. Even Lea looked at a loss for words. I made rescue-me eyes at her.

"Okay," said Lea. "Bye, Dr. Gardner."

I gave him a wave as we left. He looked disappointed.

Lea barely missed the Mercedes on my side because she had launched back into talking about the Astronaut. She wanted to keep a journal of information about him.

"Annie, please come Saturday. You can meet him. Come *on*. You are so boring."

She had a point. What was wrong with me? I had a chance to meet Christa McAuliffe and I wanted an evening alone with TV shows and potato chips.

I just didn't have any motivation lately. I wanted to sit and be still, but at the same time, I was restless. I couldn't even decide what to do after high school. Graduation was like a high, long, thick wall, like that Hadrian's Wall the English built to keep the Scottish out, or the Scottish built to keep the English out, or I built to keep my future out.

And here Christa McAuliffe was packing her panties and going to fly on the space shuttle. If she was going to space, I could get myself off my couch long enough to meet her before she did.

CHAPTER 2

I read the article again before I went to bed.

In the morning, when I was headed off to catch the bus, I grabbed the magazine and stuffed it in my purse. I was becoming as obsessed as a *Star Trek* fan. I couldn't get over how this woman seemed so ordinary but was going on this wild ride, turning her normal life into a remarkable one.

And I was going to meet her. I felt a little nervous, wondering if I could think of anything to say to her.

I'd met astronauts before. They were a part of our community, attending the local churches, joining in on cleanup days in neighborhoods, coaching swim teams, just like all the mothers and fathers of kids I knew from school. Many were aloof. But maybe they just felt awkward with small talk, like I did. Hard to believe, though. They were astronauts, after all.

In English, I was looking at the magazine photos again, wishing I had more information about Christa, wondering if the library would have other articles, when I heard my name. I looked up.

"The magazine needs to disappear, Annie. And hat and gloves off."

I pulled off my black cap, then hesitated. "But my gloves are cool, Mr. Williams." I stretched the knitted yarn to my wrists, then watched it pop back into place. One of the fingers was gone. I'd had to cut it away after it snagged on a zipper. I rubbed my skin, pale against the black of the glove.

"Annie."

Reluctantly, I pulled them off. The gloves I knitted were my own teenage security blanket, disguised as a fashion statement.

"Thank you," he said.

A hand in front shot up.

"What is it?" Mr. Williams asked. Blond-haired guys didn't normally appeal to me, but Mr. Williams did. I didn't know anyone, even my boyfriend, Mark, who was as fine as my English teacher, an opinion shared by half the students of Clear Creek High—the female half.

It wasn't just his looks, though—which were eye catching, but not over-the-top gorgeous. It was his manner, his confidence, the way he carried himself. He seemed to know the world and all about what was out there.

"Mr. Williams?" asked Theresa, a girl who threw paper wads at people she didn't like and always wore her hair in a ponytail to the side.

I thought Mr. Williams was even better looking when he scrunched his eyes in irritated anticipation of Theresa's potentially, most probably, stupid question.

"How old are you?" she asked.

Okay. Not so bad, Theresa. I glanced around. All the girls were suddenly staring at Mr. Williams with eager faces. I could see their brains waiting to do some subtraction: I'm seventeen; he's just a few years older. It could work.

He looked at me. "How old do *you* think I am?"

I laughed. "If I guess right, can I put my gloves back on?"

"Yes," he said. "You may."

I could feel my lips twitching as I tried to stop the smile. "I'd say . . . twenty-five."

He gave me a slow smile. "Your hands must stay naked."

Girls behind me giggled. The boys were probably scowling. Mr. Williams was an outrageous flirt, but nothing beyond that. He had a long-haired girlfriend working on her master's at the University of Texas. I'd seen her at school a few times, visiting him, calling him "Marty."

She always had a vintage bag thrown over her shoulder. It was well worn and all about a life I didn't have. That bag had probably grooved to Beat poets on the decline and dozed in the sun on a blanket at Woodstock.

After class, Mr. Williams asked me to stop by his desk. A friend wiggled her eyebrows at me.

"Harmless," I whispered as she walked past.

"Yes, Mr. Williams?" I asked, pulling on my gloves.

He handed me a paper. "Excellent essay, Annie."

I nodded at the A. "You only read mine?" I asked, confused by the stack of papers on his desk. No grade on the one at the top of the pile.

"I started with yours and didn't want to ruin my good mood."

I laughed, flattered. "Okay. Thanks," I said, holding up the paper.

"Your argument about Lear is solid, that Lear's epiphany has value despite his death."

"I think I read that somewhere, Mr. Williams. It's not my original thought."

"But you took it beyond the more traditional argument of Christian redemption. You *got* it, Annie, and argued it well for a . . ." He stopped and looked at me.

I laughed. "For a teenager?" His praise made me feel a little awkward, so I tried to cover it up with teasing: "And how many years has it been since you were an ignorant teenager?"

All of a sudden he looked very serious. I thought I'd gone too far in our playful bantering.

"Annie," he said. "Have you thought about where you're applying?"

"What? For college?"

"Yes, for college. I want to write you a recommendation."

"Thanks, Mr. Williams."

"Where do you want to go?"

I pulled at a piece of yarn. I wanted some new gloves. Maybe red ones. A brilliant red. I wondered if I had enough money for yarn. A string of words popped into my head: *Red yarn, color, craving color, this is going nowhere. Like me.*

Was this normal? Did normal people have random words and phrases floating around up there, interrupting them when they were trying to have normal conversations?

"Annie," he said again.

"My mom doesn't have money for college, Mr. Williams."

"You're going to hang out in Clear Lake at the movie theater all your life?"

"Hey, how did you know I worked at the theater?" I asked. "I've never seen you there."

"I want you to think about college."

"What? You want me to be an English teacher?"

"What do you want to be, Annie?"

I have an impractical dream. One that makes no money. One I'm so horrible at, it only makes me cry and wad up paper after paper.

I shrugged, hearing my grandma's voice in my head telling me not to shrug. "I like the theater."

"An actress?" he asked, looking puzzled.

"No. I mean, the movie theater. I like selling popcorn."

"And you want to work there the rest of your life?"

"I like movies a lot," I said in a teasing voice.

"Get out of here, Annie."

"Yes, Mr. Williams."

"Annie?" he asked.

"Yeah?" I asked.

"Nothing," he said, dismissing me with a wave of his hand.

Mark was waiting for me out in the crowded hall. He threw his arm around my shoulders when I came out the door. "What did *he* want?"

I shrugged.

A girl glanced at us, though probably more at Mark. Mark was only about five feet eleven, not nearly as tall as the rest of the basketball team. But his maker had put every inch of his body to good use. He looked and moved like an athlete. He wasn't cocky, but he did act like he was comfortable in his body, that it fit him perfectly.

He pulled me out of the path of a wild but friendly tussle between two freshmen. "He talks to you too much."

I laughed. "Are you jealous of Mr. Williams? Come on."

"He's too interested in you."

This made me secretly happy. And I was comfortable with secrets. "He wants me to go to college."

Mark pulled me to him, kissing the top of my head. "You wouldn't leave me, right?" He did smell good, a mixture of soap and just him, so familiar, like home should be.

But lately, I was feeling like something wasn't right— about us. I slipped away from his grasp to open my locker.

He leaned beside me, peeking at me from behind the open door. "What are you doing tonight?"

"I have a paper," I said. He swung the door back and forth, pulling my hair every now and then. "Come on, Mark." I tried not to show him just how much this irritated me.

"I miss you, Annie."

His eyes were brown and quite beautiful, but I wouldn't get drawn in. "We've been together almost every day for two years." I stared at the books in my locker. Where was I going? What was my next class? "I can't tonight."

He closed the door of the locker and gently pushed my back against the lockers, his face close. "You look so beautiful today."

Ah, he felt good, so warm and strong against the length of me. I gave him a quick kiss, but saw Mr. Williams walking down the hall. He caught my eye and didn't look away. But I did. I pushed Mark back a little. "Teacher to my left." My cheeks felt warm.

"Since when do you care about that?"

I watched Mr. Williams's back, glad he was gone. "I just don't want the hassle," I said, giving Mark a quick hug. Then I wriggled out of his arms. "Gotta go, Mark." The bell rang. "Really have to go." I turned away from his disappointed face and jogged to my next class, slipping in the door before the pad of pink slips was pulled out of the drawer.

"You almost didn't make it," whispered Lea.

I grinned. "But I did."

"Miss Porter."

Mrs. Moore was staring right at us. I cocked my head. I always thought her face had the shape of a hexagon. I wondered if math teachers ended up looking like geometrical figures, just as dog owners started looking like their pets.

I started writing down equations I didn't understand.

CHAPTER 3

I was nine when I realized that wanting to be a poet was best kept secret.

I'd found poetry on a headstone in the cemetery next to my grandma Winnie's house and was so taken with it. With one hand gripping the cool stone, I'd whispered the engraved words over and over, liking how they sounded, yearning to find the meaning created by the words, but not quite understanding. It seemed a wonderful mystery for a Sunday afternoon.

Grandma said the poem was by Emily Dickinson, and I thought it was so nice of Miss Dickinson to write the poem for the woman who died. I asked my mom if that was what I could be when I grew up, a poet who found the words for someone's life. She laughed. My aunt laughed. Then my cousins laughed. Mom said, "No, you can't. Go play."

The doorbell rang, interrupting my reminiscing.

"Could you get the door?" Mom yelled from her bedroom. "It's probably Mark."

I put down my library book of Emily Dickinson's poetry. It was dark out. I had my pj's on.

The doorbell rang again.

"Annie? Are you getting that?"

I threw on a jean jacket lying on my floor. "Got it," I called out as I went down our short hallway.

It was Mark. He leaned in, his arm on the doorframe. "Wanna come out and play?" He grinned.

I put my hand on his. "It's late."

"I gave you time to finish your paper. You got it done, right?"

"Yes. But now it's late."

"Not even ten."

I looked back over my shoulder. No Mom. I thought I'd heard her on the phone. She was on the phone a lot lately. "We have school tomorrow."

"I have a present for you."

"For me?" I asked, my hand to my chest. Mark was always giving me little things: a key ring, flowers, a Swiss Army knife, a cassette, anything. He took my hand, opening it, placing a small red heart in the center of my palm.

"For your charm bracelet," he said.

"Ooh, so pretty," I said, caressing the metal and admiring the color. Mark knew I liked color. "Thank you."

"Come out and look at the stars with me, Annie." He touched my cheek and gave me a gentle kiss. A surge of delight shot through me. He knew how to woo me.

I put my heart in my pocket and let Mark lead me out onto the cool grass.

My mom and dad and I had spent a lot of time in our yard watching the stars. Mom would spread out a blanket and the three of us would lie down on it, with me in the middle. Dad would show us Polaris and Venus, the constellations Orion and Cassiopeia, and tell us stories about them. Over the years, I'd listen to him, watching him point out the stars, and think I had the smartest father in the whole world.

When my parents split up, something inside of me ripped open. I didn't realize it at first because I was only eleven. But I carried around an empty feeling that seemed to stretch from the pit of my stomach to right behind my eyes.

No one wanted to look at the stars anymore. But I did it anyway. It was hard at first, not so much because I was alone, but because I'd remember what it'd been like to have my mother on one side of me and my father on the other. Those first few nights, the sky felt as empty as what had opened up inside me.

But the stars were beyond beautiful and held such promise. And they were constant. Then Mark came along and would look at the stars with me. That empty feeling inside me wasn't completely gone, but his love had pushed it to a small corner of my heart. I loved him for that.

He and I sat down cross-legged, looking at one another. He took my chin in his hand and gave me a slow, sweet kiss.

I pulled back and grinned. "This is looking at the stars?"

He laughed and fell backward onto the grass, with his arms out. I lay beside him, using his arm as a pillow. We looked up.

We stared and stared, not saying anything for a few moments.

"You know what Van Gogh said about the stars?" I asked him.

"The painter?"

"Yeah, I found a book of his letters the other day. He said: 'For my part I know nothing with any certainty, but the sight of the stars makes me dream.'" I turned my head to look over at Mark, tears pricking my eyes. "Isn't that so lovely and true?"

"It is," he said, squeezing my shoulder, still looking up.

Van Gogh saw so much in the sky.

For me, the stars shone wonder and hope—the unknowable in an amazing night sky. A simple image, really: white twinkling lights against a background of deep black. But it was more than that. It was what it suggested. It showed us what was beyond us, but also what was inside of us. It reflected back our souls.

I wished Van Gogh was beside me now. I couldn't tell Mark the way I felt about the stars, but after reading Van Gogh's letters, I thought the painter might understand. His words had made me feel less alone.

CHAPTER 4

$\mathbf{M}$uch nicer than the bus!" I said, slipping into the seat, welcoming my ride to school. "You are the best boyfriend."

Mark gave me a kiss, smiling and looking into my eyes for a moment. He grabbed my hand and backed out of the driveway.

"It's nice getting into a warm car on a cold morning," I said, unbuttoning my coat.

Mark smirked and shook his head. "It's probably fifty-five degrees out, Annie."

"That's cold!" I ignored him. He and I never agreed about the weather. "One more day until Friday, and then finally the weekend will be here. Yes!"

"We're early. Want a doughnut?"

"Doughnuts and coffee!" I'd been drinking coffee since my grandmother had been sneaking it to me.

The radio was on, the volume low, but I could still make out the song "Wouldn't It Be Nice" coming out of the speakers. Mark switched to another station.

"Hey! I like that," I told him.

"Since when have you liked the Beach Boys?" But he flipped the song back on. I started singing along to it. I had the most awful singing voice in the world. You know your boyfriend loves you when he lets you sing songs he doesn't care for sung in an off-key voice, first thing in the morning.

I belted out the chorus, glancing over at him with a smile.

He laughed. "Remember when we used to talk about getting married and how we'd live in Hawaii and I'd surf and you'd read while I surfed?"

"And we would work here and there for a little money?"

"And just go from beach to beach, until we'd seen them all?"

"And then we'd start all over again," I said.

He nodded.

"Hey," I asked, pulling my stolen copy from my purse, "you want me to read to you from *People* magazine?"

"Since when have you started carrying *People* around with you?"

"This article about Christa McAuliffe is fascinating."

"It must be. You've been talking about her for days."

"Have I?" I asked. "You would like her, Mark. It says she's interested in how 'the common people lived through the ages.'" I looked up at him. "Are you listening?"

"Hey, we're here. What do you want?"

We ended up getting two coffees and two dozen doughnut holes. *Sugar and oil, almost as good as salt and oil,* I thought. The doughnuts were warm and sweet, and the coffee was hot and milky and sweet. We'd finished the doughnuts off by the time we pulled into the school parking lot.

Lea ran toward us as we walked toward the building. "I've been waiting for you two!" She broke our hands apart and got in the middle of us, throwing her arms around us both. She touched Mark's cheek with her hand and he jumped back.

"Get some gloves, woman. Make her some, Annie."

"No way," I said, tugging at my own black ones. "She would just lose them."

"I would," said Lea, nodding.

"But you're rich," said Mark. "Your parents would buy you more."

Lea started hitting him on the shoulder.

"Ow. Ow."

"Stop being that way!" Lea told him. "Stop it now!"

I couldn't help but laugh.

"What are you laughing at?" asked Mark. "Want to be tickled?" He knew how ticklish I was; just the thought of it made my skin laugh somewhat madly.

"No, no." He reached across Lea and kissed me. His lips were sweet from the doughnut sugar.

"Okay," said Lea, "I'm gone." She started walking backward. "My house, Saturday night, Annie?"

"Yes!" I yelled as Lea ran off. I looked up at Mark and saw his face. Not again. "Mark, what's wrong?"

"You're going to her house on Saturday?"

"Yeah. I'll see you Friday night. And all day Saturday."

"At work? You'll see me at work?"

"Mark—"

"I gotta go, Annie." And then he was gone, and I was staring at his back moving away.

Ducked head. Hands in pockets. My jealous boy.

I wouldn't call him back. In a way, it was a relief not to have to argue with him. He was probably hurt Lea hadn't invited him over too. Sometimes I felt torn between the two of them. When the three of us were together, I couldn't make either one of them happy.

But a guilty thought needled at me. Mark hadn't always been this insecure about us. It was partly my fault. Senior year was making me withdraw, not just from Mark, but from others too. My friends were looking to the future. And I wanted to cocoon in my house.

I liked my little house, my life with Mom. I liked that my dad hung out there. It felt as if we were still together in a way.

At least I was getting out of the house on Saturday to meet Christa McAuliffe. I had this feeling it was important for me to go. I wanted to know what kind of person went from teacher to teachernaut. I'd always seen teachers as practical people who wanted their feet on the ground.

Of course I was nervous about meeting her. I didn't think I had it in me to get strapped into a seat in a rocket to be hurled into space. It didn't seem real. That was probably why all these conspiracy theorists thought the moon launch was faked. To them, that level of deceit was a more likely possibility.

I walked slowly. I enjoyed the quiet of the parking lot now that most everyone was already inside, driven in by the cold and the lateness. The wind felt good. It was cold, but not bitterly so, and blew gently, like whispered tiptoes against my ears.

I envied the wind: moving, but with stillness at its center. But of course, the wind couldn't be moving and be still. So I wasn't sure what I meant. Maybe that stillness was a sense of peace, or a certainty—stillness in purpose. I couldn't find the right words. I'd try to capture the feeling in a few lines later.

I didn't tell anyone I wrote poems. People thought poetry was a waste of time. It was no longer popular, not practical, and to some, as elusive as a moon landing.

Most likely, though, they'd think I didn't have the talent. That was what I thought. Poetry was for the Walt Whitmans, the Ezra Pounds, the Marianne Moores—not for a regular girl living in Texas. One of the masses, one of the millions. You either were born with the gift or not.

And there was something else too. A poet couldn't keep herself at a distance from her own poetry—at least if her poems were to say something new. Van Gogh felt paintings came from a painter's soul. I wondered if he'd felt he was leaving behind pieces of Vincent on each of his canvases.

I thought it must take courage to be that kind of painter, that kind of poet. It was a different kind of courage than launching into space. But it was still courage.

CHAPTER 5

After school, I came home to an empty house and went straight for the kitchen. I pulled out the potato chips, opened the bag, and crunched into their yummy saltiness.

I wanted to have them finished before Mom got home to complain about the weight I was gaining. She didn't have to nag me about it. I knew I was gaining. I couldn't help it that salt and oil was such a delicious combination. And she didn't make losing weight any easier by baking all the time.

Grabbing a blanket, I settled onto the couch to watch cartoons. The screen was fuzzy, but not too bad. After that show ended, I grabbed the pliers to change the channel. Dad had broken the knob last year when he was over, and we'd never repaired it.

I watched reruns of *MASH* and *WKRP*, finishing off the chips and licking my fingers. What could be better than this? It was getting a little chilly now that the sun was sinking, so I flipped on the heat.

The front door swung open. My father burst in and plopped

down in the chair with the stuffing hanging out. He thought of it as his chair, even though this wasn't his house and that wasn't his chair. "Hi, Annie."

"What's up, Dad?"

"Any chips left?"

I peered in the bag. "Not a one. Not even a crumb."

"You're a heartless girl."

"But full," I said, patting my stomach.

"Where's Mark?" he asked. "I'm surprised he's not here. He's always here."

He's *always here*? I thought. "He's got basketball."

Dad studied me. "You two are getting awfully close."

I looked away. "Mm-hmm."

"I mean, have you even dated anyone else? Ever?"

"Nope."

"Well, I don't think you should settle down right away."

"I'm not settling down," I said, peeved. I didn't need relationship advice from my divorced father.

"Humph. I wouldn't be surprised if that boy buys you a ring for Christmas."

"Oh, Dad," I said, but I had a sinking feeling in my stomach.

"It's true. That boy's smitten."

"Subject will be changed now, please," I said.

"You should date more. There's this guy, Tommy, at the plant—"

"I thought you liked Mark," I interrupted.

"Sure, I like Mark. But what do you two have in common?"

"Let's not do this, all right?" I turned back to the TV.

"Your mom's not home yet?"

"Nope." Dad had a job at a chemical plant and had for years, but he worked odd hours. He didn't understand the routine structure of office work.

He didn't answer, just stared at the screen. He got up, went through the swinging door into the kitchen, and came back with some cold chicken.

"Mom's not going to like you eating that."

"We'll tell her you ate it," he said, grinning. He pointed a chicken leg at the screen. "Find something good on."

I was a little irritated. Today, I'd wanted to be alone, just me and the TV. "Don't you have some place to be, Dad?"

"Hey, look," he said. "There's that teacher from Concord."

"What?" I asked, my head whipping around. "Oh, shhh," I said, running to the set and turning up the volume. I sat down on the floor in front of the TV so Dad's talking wouldn't keep me from hearing. Christa McAuliffe was being interviewed by a local television reporter.

There was a knock at the door. I barely looked up. Christa was in the middle of a sentence.

"Come in!" Dad yelled.

I glanced up from the TV. "Mark!" I said. "I thought you had basketball."

"Canceled," he said, kissing the top of my head. "Hey, Jesse." He sat on the floor beside me. I looked back at the TV. They were replaying a shuttle launch.

"Look at that shuttle go," Dad said. "God, it's beautiful."

Orange fire, blue sky, rising white.

It was a familiar sight, at least on TV. The reporter was saying that Christa's mission in January would be the twenty-fifth flight of the shuttle. I leaned in to watch the shuttle roll over on its back as it climbed in the sky and wondered why it did that.

And for the first time, I wondered what it would be like to actually be in the shuttle. What did the astronauts feel? What did they see? What were they thinking? I couldn't even imagine it.

"What's the thrust of those engines, Mark?" Dad asked, a kidlike grin on his face. Dad really got excited about things. I liked that about him.

Mark fingered my new charm, now hooked permanently to my bracelet. "I'm not that interested in the space program, Jesse. I have to be around those NASA kids all day. They're full of themselves."

"Lea isn't," I said defensively.

"Lea's different," said Mark. "But a lot of them don't like hanging out with blue-collar kids. To them, you're not as good as they are if your parents didn't go to college. You didn't go to college, Jesse. You didn't need that." Mark glanced at me, like he was checking for my response.

"Damn, Mark, I *am* an idiot," Dad said, letting out a loud laugh.

"You're not either," I said, irritated with both of them. "You can tear up a car and put it back together. You can fix anything that breaks at all. That's not stupid."

"Well, thanks, Annie," he said, looking pleased.

"And your art car is very cool, Dad."

His ears blushed pink, and he gave a shy grin to the floor. My dad was an odd combination of Texan and beatnik hippie. He fished, he hunted, he read Beat poetry, and he'd protested against the war. He loved the poem "Howl," which many labeled profane, but he didn't like women swearing.

I heard the jangle of keys.

Dad's eyes swung to the door. "Uh-oh."

He said that, but I knew he could've left a while ago. My dad was still hung up on my mom. She'd wanted the divorce, not him. But I knew from my aunts that he'd run around on her.

In some ways, he'd never really left, though. With his odd work schedule, he'd been able to look after me when my mom or my grandma couldn't, keeping me company after school.

Mom stopped in the doorway, wearing the high heels and nylon hose she hated, looking at Dad. She hadn't seemed to mind him hanging around all these years, until recently. Donald was bringing lots of changes into our lives.

"Hi, Mags," Dad said, gazing at her warily.

"Hi," Mom said, clutching a bunch of purple tulips in one hand.

Good, I thought. *Flowers usually cheered her. Maybe she wouldn't get annoyed with Dad.*

She threw her keys on the table by the door. "Nowhere to be, Jesse?"

"Just visiting with my daughter," Dad told her.

"And eating my food?" she asked, glancing at his plate.

"Gotta go." He stood. "See ya, Annie."

"Bye, Dad," I said.

The door slammed as Mark yelled out a good-bye.

"It's so hot in here," Mom said. "Annie, turn the heat down.

I can't afford to pay for beach weather. And put these tulips in water, please." She laid them down on the coffee table.

I didn't like being ordered around, so I waited an extra two beats before getting up and grabbing the flowers.

"Start peeling potatoes," Mom yelled from the hallway.

Mark followed me into the kitchen.

I chose a ceramic glazed vase from the many under the sink and began filling it with water. Mom used to make ceramics in the garage, hoping to escape secretary work by opening up her own business. She just ended up exhausted.

"What's with your parents?" Mark asked quietly. "They're usually friendly."

I shrugged. "Things change."

I put the vase on the table and the flowers into the vase. Mom was right. Fresh flowers did brighten the kitchen. Mark sat down while I arranged the tulips.

"Was basketball really canceled?" I asked, rubbing one of the petals, so pretty, the purple so rich. "Or did you skip again?"

He gave me a look.

"You're going to get thrown off the team," I told him. He didn't say anything. I stared at him. "You *want* to get thrown off the team, don't you?"

"What does it matter?" he asked.

I sat down beside him, taking his hand. "But you love basketball. You've been on the school team since, what, the seventh grade?"

"Sixth." He shrugged. "I don't like sitting on the bench."

"But, Mark, it's your senior year. Don't you want to stick with it, finish it out?"

"I don't have time for it."

"That's because you're working too many hours at the theater."

"I need the money. Bill and I want to take another surfing trip." He grinned. "Costa Rica."

"That'll be fun," I said, wondering why I was so disappointed. "Expensive." I got up, pulled out the potatoes.

"That's why I'm saving up," he said, coming over to me at the sink. "I'm thinking about getting a second job, maybe as a mechanic."

"A second job. Wow."

"What's wrong, Annie?" he asked, tucking my hair behind my ear and looking into my face.

"I don't know. It's the basketball. I wish you wouldn't quit." I realized I was disappointed he could give up something he loved so easily. I couldn't give up writing that easily.

He leaned against the counter as I washed the potatoes. "I didn't know that basketball was that important to you."

"It's just that . . . I liked that you liked it so much. You're so happy when you're on the court. You like . . . glow or something."

He grinned. "I glow?"

I laughed and wrapped an arm around his waist. I liked the way we fit together. He squeezed me tight, lifting me up off the floor.

"Whooaa," I said. When he set me back down, I looked up at him and we kissed. His lips felt warm. I cuddled in closer.

"You know, Annie," he said in my ear, "people sometimes still end up together."

I leaned back to look at him. "What do you mean?"

"I mean, people sometimes fall in love in high school and get married after."

"And love each other forever?" I asked.

He answered with a lingering kiss.

Part of me really wanted this.

CHAPTER 6

On Saturday, Mom dropped me off early at Lea's. She wanted time to get ready for her date with Donald. Mom never used to wear makeup, but she was wearing blush and mascara now. At least her hair was still long and straight, the way she'd worn it for years.

Mom didn't really ignore trends like Lea did; she just wasn't aware of them. She didn't read popular magazines and didn't understand my obsession with TV. I liked her easy style, with its leftover hippie vibe. It made me see how she and Dad fit together at one time. I hoped she wasn't changing.

Donald was divorced with older kids he rarely saw. He was quiet, but he laughed at subtle humor, which I liked about him.

The thing is, though, he didn't seem anything like my mom. She was quiet, like him. But she was different, special. She had a quirky perceptiveness.

I looked over at her. "What's wrong?"

"Nothing." She glanced at me. "Why?"

"You're quiet. And you're drumming your fingers on the steering wheel." Her fingers were long and thin and always capable and busy.

"Oh," she said, stopping. "Sorry."

"I'm just wondering what you're thinking about."

She hesitated. "You, actually."

"Oh," I said, looking out the window. "Sorry I asked."

"Annie."

"I really don't want to know anything I've done wrong."

"I was thinking about next year."

I twisted my long hair into a bun, then let it go. Why had I asked? I should have known better.

"Annie?"

"What, Mom?"

"I know you don't want to talk about this."

I looked out the window. Here it comes.

"But we need to, honey. You need to figure out what we're doing next year."

We're doing? How was it we? "It's only November."

"Well, have you at least thought about your plans?" she asked.

"Sure I have."

"Do you know if you want to apply somewhere?"

I shrugged. "I don't know."

"So you want to stay in Clear Lake and work?" she asked.

That didn't sound right to me either, so I shook my head, not having any answers. She was quiet then as we drove over the brown swampy creeks to the west of the lake, but I knew she was getting ready to say something else.

We passed some of the newer condominiums at the edge of the creeks, and I wondered what it would be like to live in one. The area was changing rapidly as the shuttle program took off, becoming something very different from the small prairie towns my grandparents and great-grandparents had been born in. Very few of my relatives had ever left, and those that did usually came back. Mom sure wanted me to leave. But I didn't know what I wanted. New lines ran through my head:

I yearn to leave, yearn to stay:
Hey, Mom, I know!
I'll split myself apart,
Run with my legs,
Leave behind my heart.

"Annie, it's just that, if you're going," Mom said, "then you need to get your applications ready."

"I don't know yet."

"Well, why don't you send them in?" she asked. "Then you can decide later if you want to go."

I sighed. "It costs money to apply."

"At least fill out the applications. Be ready."

"Let's just drop it right now, Mom." All that the parents and teachers of seniors seemed to think about was college. This was my life, not theirs. That was the good thing about graduating from high school. No one could tell me what to do.

"Annie," said Mom, glancing over at me, "don't get stuck here like I did. You need to get out of here and go someplace else."

"Teenagers in Someplace Else are talking about how they want to go someplace else. So what's the point?"

She opened her mouth to say something else, but then stopped and went back to drumming on the wheel, all the way to Lea's. And then I thought I got the rhythm of her song: *What am I, am I, going to do, to do, about An-nie?*

CHAPTER 7

"Hey," Lea said, standing in the doorway. "You're late." She held up a pair of tweezers.

"Have you seen Madonna's eyebrows?" I asked. "Thick." Lea was a big Madonna fan. We'd gone to see *Desperately Seeking Susan* three times.

"Since when have you wanted to look like Madonna?" she asked, shutting the door behind me. "Although you are wearing fingerless gloves now."

I laughed, raising my hand and pointing to the one gloveless finger. "It snagged. It's not on purpose."

"All right, no plucking your eyebrows. You can paint my toenails instead."

"My day is made," I said, following her up the stairs.

Lea's house was in one of the first NASA neighborhoods in Clear Lake. Her parents recently updated the 1960s house. It was now larger with more windows. They'd bought all the furniture from one store, probably from one display, even the pictures on the wall. It was pretty. It was perfect. It was filled with light.

"Who's here?" I asked, as Lea closed her door.

"Just Mom and Dad."

Lea had two older brothers, away at college at A&M. She didn't want to follow in their footsteps because she said College Station was in the middle of nowhere. So she'd talked her parents into letting her apply to the University of Texas at Austin.

"The guests get here soon, though," said Lea, pulling out some pink polish. "And then you get to meet the Astronaut."

And meet Christa, I thought, taking the bottle from her. "Pink, Lea? Pink? I don't see you and think pink."

"They're not your nails," she said, pulling off her socks.

We settled onto the comfy thick carpet, with Lea's feet safely on towels because she knew I wasn't very good at this.

"Try not to get it too much out of the lines," said Lea.

"What are we, coloring?"

"Focus," said Lea, pointing at her nails.

I shook the polish, giving Lea an evil laugh. "Oh, I'll focus. Just trust, grasshopper. Close your eyes and trust."

Lea pointed at me. "You are scary, Annie Porter."

"Hey, do you think I'm related to Cole?"

"Cole who?"

"Cole Porter, you nimwit."

"Does he go to Clear Creek?"

I shook my head. "Never mind."

"Hey!" yelled Lea, pointing. "You're getting it on my skin."

"You're getting under my skin," I mumbled. "Hold still."

She was quiet for a moment. "You're nervous about tonight," she said. "I can tell."

I glanced up at her. "And how can you tell?" I asked, try-ing to pretend I wasn't.

"You get cranky when you're nervous."

It was hard to hide stuff from Lea. "I've never met anyone famous before."

"You've met astronauts."

"Yeah," I agreed, "but this seems different." Even though I'd felt awkward and tongue-tied those times too. There were many astronauts, but only one Christa.

"I won't let them eat you up," Lea said quietly.

I paused, something catching at my too-soft heart, know-ing that she meant it. I'd been comfortable with Lea from the moment I'd met her. She was so direct and open. She wasn't polite to your face and then trashing you behind your back. If she trashed you, it was to your face. So you always knew where you stood with her.

And for the two of us, it'd been like sisters from the start. Sometimes she was the big sister, sometimes I was, sometimes neither, but we'd been there for each other, no one else get-ting between us. Except for Mark. But even that had gotten better with time.

"Annie," Lea said, "you can talk to me, you know. About anything."

"I know." I dipped the brush back into the bottle of pink. Lea took her foot back.

"Hey!" I chastised. I pointed the pink brush at Lea's foot. "I've got to do those two toes." But she was looking at me with a serious face. "What, Lea?"

"I tell you everything, you know that?"

"I know."

"So why are you so secretive? Don't you trust me?"

"My life is pretty secret free." The poetry thing didn't count. That was private.

"You've been very quiet lately, Annie. Something's different. Mark's noticed too."

I looked at her. "You and Mark have talked about me?"

"We're worried."

"You should've just asked me. You didn't have to talk to Mark." That explained why he'd been hovering so much lately.

"It wasn't like that," she said. "I didn't go to him. We were just talking, and it came up."

"Right," I said, annoyed. "Neither of you should worry. It's fine. I'm fine. No more worrying about me."

But as was Lea's way, she ignored everything I said. "Is it Mark? Your parents? Is it because we're graduating?"

I sighed. "Oh, Lea. You're such a pain!"

"Talk to me!"

"I don't know. Things are different this year. I'm just trying to figure out how I fit into things." I pulled her foot back onto the towel, set on finishing her toes.

"Annie, you're smart."

"You're smart."

"But you're different."

"You are very different," I said.

"But you know all about dead writers," she said. "And you love cemeteries. And you're always quoting obscure lines of poetry that nobody cares about."

I laughed. "That's your proof of my genius?"

"And you think an *awful* lot. It's a rare kind of weirdness you have. You're going to do something special with your life."

I gripped her ankle trying to keep her still. "You're the only one who thinks so, Lea."

"Mr. Williams thinks so, unless he just wants your body."

"A girl can dream," I said.

"If I had your curves instead of my skinny butt, then good-looking English teachers might chase me."

"Stop moving around," I said.

"You're hurting me! Give me the brush," Lea ordered, palm out.

"Fine." I passed her the brush and the polish and lay back on the floor.

Lea hummed while she painted, and I stared at the ceiling.

She screwed the top back on the bottle and put it aside. She folded up the towel and pushed it away. Then she lay beside me.

"I'm not serious about things like you are, Annie. I just want to have *fun*."

Then we were both quiet and listened to Lea's *Like a Virgin* record over and over until we were called for dinner.

CHAPTER 8

The first thing that struck me about Christa McAuliffe was how natural she was and how much she seemed to be that person I'd seen on television. That kind of surprised me. I thought there would be a difference, that when people were on TV they put some other public person out there to hide behind. But Christa radiated genuineness.

Twelve people, including Lea and me, were at dinner. Some of the Taylors' NASA friends were there, everyone in jeans. I thought a couple might be astronauts, but I wasn't sure.

We stood around talking for a bit before supper, the adults drinking beer. Lea and I were at the edge of a circle of NASA nerds—I mean, engineers—who were talking to Christa. She had a quick smile. Everyone gravitated toward her.

It was kind of cool that I'd just read about her and seen her on TV and now here she was. I could glimpse a little bit of her charisma, but I wanted to talk with her. I wanted to find out what NASA saw in her, why they chose her out of the eleven thousand teachers who applied.

Lea pulled me to the side. "Isn't he cute?" she said, almost squealing.

"Who?" I asked.

"The Astronaut," she said.

"So he's here?" I asked, looking over my shoulder at Christa. I wanted to make my way back over there, but Lea's hand was on my arm, anchoring me to one piece of carpet.

"Him," she said, pointing to a guy with a buzz cut. He looked younger than I thought he'd be, maybe mid-to-late twenties. He was standing by a woman with a perm of long curly hair. She was saying something, and he was listening, really listening, all of his attention on her.

"He *is* cute," I said, although cute sounded like the wrong word for the Astronaut. "I can see why you've got a crush. But he's got to be twenty-six or twenty-seven."

"I think this might be a real possibility for me."

"Seriously, Lea? Your parents won't let you go out with somebody that age. And anyway, he looks like he's really into that woman."

"I'm in love."

"Right." I looked back at the Astronaut. He was laughing, his eyes lit up. "Have you even talked to him, Lea?"

"Come with me," she said, pulling me behind her. We almost knocked over a lamp trying to squeeze our way by a couple of people to get to him. He took a quick glance at us in the middle of a sentence. Something made him look back at Lea. She was grinning.

"Hi," Lea said.

"Hi," he said. He seemed very astronaut-y to me. Like he

might've actually driven up in a T-38, one of those NASA jets, and parked it outside in the driveway.

"Remember me? I'm Lea. This is Annie."

I gave a nervous little wave.

"Hey!" he said. "I'm—"

"I know who you are," said Lea. "We've met before."

"Yeah," he said, looking uncomfortable. "You're Jim's daughter?"

"Right," said Lea. "When do you fly? On the shuttle?"

"I haven't been assigned a mission yet."

"I'm so sorry," said Lea, looking like someone died.

He laughed. "I just finished training."

"Really?" asked Lea, moving closer. "How long did you train for?"

He glanced over at the woman he'd been talking to, as if he expected her to rescue him. She had big blue eyes and looked patiently amused. "A year."

Mrs. Taylor was at Lea's elbow. "Can you girls help me in the kitchen?"

Lea looked back and forth between her mom and the Astronaut. "Mom—"

"Lea."

She pressed her lips together, working them while she thought. "Excuse me. I have to go help my mommy." She dragged me into the kitchen with her. "Isn't he something?"

"I think you need to back off the Astronaut."

"Back off?" she asked. "No way."

Dinner was all very casual. We had chicken and rice. Lea's mother used their everyday family plates, but we ate on the large dining room table. Lea tried to get us seats by the

Astronaut, but I hung back. I wanted to sit by Christa. I'd come to this dinner to meet her. I wasn't going to be shy Annie and miss the chance to talk to her.

Lea's mom directed Christa to one end of the table. I followed and sat down on her right. Lea was on my other side.

Christa smiled at me. "Hi, I'm Christa McAuliffe."

"I'm Annie Porter," I said. "I'm a friend of Lea's." I pointed at Lea. "Her friend."

"It's nice to meet you," said Christa. "Lea, your mom talks about you a lot."

"Uh-oh," said Lea.

Christa laughed. "The good stuff."

Mr. Taylor, at the other end of the table, passed a bowl of broccoli to the Astronaut on his left. "Dig in, everybody. Lots of food here."

I took a sip of iced tea, trying to think of something to say. I should have written out a list of questions beforehand.

Lea picked up the bowl of rice, scooping some onto her plate, and launched right into asking Christa, "So you aren't scared to fly on the space shuttle?"

Mrs. Taylor gave Lea a mom look, but Christa didn't seem surprised by the question. "Oh, no. It's not like the early missions when the astronauts had no control." She took the rice from me. "Thank you, Annie."

Her voice sounded exactly like I thought a New Englander's would. My Texas twang must be hurting her ears. My accent wasn't as strong as my parents', and theirs weren't as strong as their parents', but we still had them. Lea's family didn't, though.

Christa's face was serious, but open. "Now they can make

emergency landings or orbit the earth once before landing. There's a lot less to worry about." She grinned at Lea. "But you're a NASA kid. You know this!"

"Not really," said Lea.

"Christa's right," said Mr. Taylor. "Some say we're too conservative."

"And never get off the ground because of it," added one of the engineers. "The press won't let up about it. They expect it to be like flying airplanes."

"Things do go wrong," said the engineer with the serious eyes. "Look at the Apollo 1 fire."

"But problems are rare," said Mrs. Taylor, looking like an agitated hostess. "Incredible when you think about the complexity—"

"But Apollo 13—," continued Serious Eyes.

Mr. Taylor cut him off: "Christa, did Helen ever tell you what she said to Ken Mattingly?" Mrs. Taylor laughed.

"Who's Ken Mattingly?" I asked shyly, taking a bite of my chicken.

"He was the astronaut," said Christa, "who was originally on the Apollo 13 crew."

"Oh," I said, "that's the flight when they said, 'Houston, we've had a problem.'"

"Exactly," said Mr. Taylor. "And there *was* a problem. Anyway, they bumped Ken because they said he'd been exposed to German measles. He must have been so disappointed. So, Lea, your mom and I meet Ken a few years ago, and your mom asks him if he was relieved he was bumped off that flight."

Long-Curly-Hair Lady laughed. "What did he say?"

Mrs. Taylor played with her napkin. "He gave me an amused smirk, then looked off and didn't say anything. Everyone around me acted a little embarrassed, as if I'd committed a serious *faux pas*." She shook her head. "I don't think he minded."

"Oh, Mom," said Lea.

"That's a good story," Christa said.

While everyone was laughing, I saw an opportunity. "What do you teach?" I asked Christa quietly.

"I teach an economics course," she said, her curly brown hair soft against her open face. "And American history to eleventh and twelfth graders. I also teach a course I developed called The American Woman, which is social history."

"Social history," I repeated, wishing I could think of something memorable and profound to say to her. "Like what went on in the homes and in the communities?"

"That's right. Social history gives my students an awareness of what the whole society was doing at a particular time in history. I use diaries and personal letters and travel accounts as sources, like those left by the pioneer travelers of the Conestoga wagon days."

"I read you're going to keep a journal? Like those pioneer women did?" I wondered if she liked to write.

Christa paused. "I'm not sure if I'm going to do that now. But I do think there's so much we wouldn't know about history if it weren't for those journals."

"I'd take your class," I told her.

"What grade are you in?" She seemed genuinely interested.

"We're seniors," said Lea.

"That's exciting," Christa said. "Senior year is a special year. It's the beginning of what you're going to be doing in life. Any plans yet?"

"Lea's been accepted to UT," said Mr. Taylor.

"What are you going to study, Lea?" Christa asked.

"I'm undecided."

Lea was being coy. She was exceptionally gifted at math, which she casually accepted. I knew she would never ever admit it, but she liked doing math homework while she watched old movies.

"You'll figure it out," Christa said.

"She'd better and quickly while she's spending my money," said Mr. Taylor.

"You mean our money," said Mrs. Taylor, sliding him a look.

Lea grabbed my arm, while looking at Christa. "I want Annie to come with me to UT. But I can't convince her."

"I'm not sure what I'm going to do," I said.

Christa nodded. "So many choices."

"Or just one!" announced Lea, hitting me on the arm. "Go to UT with me!"

Christa smiled at me. "You must be looking at all the career opportunities and colleges and saying, 'What am I gonna do? What do I want to do?'"

"It can be confusing," I admitted. "And a little scary." I laughed. "That probably seems pretty wimpy considering what you're doing." I looked at her shyly.

"I say reach for it, Annie. You know, go for it, push yourself as far as you can, because if I can get this far, you can do it too."

There was something about her that made you want to do just that. Perhaps because she wasn't telling you to do something she would never do. I mean, look at what she was doing.

"Do you think you'll continue teaching after all this?" I asked her.

"The teacher in space," she said, buttering a roll, "has got to get back into the classroom. And I can't wait. I want to show my students how the space program connects with them, how it belongs to them."

Now that I met her, it was easy to see why NASA selected her. She was confident, very sure of herself. And she had my dad's optimism and excitement about life, but without his particular brand of craziness and laziness. She was like the stars, shining with possibility.

"So you'll still be teaching in, say, ten years?" I asked her.

"What could you possibly do," Lea chimed in, "that'd compare to flying into space?"

"I think I'll be in New Hampshire and in education," Christa said, without hesitation. "But I want to have a bigger impact on how the system works, so maybe in curriculum development or administration."

"But how could you possibly make a bigger impact in education than you can with this mission?" Lea asked.

Christa's eyes shone. "I'm not sure, but I can't wait to find out."

Oh man. Look at her. She was lit up. I wanted to feel that

enthusiasm inside me. I felt so apathetic when I was supposed to be excited about graduation and life, about *something*. Did you have to be born with that? Was Christa like that as a toddler, climbing up ladders, counters, anything, so she could see what was up there?

Lea and I helped her parents serve coffee and chocolate cake. Lea gave the Astronaut a huge piece of cake, twice the size of the others. He blushed when she put it down in front of him.

Right after we settled back down with our own desserts, Lea began to riddle Christa with questions. "Didn't you get to meet the president? And go on *The Tonight Show*? What was it like meeting Johnny Carson?"

"Come on, Lea," Mrs. Taylor said, waving a fork of chocolate cake at her.

"What?" asked Lea, palms up. "Okay, I won't ask that." Her eyes went up to the ceiling like there were questions there. "Let me see."

Lea was the right person to have at a dinner party because she could always think of something to say. She put people at ease. Even now, everyone was smiling at her, even Serious Eyes, who had pushed back his chair and thrown a leg up, his ankle resting on his knee. The Astronaut was watching her with a smile on his face (and his plate almost empty of cake). I thought part of the key to Lea's charm was that she never cared how ridiculous she looked to others.

"Oh! I know!" Lea said, looking at Christa. "Where's your husband?"

Christa grinned. "Back in New Hampshire with our two children. And Johnny's very nice."

"I saw a picture of you with your family in *People* magazine," I said.

"Did you?" she asked, her face soft. "I am homesick. I miss my kids and my husband."

Lea pushed her plate forward and folded her arms on the table. "How long have you been married?"

"Steve and I got married after college, but we were high school sweethearts."

"No!" said Lea.

Christa laughed, nodding her head. "Oh yes. We started dating when we were sophomores. My father thought fifteen was too young to get serious and wanted me to date other boys. But I wanted to be with Steve."

"Just like Annie and her boyfriend!" Lea exclaimed.

Christa glanced at me like she might ask a question about that, but Lea leaned over me and asked, "What was your wedding like?"

I thought Christa would be tired of the questions, but perhaps all the press conferences and interviews had prepared her for people like Lea.

"I wore daisies in my hair," she said.

"Aww," said Lea.

"The reception was in my parents' backyard." Christa laughed. "The Trolls played while we danced until dusk."

"The Trolls?" I asked, smiling.

"A local rock band. After it was over, Steve and I drove away in our orange VW bug with a trailer attached to it. Tin cans were tied to the bumper, clanging behind us."

Lea sighed. I laughed at her. "What?" she asked me. "Leave me alone. I *love* this stuff."

"So, was flying in space," I asked Christa, "just a wild dream you had all these years?"

"Any dream can come true if you have the courage to work at it."

"Well, you have to be a good student too," said Serious Eyes. "School's important in helping us realize our dreams."

Christa looked at him directly. "I would never tell a student, 'Well, you're only a C student in English, so you'll never be a poet.' You have to dream. We all have to dream. Dreaming's okay."

I stared at her for a moment. I knew there was no way she could know I wanted to be a poet. I hadn't told anyone that. I felt like she'd read my mind, or I was getting another cosmic message, Earth to Annie. Snap, snap. I took a sip of my coffee and thought about poetry and me.

The dinner was over too soon. Christa pulled me aside right before she left. "I enjoyed meeting you, Annie."

"Me too," I said.

"Listen," she said. "Would you like to come play volleyball at the space center?"

I couldn't help but laugh. "What?"

She laughed too. "I'm playing at the recreation center at JSC on Tuesday night with some engineers. I thought you and Lea might want to come."

"Can we get on-site?"

"Oh, sure. Use one of Lea's parents' cars. They have an on-site sticker."

This was probably not a good idea. I didn't know much about volleyball—I'd only played the few times in PE when they'd forced me to. But I knew I shouldn't turn down invitations from Christa McAuliffe.

So I did a very un-Annie-like thing and said, "We'll come. Sure we'll come."

The room seemed to sag a little once Christa was gone, but a little of her excitement was left behind. I could sense it in the Taylors, who were smiling and laughing as they cleaned the kitchen together, talking about Christa and her upcoming flight.

Christa's students must love her.

CHAPTER 9

The next morning, Mark picked me up from Lea's. I wanted so much to tell him about meeting Christa. I was still spilling over with excitement about the evening. But I hesitated. I knew he wouldn't be interested. And that would make me feel disappointed. And I didn't want to feel disappointed.

Dad's words nagged at me, but he was wrong. Mark and I had things in common. We did.

"You want to go home?" Mark asked.

I shook my head. "I want to go over the drawbridge."

Mark grinned. "That's my Annie."

As we drove across the bridge, I looked out at the bay. Seagulls swooped down on the many boats coming back in from an early Sunday morning hauling in shrimp. Sailboats lined up on the lake side, waiting to get out.

We drove and drove.

I loved this place. So many Northerners came down and complained about the heat and the hurricanes, and especially the lack of hills. But there was something peaceful and open about seeing the horizon in front of you, like you were on the edge of the Earth and the world began and ended right here.

I couldn't compare it to anywhere else because I'd never been anyplace else, except for the occasional weekend camping trip. I wanted to travel, but I hadn't had the opportunity to, not like Lea, whose family went skiing every winter. What I really wanted to do was see the shuttle launch, Christa's shuttle launch, in January. But it was impossible. I had no money, no ride, and no time off from school.

We drove out to the island of Galveston, about thirty miles south of Clear Lake. We ended up at the beach house of a surfing friend of Mark's.

I went out to the water's edge and watched the waves while the guys pulled on wet suits. Mark looked good, all slick in black. The wet suit clung to his body, outlining all his muscles. One would think he was always at the gym, although he never was. He just played and worked.

He waved one wet suit–black arm toward the ocean. "Hey, Annie, look at those swells."

I glanced at the brown waves spitting up white as they hit the sandy shore. "Kind of mushy, Mark." I grinned at him.

He laughed. "I'll find my wave. You watch me, babe." He leaned forward, giving me a peck. "We won't be in long."

"Go," I said.

I settled in the sand, wrapped in my winter coat, watching them paddle out.

Mark was the first one up. I loved to watch him surf. His body looked loose, but in control, joyful in the turns. He rode the wave not quite all the way out, then jerked his board toward the crest, and dove into the wave. He came up laughing. He was so happy here.

The sound of the surf filled my ears. I wondered how I'd feel if I didn't live close to water, particularly the ocean. The birds squawked at me, but I had nothing to feed them. I watched Mark and wondered if he could really be in love with me if he wasn't interested in what I liked or what I thought. I scooped up sand into hills of doubt.

CHAPTER 10

I mailed the scary white envelope the next day.
My own little launch.

CHAPTER 11

Christa had a training session before the volleyball game. Lea's mother suggested we come over to JSC early so we could peek in on the session. Lea wasn't too interested, but I talked her into it.

Lea's mother explained that the astronauts prepared for their flight by being trained in simulations. Instructors would set up scenarios where the crew would go through their normal checklists but be surprised by failures along the way. The goal was to get the crew working well as a team so they could confidently handle a real in-flight emergency.

I went home with Lea after school, and then we drove over to the space center about five o'clock. Her neighborhood was about five minutes from the front gate of the center, just across the very busy four-lane NASA Road One.

Many NASA employees were on their way out. This cool uniformed guard was on duty at the front. He did these wild gesticulations, waving people in and out of the center. He'd drop down on one knee and circle his arm around with exaggerated motions, pointing us in the right direction. He motioned us to a parking lot across from the guard station so we could get a badge.

We waited outside for Lea's mom, watching the guard while Lea harassed me.

"Oh, come on, Annie. You know you and Mark are getting married."

"I don't think so, Lea."

"Every day I wonder if I'm going to wake up to a phone call from you saying, 'We're in Vegas and we eloped!'"

I hit her arm, smiling. "Stop."

"You're right. You wouldn't leave Texas. So you'll call from just up the road in the little town of Cut and Shoot."

I laughed. "I'm not getting married at eighteen."

"Why not? Elizabeth Taylor—"

"Your twin," I interjected.

"—married Nicky Hilton at eighteen. And, oh, oh, look at Loretta Lynn and her husband Mooney. She was thirteen. I know because I saw *Coal Miner's Daughter*."

"Yeah, Jerry Lee Lewis's wife was thirteen too," I said.

"Whoever he is."

And she was a distant cousin.

"Not to mention Edgar Allan Poe's wife was also thirteen and his *first* cousin."

"No! Ew."

"It's true," I said. "And Percy Shelley married sixteen-year-old Harriet."

"Bo-ring, Annie. Have no idea who that is and don't want to."

"Yeah, you do. He's a poet."

"Bo-ring," she repeated.

"Then he left Harriet for sixteen-year-old Mary, who he later married and then she wrote *Frankenstein*."

"Harriet wrote *Frankenstein*?" Lea asked.

"No! Mary Shelley wrote *Frankenstein*. Harriet drowned herself."

"Still boring."

"Why is it my literary references are boring and your 1950s movie actresses are not?"

"It *is* an intriguing question." She sighed. "I guess we've proven we are old maids at eighteen."

"Maybe I *should* marry Mark."

"It would make him happy," she said.

"But on the other hand, Elizabeth Barrett Browning was forty when she married Robert Browning," I said. "And Emily Dickinson never made it to the altar."

"And such a cheery gal Emily was."

"She did need to get out more," I said.

"Like you."

When Mrs. Taylor got there, we went into the small building and filled out paperwork and got temporary black-and-white badges to wear.

We were back in the car, driving past the long Saturn V rocket lying on the ground to the left of us, many 1960s-era buildings, and shady oak trees. Johnson Space Center felt a little like a college campus. Mrs. Taylor said most of the buildings surrounded three man-made ponds, where many birds—including a blue heron—liked to hang out. We were headed to a building a little off from the ponds that housed the Shuttle Mission Simulators, or SMS.

Mrs. Taylor inserted her NASA badge into a card reader and punched in some numbers. Once we were through the door, a guard at a duty desk checked our badges and waved us through.

Inside and out, Building 5 looked very much like a standard government office building, with linoleum floors and drab yellowish walls. But patches from each shuttle flight and photos of the astronauts hung in the hallway. I already knew that a patch was designed for each mission and that the symbols selected for it had meaning for the crew. It was neat to see the patches all lined up, taking us through the history of shuttle flight.

We entered a fairly small room on our left. Along one side of the wall, there were men and women sitting at a row of consoles, keyboards at their fingertips, looking up at monitors above them. They had headsets on.

"Those are the instructors," Mrs. Taylor whispered over the hum of computer noise.

"What are they doing?" asked Lea, a little too loudly. One of the instructors glanced around to look at us, but then went back to what she was doing.

"Shh, Lea," said her mom. "Don't interrupt. They're following a preplanned script for the training session and need to listen to the crew's reactions, and to talk to them."

"Where's the crew?" asked Lea, her voice only slightly lowered. "Is Christa with them?"

Mrs. Taylor led us back out into the hallway. "The astronauts are in the simulator, which is in an area behind the instructor rooms along this hallway."

"Let's go there," said Lea.

Mrs. Taylor shook her head. "We can't go back there."

"What is a simulator?" I asked.

"It's a mock-up of the crew cabin, with all the switches, controls, and displays of the orbiter, and also simulated out-the-window views. There are two simulators in a large open area: the fixed-base simulator, which doesn't move, but is elevated, and the motion-base one, which can simulate the motions of all phases of flight, from launch to descent. For this particular sim," she said, gesturing to the room, "the crew's in the fixed-base trainer."

I peeked back in. "What are the instructors doing?"

"They're in control of the session. Right now, they're running a post-insertion ops sim."

" 'Ops' is NASA talk for operations," Lea said, nodding at me.

"Post-insertion operations?" I asked.

"Right," Mrs. Taylor said. "The entire crew is needed for this sim. Christa doesn't usually do many of these, but she needs to be here for this one. One of the objectives is to make sure the crew is working well together. Each has his own job to do, but it's also important they manage anomalous situations well as a team."

Lea looked at me. " 'Anomalous' is NASA talk for things are going very wrong."

"And so these instructors make sure things go very wrong?" I asked, pointing in the room.

"They put in malfunctions of different systems," said Mrs. Taylor. "There are thousands of failures they can use. See, that instructor there, touching the light pen to the screen. She's inserting a malfunction. The crew will see indications of the failure on their displays and will need to figure out how to respond."

"But . . . what kind of failures?"

"For this training session, they won't have any issues that would cause an abort or a major change to the mission. They want to take the crew through a complete launch sequence and the preparation for orbit operations. The training guys might fail a sensor of one of the orbiter systems or cause a minor leak that wouldn't have a major impact."

"Do they ever simulate really big failures," I asked, "something that might go really wrong?"

Mrs. Taylor thought for a moment. "They train for things the astronauts can do something about."

"How long does the training session last?" Lea asked, looking at her watch.

"About five hours."

"Five hours!"

"Lower your voice, Lea," said Mrs. Taylor. "They're at the end of the session now."

"Oh," Lea said.

It wasn't long before Christa came out.

"Hi, Christa," I said.

"Hi, Annie," she said. I was pleased she remembered my name. It'd only been a few days since I'd seen her, but I knew she'd met so many people in the last few months: newspaper reporters and photographers, NASA engineers and astronauts, and even President Reagan, whom she met at a White House dinner.

She gave us a tired smile and pushed her purse up farther on her shoulder. Her schedule must be draining. I wondered how she was going to play volleyball.

"Hi, Christa!" said Lea. "You're wearing normal clothes."

"What did you think she'd be wearing?" I asked.

"Those pretty sky blue flight suits."

"Christa," said Mrs. Taylor, ignoring Lea, "can you take the girls from here? I've got to get back to my office."

"Sure. I've got them."

"Thanks, Christa. Y'all have fun."

On the way out to her car, Christa asked if either of us played on a volleyball team.

A team? How good were these people? I should have known: this team was probably made up of overachieving engineers who overachieved at volleyball too. A shot of nerves hit me. I should have told her I didn't know how to play.

"Neither of us has been on a team," Lea was saying, knowing full well I had a hard time telling the difference between a soccer ball and a volleyball.

Lea got in the backseat of the car, gesturing for me to get in the front with Christa. She knew how fascinated I was by her. I slid into the copilot seat, wondering if I should tell Christa about my lack of volleyball experience. Here she was bringing us to play with her friends and I didn't even know how to play.

"I'm not that good at sports—," I began.

"Yes, you are!" Lea said. "You're really good at tennis, Annie."

Christa glanced over at me as she pulled out of the parking lot. "Do you play tennis, Annie?"

"I just hit the ball around. I practice against the backboard a lot." That sounded pretty sad, probably because it was pretty sad.

And it had been months since I'd done that, I realized. I used to love to be outside, under a blue bowl of a sky, loving the feel of the ball as it bounced against the strings of the racket.

"She could have made the school team if she'd tried out," Lea said, leaning forward in between the seats. She kept talking about how I would have been this great tennis player if I'd only tried. She had me winning the Olympics by the time we pulled up to the Gilruth Center.

CHAPTER 12

Are those deer?" I asked, seeing brown forms in among the trees.

Lea looked in the direction I was pointing. "Dad said there were deer out here. One night, when he was working late, he almost walked into one on a sidewalk close to his building."

The employees' recreational center was made up of baseball fields, a large grassy area with trees, a nice-sized pavilion, and one building with a gymnasium and locker rooms. People in sweats, some in shorts, were running alongside the road in front of the building.

"Armand Bayou Nature Center backs up to here," Christa told us. "Joggers hit a dirt road right behind those trees," she said, pointing. "The road borders the nature center." She laughed. "But you probably already knew that."

I shook my head. "I've never been on-site before. I mostly hang out on my side of the lake."

Christa had to change, so she went into the locker room. Lea and I waited in the gymnasium, which looked just like any other gymnasium.

We sat on the floor, leaning against the wall, watching some of the engineers playing around with the volleyball. The net was already set up. One of the guys went up for a ball and spiked it over the net.

I was getting nervous.

"Mind if I join them?" asked Lea.

"No, go, go," I said, waving her on.

She jumped up and walked over to the three guys warming up. "Hi, I'm Lea," I heard her say. "Christa invited us."

I smiled. Meeting new people was easy for Lea. I'd always wished some of it would rub off on me.

Lea started playing. She wasn't as good as the guys, but she got in some good hits. Her serve was pretty decent too. She threw the ball up in the air and came down on it hard, most of the time getting it over the net on the first try.

Christa came out of the locker room. A group of three others—two women and a guy—walked through the door. They all called out to one another. It was obvious they'd known each other awhile, either through this volleyball league or through working together at the space center.

Christa came over to me. "Did you want to play, Annie?"

Other people walked up, throwing bags and purses on the sidelines. "You've got enough on your team. I'll just watch."

"We can rotate you in."

"Maybe later."

She smiled and went back out to the court. The game started.

Each team had extra players, so they rotated people into the game between points. Some of them were pretty good, some very good. A girl with frizzy brown hair couldn't play well, but the others didn't seem to mind—except for a guy with glasses. He fussed at her once for missing an easy shot. She just laughed. I figured out later they were dating.

Everyone was having fun, and no one more than Christa. She seemed to have a new surge of energy, leaping up to shoot the ball over the net. I realized she didn't know very many of these people, but she was laughing, and congratulating them when they made a good play. Like Lea did.

I wondered what it must be like to be so comfortable in your own skin that you could just blend in seamlessly with others. Christa excelled at that. She was so natural and sure of herself. It must be so freeing: to be able to always be yourself. You wouldn't have to hide anything away, out of fear that others might not like what they see.

I stood and leaned against the wall, watching.

Lea had been right about me. I hadn't wanted to try out for the tennis team. I hadn't wanted to mess up in front of anyone, so I didn't even try—even though I loved tennis.

I went over to the two women sitting on a bench on the sidelines, talking and waiting for their turn. I sat by them.

"Hey," one asked, "you're Christa's friend, right?"

I smiled, liking the sound of that. "Yeah."

"Did you want to play?" she asked, gesturing to the court.

My heart was speeding up. "Yeah."

"What's your name?"

"Annie."

The woman called out. "Hey, y'all, Annie wants to play. Put her in."

"Annie!" yelled out Lea happily.

The guy with glasses ran out. "Take my place. I need a break."

I walked out on the court. "Where do I stand, Lea?"

"Right here," said Christa, pointing next to her in the back.

I moved to the spot, trying to remember how to play. I'd seen how the others hit, some of them going low, bumping the ball back up with a two-handed fist, others pushing the ball up with their open hands, setting it up for another player to spike over the net. I just wanted to get the ball over.

Standing here, though, waiting for the serve, I realized I just wanted the ball to go someplace else.

"This guy's got a killer serve," Christa told me. "Watch out for it."

As the ball flew toward us, I realized I wasn't going to get my wish: it was coming right for me. Reflexively, I raised my hands to hit it, and the ball smashed into my nose.

My hands went to my face. It *hurt*.

"Annie!" I heard Lea yell. She was right beside me.

I looked at my hand. No blood. Good. I tended to have nose-bleeds. But it still really hurt. I pressed on my nose with both hands, wiggling it around gently. I didn't think it was broken.

The other players crowded around me. A woman with long blond hair hit the server on the arm. "God! You didn't have to give the girl a facial."

"I didn't mean to," said the guy, leaning in to me. "Are you all right?"

I felt the heat rise in my face. The attention was freaking me out. "I'm okay." Christa was looking at me with concern. I repeated, "I'm okay."

All these eyes were on me. I was trying to figure out how to retreat to the sidelines without looking like a complete dork. "Are you sure you're all right?" asked Lea, her hand gently touching my nose. "It's red." I just wanted her to go back to her spot and for everyone to stop staring at me.

"She's okay," said Christa, clapping her hands. "Get the ball, Annie? It's behind you." And with that, everyone went back to their positions, like Christa was the teacher and we were the students. I picked up the ball, and Christa pointed for me to throw it back to the server. "Thanks, Annie," she said. "Let's play."

I missed every ball that came at me. Since Christa was beside me, I thought she might run in and take my balls so that the team wouldn't lose the points, but she didn't. Instead, she showed me how to position myself to take a lower ball and how to set the ball with my fingertips.

As we rotated around the court, I knew it was soon going to be my turn to serve. I couldn't do it. I wouldn't get a serve over the net. The serving line was too far back.

As I was waiting for the other team to serve, I wasn't thinking about the ball coming over the net. I was thinking about how I was going to rotate myself out after the next point.

I looked up, and the serve was coming right at me again, and I swear I saw guilt on the server's face. The ball was flying in hard and fast. I leaped up, stretching out my arms, and the ball bounced against them and went right back over the net. The other team was so surprised I'd returned it they watched the ball drop to the ground without moving.

"Nice shot!" Christa yelled, holding up her hands to me. I slapped them, elation shooting through me.

"Yes, Annie!" Lea yelled out, slapping my arm.

After that, I got the courage to serve. And missed both tries. But it didn't matter much. I was still a little high from my score. I said I needed water and took a break.

On the sidelines, after having played, I was into the game, cheering "my" team on. I talked to the people being subbed in and out, who were all very friendly and having a good time. I knew I'd played lousy, but at least I'd played.

Christa came out of the game and sat down beside me. "Having fun?" she asked, wiping her face with a towel.

"I am, actually." Then I realized what I'd said. "Not that I didn't think I would." I laughed. "Okay, I guess you've figured out I don't know how to play volleyball."

"It's the fun of it, right?"

I nodded, looking back at her. "Why aren't you exhausted, with all you do?"

"I *am* tired." She held her hair up and fanned her neck. "But I'm having a blast. I don't want to miss any of it."

I was so in awe of her, I had to ask: "Where do you get your courage? Where does that come from?"

Her eyebrows went up. "To fly in space?"

"That, and just . . . to live your life the way you do." I shrugged, feeling awkward, trying to find the words. "You know, being so . . . authentic, I guess." I bit my lip.

She looked at me. "You don't feel you're authentic?"

"I don't know." But of course, I did know. "I feel different from other people, from my friends even."

"There's only one you, Annie. That's what you have to offer."

"Yeah," I said, knowing she was right, but wondering why it was so hard for me to live that way.

"What do you enjoy, Annie? Is there something you're curious about? Want to know more about?"

I took a breath. I suddenly felt the need to tell this woman I hardly knew my secret. There was something about her that made me trust her. "I like reading poetry and . . . writing it." And just like that, my secret was out. I felt so relieved saying it out loud, like a big stack of thick poetry books was lifted off my chest.

And she didn't laugh at me. "That's wonderful, Annie."

"I'm not sure if poetry is a very practical thing to study in college." I couldn't tell this very brave woman I was afraid of being a poet, fearful of leaving bits of my soul in the poems I wrote and letting people see what was inside of me. "But I could teach, and I've been thinking about that. You like teaching."

"I love teaching. I'm a teacher. When I was in the classroom, I felt like I was doing exactly what I wanted to be doing."

What a rush, I thought, *to be able to do what you love every day.* "Will you go back to it? After all this."

"Definitely."

"I hope they show the launch on TV. I want to see it."

What I really wanted was to *go* to the launch. It struck me as pathetically funny that Christa had made her dream of launching into space come true, and I couldn't even get myself over to Florida to see it. Okay, there was Mom, school, and money. Still, as my grandma would say, where was my gumption?

"I'd like to hear from you, Annie. I don't have a lot of extra time right now. You should see the stack of manuals they gave me to read!" She laughed. "But afterward, when things calm down, I'd like to talk to you more. Will you write to me?"

"I'd like that."

We went back to watching the game. Lea stayed in, bouncing around the court, half bunny, half butterfly. By the end of the game, she was like a part of the team.

Afterward, Christa drove us to Lea's car.

"Wait, Annie," said Christa as I opened the door.

She took a piece of paper and pen out of her purse. "This is my address in Concord," she said as she wrote. She handed the paper to me. "Write to me."

I stared at the address, thrilled. She gave me a hug before I got out of the car. Lea came around to Christa's side, and Christa squeezed her hand. "You write me too, Lea."

"Good luck!" said Lea. "We'll see you after your flight!"

We waved to her as she drove off.

"Lea, would you do something for me?" I asked.

"Anything," she said.

"Your dad was talking about how you can request a car pass that'll get you on-site at Kennedy Space Center to see a launch. Could he get me one?"

She grabbed my arm. "Are you going?" she asked excitedly.

"Once I convince my mom."

CHAPTER 13

I began to follow Christa's journey in the newspapers, through reports from Lea's parents, and on the TV news. I wished we could have another evening at the Taylors', but I knew Christa didn't have the time for that.

Christmas was in a few weeks. And after that, it wouldn't be long before Christa and the rest of the crew would go off to Cape Canaveral, which used to be called Cape Kennedy. Cape Canaveral was actually the Air Force base and shuttles were launched from Kennedy Space Center right next door. Most NASA people just called it The Cape. The crew would be put in isolation a week before the launch, which was in January. Not long now.

I wanted to go. *Badly.*

Lea's father hadn't heard back about the launch pass. I was waiting for that news before I asked my mom. But that was an excuse. If I couldn't get a pass, I'd still be able to see the lift-off from a place close by the Kennedy Space Center, maybe on a beach in Cocoa Beach. So the only reason I was delaying talking to Mom was because I was a big fat coward, as Lea said.

But right now, I couldn't bear to hear the word no. The longer I put off asking Mom, the longer I could pretend I was actually going.

- - - - -

I checked the mailbox daily. Nothing for me.

CHAPTER 14

And then, luck arrived: Lea's dad got the launch pass.

I was on the phone with Lea, and after she'd told me the good news, she started babbling about the Astronaut and how she'd found out he was from Iowa. I twisted the long phone cord around my finger, not really listening to her. I had to ask Mom about the trip. No turning back. Finally, Lea had to go, and we hung up.

It was Saturday, and Mom was spending the day with Donald. As soon as she got home, I'd ask her about the trip. I danced a little jig in the kitchen.

I grabbed my knitting needles and my new hot pink yarn and plopped down on the couch. I wondered what Lea would say when she saw her new gloves and if she'd wear them. I'd also bought a deep red yarn for me. I tied a slipknot and began casting stitches.

I tried to slide into the calm of knitting, but I was restless. Where was Mom?

I got out a crisp piece of paper and wrote down a jumble of words. I read over the poem. Ugh. I crumpled it up and threw the paper in the fireplace, where it settled with many other crumpled pieces of paper. *Poems to ashes, dreams to dust.*

Mom walked in. "Hey, Annie." Her cheeks were flushed.

"Hi! Where've you been?" I asked, in the friendliest voice I could manage. I wanted her in a good mood so she'd say, *Yes, Annie, you may go to the launch. Is there anything else I can get you?*

"At brunch at the Galvez. Then we took a walk on the beach."

"Brrr," I said. "Kind of cold."

She was all aglow. My mom was in love and it was changing her. "We talked about you while we walked actually." She sat on the couch with me.

"Uh-huh," I said, picking up my knitting again.

"Donald," said Mom carefully, "has offered to help pay for your college."

"What?" I looked up. "No."

"He offered, Annie. And he's got the money."

"So?" I asked, no longer feeling friendly. "Do we take money from someone just because he has it? It's not my money, Mom."

"He *wants* to help."

"And I don't want him to." I stood.

Mom held out a white bag.

"What's this?" I asked.

"Leftover shrimp."

I took it. "Did you get some tartar?"

"It's in there too."

"Thanks," I said, swinging through the doors into the kitchen and settling at the table. Mom followed me in.

I opened the bag and my book of Sylvia Plath poems lying on the table. Perfect. I felt like Sylvia Plath right now.

I could feel Mom staring. I heard her open the cabinet, then the refrigerator. She sat at the table with me. I ignored her while I peeled the fresh shrimp and dipped it in the sauce. Finally, I closed the book. "What, Mom?"

"Nothing, Annie. I'm just drinking my orange juice."

I watched her play with the Fiesta bowls on the table. Mom collected old bowls, all sizes and colors. "Mom. I have something to ask you."

"Shoot," she said.

"I would really like to do something, and I'd like it if you said yes."

Mom put down her juice. "What?"

"Well, you know I met Christa McAuliffe?"

She took one of the cold shrimp out of the bag. "Right."

"Her shuttle flight is in a few weeks."

"Is it? There are so many now."

"I've never seen a launch. I've never even been out of Texas."

Mom put down the shrimp. "Annie."

"I want to go to Christa's launch."

"Annie," Mom began, shaking her head. "I can't take off work. You know I don't have any vacation time. I had to use it to tend to Grandma when she was ill."

"I was hoping you'd let Dad take me."

"Dad?"

"Yeah."

Mom sat back in her chair. "I didn't see that coming."

"I really want to go."

"But with your dad, Annie?" she asked, standing, "All the way to Florida?"

"I know he's a mess, Mom. But I'm not. I'm eighteen. I'm not a mess."

"No, you're not." She put her hands on her hips and studied the linoleum floor. "He'll get you into all kinds of trouble."

"I can handle it."

"You don't even know, Annie," she said, shaking her head. "What money are you going to use?"

I felt a little bit of hope then. "I have a little money."

"No!" said Mom. "That's a start for . . . your future. No."

"I'll figure it out."

"Figure it out? The launch is in, what, a month?"

"January 22."

"And you'll miss school."

"Yeah," I said.

"I'll have to call the school."

I tried not to smile. "Yeah."

"I just don't know, Annie," she said, then left the room.

I took a sip of her orange juice.

Mom didn't come out of her room much that night. She was mostly on the phone; I could hear her talking. I knew it was probably Donald.

I stayed in the den, hoping to catch her before she went to bed. She came out briefly while the news was on. She got a glass of water and asked where Mark was.

"He has a game," I said, so glad he hadn't quit the basketball team yet.

Mom kissed me on the head and said good night. I turned off the TV and went to bed.

I fell asleep while reading the poem *The Waste Land*.

- - - - -

I sat up in bed, trying to wake up. My book fell to the floor. "Mom?"

"Yes, it's me."

I blinked my eyes. "What time is it?"

"I don't know." She stood in my doorway, her hand on the knob. "If I let you go, you have to promise me something."

I was really awake now. "What?"

"That you'll think about going to college."

I tried not to grin. "Okay. I'll think about it." That was easy. I might not talk to anyone about going to college, but I thought about it all the time.

"And that you'll take Don's money for college, if you decide to go. And you'll take his money for this trip. He's got it. He wants to help."

"Did you call him and talk to him, Mom, about this?" I asked.

"Annie. Those are the conditions."

She closed the door quietly. She couldn't see it, but she was wrong about Donald's money. I shouldn't take it. But she'd see that eventually.

I shot up on the bed, jumped up and down a couple of times, my heart pounding. I fell back down, lying like a log, my head against the pillow. I couldn't believe it. She'd said yes. I'd asked, and she'd said yes.

CHAPTER 15

I checked the mailbox again.

Nothing.

I wouldn't lose hope. Reach for it, Christa had said. Reach as far as you can.

CHAPTER 16

The next day at school, all I could think about was the trip. I didn't want to get ahead of myself, but I was almost positive Dad would take me. I was ready to have *fun*, as Lea would say, and get away from real life for a while. I started asking friends at school if they knew anyone who'd seen a shuttle launch.

When I found someone that had, I waited for him after his art class.

"What was it like?" I asked.

"Cool. It was cool."

"But I mean, what did it look like?" I asked.

"It blasted off. It was loud. It was cool."

"Uh, thanks."

Mark gave me a ride home after school. If Dad didn't show, I was going to call him, but I wasn't surprised when he walked in the door. I wanted for him to get settled before I asked, but I burst out with the question when he sat down.

Dad looked startled. "Are you serious, Annie?"

"Mom said we could go, if you can take me."

"Go with my daughter on a trip? You bet!" Dad laughed.

I didn't expect him to be so excited about it. I wanted to hug his neck.

"We'll make it a road trip," Dad said, "sleeping in campsites on the way. Hey, man, I haven't slept on a beach in years. We could stop in Pensacola. Beautiful place. And you sure your mom agreed?"

"Yes," I said, clapping my hands.

"When is the launch?" asked Mark.

"Just a few weeks," I said, reaching over to squeeze his hand. I felt guilty that I hadn't talked to him about it, but I was so excited and didn't want him to be unhappy and ruin my good mood. He didn't look pleased. "We'll only be gone four days, maybe five."

He nodded.

"We'll take my gear and camp out on beaches along the way," Dad said.

"We won't eat any more food on the road than we would here," I said, "so that's not any more money."

He nodded. "That's right. All we need is money for food and gas and a KOA campground. It won't be much."

"I've got some money," I said.

"It'd be fun to take the Beatmobile," he said.

"Dad."

"What?" he asked.

"I'm not driving all the way to Florida in an art car."

"I thought you liked the Beatmobile."

Dad's contradictions merged for his art car. His car was a "tribute to the Beat generation," but he was equally proud of being a Texan. So he'd painted the car a deep black, and on the hood, he got a talented friend to do portraits of the writer Jack Kerouac and the poet Allen Ginsberg. He'd been collecting Beat paraphernalia—poems, buttons, T-shirts, book covers—and he made a collage of these things on the car doors. To top it off, on the roof of the car, he painted a red, white, and blue Texas flag. Patriotism, but with a rebellious, cool streak.

"The Beatmobile is cool, Dad, but it's not the most reliable car. Can we take your truck?"

He looked disappointed. Then he started laughing again. "And you're sure your mom said yes?"

"Yes, Dad, she said yes."

Dad grinned. "We're going to have us a time, Annie. We'll have us an adventure like Jack Kerouac and Neal Cassady."

"Not really, Dad."

"Who are they?" asked Mark, looking grumpy.

"Kerouac wrote a novel called *On the Road*—," I began.

"Not really a novel," interrupted Dad. "Very autobiographical."

"You didn't even finish it," I said.

"I did. I just skimmed the second part. I didn't like that part much. But it's a great book, Mark. The manifesto of the Beats."

Poor Mark. Dad was on a roll. I closed my eyes and let him talk. The stars had aligned: *Cape Canaveral, here I come.*

CHAPTER 17

I checked the mailbox. A lone letter. I grabbed it.

It was my own envelope, with my own name, my own address written on it in my own handwriting. The envelope had creases where I had folded it carefully to put in the envelope I mailed.

A rejection.

I sat on the curb, pulling my coat around me.

CHAPTER 18

The kitchen was warm and a heaven of baking smells. Mom was baking, and I was eating what she baked, at least some of it. She wouldn't let me touch the pies, which were for Donald's office party.

That was so unfair. Their perfect flaky crusts edged over the sides of red ceramic pie pans, tempting me. When Mom wasn't looking, I pinched off a piece. I loved crust. I needed to bake a pie crust and just eat that. I should write a poem about a pie crust with no filling. It could be a metaphor; for what I didn't know.

It was a nice afternoon, with just the two of us. We talked about baking, about the family, about nothing really. It was nice. The moment felt right for me to ask her what was on my mind. "Mom, why is it so important to you for me to take Donald's money?"

Mom rolled her shoulders. "Two reasons, I guess."

"Okay. Shoot."

She was thinking. I tried to be patient. "First, I want you to do what I never got to do."

"Right. Go to college."

"Partly. But yes, mainly. And, Annie, money is an issue for us. And for you to get offered this money . . . honey, do you realize how your life opens up with possibility because of that? College will do that for you."

"But what if I don't want to go, Mom?"

"But why, why wouldn't you?" she asked, throwing a hand up in the air. And with that, our peaceful afternoon was ruined. Why did I try?

"I think *you* want to go," I said. "So you're trying to live through me."

"Annie. No. I want you to have a chance to see what's out there."

"Out where?" I asked. "You know, we live just thirty minutes from a city of two million. A very international city."

"Isn't there something you want to see besides Texas?"

"Sure," I said. "But I don't think I have to go to college to do that."

She bit into a cookie.

"Mom, just because *you* want something doesn't mean that I want it."

"Let me ask you, Annie. Why don't you want to go to college? Why don't you want to leave Clear Lake? Is it Mark?"

I shook my head, then shrugged.

"So it is Mark?"

I felt like crying. I was so frustrated. Even if I wanted to go somewhere, where would I go?

And there was Mark, who loved me, who wanted to be with me. That felt good and certain. I could rely on him. He'd always be there for me, no matter what went wrong.

I couldn't say any of this to Mom.

"Annie?"

I closed my eyes until I felt calmer. "Mom, I'll take the money for Florida from Donald. But can we just put off the other decision until later?"

"You mean about him paying for college?"

And me actually going to college. "Yes."

"Sure," she said, getting up to answer the ringing phone. It was Donald.

It was only later that I realized she didn't tell me the second reason why she wanted me to take the money.

PART TWO

"If anything, the overriding emotion is gonna just be excitement."
—Christa McAuliffe

CHAPTER 19

Two things jumped out at me when Dad pulled up. First, he was in the Beatmobile. But before I had time to get mad about that, I noticed the second thing. He wasn't the one driving the car. Mark realized it too. So did Mom.

When Dad got out, Mark asked: "Who's he?"

The driver's door swung open. A guy with dark wavy hair stepped out, resting his arms on the car hood. He gave a friendly wave. Then, he smiled. I felt my stomach do sweet, chaotic flips. He was cute. Really cute.

"Yeah, Jesse. Who's he?" Mom asked.

His smile was like magic. It made you want to grin back at him, which I thought I might be doing. His sunglasses covered his eyes. So I couldn't tell their color, but I didn't think it mattered.

I tried to step forward to mutter hi or something intelligible, but felt a motherly grip on my shoulder and a boyfriend's hand pulling on mine. But I couldn't stop looking at the guy's smile. It was so . . . welcoming. It made me giddy. Mark's hand tightened.

"Who is this?" I heard Mom ask again.

An unexpected scowl turned down Mom's lips and up her eyebrows, giving her face an odd, fractured look.

"Huh?" Dad asked, looking up. He'd been throwing old tennis shoes from the backseat to the trunk, and old french fries onto the grass. I realized Mom must be in shock because she said nothing about the limp fries hanging out on her lawn. Her eyes still bore into Dad's.

"What, Mags? What?"

"The boy," said Mom, waving. "Who's the boy?"

But this guy wasn't a boy. He was out of high school, for sure, probably graduated for a few years. His grin didn't fade, just kind of slid into an amused smile, while he glanced down. He looked back at Mom, a little shyly. It was adorable.

"What are you staring at?" asked Mark.

I looked at Mark, trying to place him. Then I felt the heat flow up into my face. I *had* been staring. I looked back at the guy. But he was just so incredible. No one, not even Mr. Williams when he defied the principal and wore his jeans to school, looked quite so incredible.

"This is Tommy," said Dad, casually throwing a hand his way.

Mom stepped forward. "And you're dropping him off?"

"Yeah," said Dad, laughing, "in Florida."

"He's not going with you," said Mom. Not a question.

"Yeah, he is, Mags. He's helping me drive." He shrugged. "And he wants to see the launch of the space shuttle, don't you, Tommy?"

Tommy took off his sunglasses. "Nice to meet y'all."

His eyes were blue. Not that it mattered.

"Can I talk to you?" Mom asked, grabbing Dad by the arm. She started pulling him over to the side.

"What?" Dad asked, brushing her off. But he followed her. Mom began talking frantically. She never talked frantically. I didn't understand why she felt the need to drag Dad to the side, when she wasn't lowering her voice.

"We can hear you, Mom," I yelled, but she didn't get any quieter.

I caught Tommy's eye, and he gave me a little shrug. "Hi," I said. "I'm Annie. Sorry about them."

"Can I talk to you?" Mark asked.

"Sure."

He led me to the door by the hand he'd not let go since Dad had driven up. He opened the door, like he was heading inside, but I stopped on the front step. "What's going on?"

"You're not getting in that car."

"What?" I pulled my hand out of his. "Mark, don't get crazy."

"You think I'm going to let my girlfriend go off with . . . him?"

"Let? You're not going to *let* me?"

"Don't start with that, Annie. You know what I mean. If I was going . . . surfing with a hot chick, you wouldn't want me to go."

"I don't think I'd mind. I trust you."

Mark's mouth set into a firm, straight line. He looked down, shaking his head. "Annie, you're not going." His voice was tight, angry.

"I am going."

With that, he hit the door with his fist so hard that the bang made Mom and Dad turn toward us. I stepped back from his anger. Tommy came around the side of the Beatmobile, but Mark started walking straight toward his own car. And just then, Donald drove up.

"Mark!" I yelled. "Come back, Mark!" I saw my neighbor down the street out in her yard. I swore she had binoculars in her hand.

Mark didn't say a word, just kept walking. He looked up at Tommy when he passed him by. Mark's back was to me, so I couldn't see his face, but I could tell from Tommy's raised eyebrows Mark had shot him some look.

Tommy shook his head and said something too low to be heard.

Donald, who had parked on the street, was getting out of his car. What was everybody doing here? Didn't anyone work a full day anymore?

Dad looked like he might say something to Mark, but when he saw Donald, he stopped, then started walking away from Mom to the Beatmobile.

"Ready to go?" he said to me, grabbing my bag off the driveway.

Mark's car tore down the street, tires screeching on the road. Our neighbor scuttled back into her house.

"Yeah," I said quietly. "Ready."

Donald walked over to me, pulling out his wallet. "I'm so glad you agreed to let me help with this trip, Annie."

Oh no.

"What? She doesn't need your money," Dad said.

"How are you paying for gas and food?" Mom asked.

"Me and Tommy are paying. And Annie's pitching in some."

"Yeah," said Mom, taking the bills out of Donald's hand and giving them to me. "This is the money."

"He," Dad began, "is not paying for my daughter." He stuffed the bills back in Mom's hand, ignoring Donald. "Annie said she had money."

"Dad. This is the money."

"What about your movie-theater money? You've been working there for two years, Annie. You never buy anything. I know you have money saved up."

"That's for college, Jesse. It's just like you—"

"Mom," I interrupted.

"He should be paying for something, Annie."

"All I know is that she's my daughter, and HE isn't paying for her."

I took the money from Mom. "Yeah, he is, Dad," I said. "Now get in the car."

"Annie."

"Get in the car, Dad."

"Well, dammit. This trip has gotten off to a great start," he said sarcastically, like a little kid. He slid into the passenger seat, and I slid into the back.

I rolled down the window. "See you soon, Mom."

Mom's mouth twisted a little. "Annie."

"I'll be back soon, Mom. We're driving back right after the launch on Saturday. I'll be home Sunday night or early Monday morning."

"I don't understand why you had to leave this evening," she said.

"Because I like to drive at night," Dad said, but his window wasn't down so I hoped she hadn't heard him.

Mom looked so concerned. "Call me, Annie, when you get to Cocoa Beach so I'll know you got there safely." She glanced over at Dad.

"I will."

"Don't forget."

"I won't, Mom." I saw Tommy looking at me in the rearview mirror. He hadn't started the car yet. "We have to go, Mom."

"Call."

"I won't forget."

"Let's go," Dad said.

Tommy's hand was on the ignition, but he glanced back at me. I nodded at him. The car started up.

Mom was gesturing with her eyes toward Donald.

"Yeah, thanks, Donald," I said.

"Sure, Annie. Have a good time. Should be quite a show."

I waved my hand out the window as we drove away. Tommy slid in a Van Morrison cassette and cranked up the volume.

Dad smiled. "Yeah! Thank you, kid."

We took the Kemah Bridge. To the east of us, a blue sky stretched out over the bay. Like Van Gogh, I didn't think I could ever tire of a blue sky.

CHAPTER 20

I couldn't hear what Tommy and Dad were saying. The music was loud, still, and the windows were down, still. That was fine for a while, even wild and fun, but when we got to Beaumont, I hit Dad on the arm. "Hey."

"What is it?"

"Your music—*pftt*—is loud—*pftt*," I said, trying to keep my hair out of my mouth while I talked.

"What?" he asked, turning down "Have You Ever Seen the Rain?"

"John Fogerty is singing way too loud. And I'm cold," I said, pulling at my red gloves. "The sun has almost set, if you haven't noticed."

"Sure," said Tommy, rolling up his window.

Dad started cranking up his as well. I combed my hair with my fingers, trying to smooth it back down so it was somewhat flat on my head.

"Sorry about that," said Tommy, looking at me in the mirror. "I forget that others don't like it as cold as I do."

"It's fine," I said. "How's my hair?"

He laughed. "A little unkempt."

Unkempt. Unkempt. I couldn't get the word out of my head. Tommy, my father's fine friend, had used the word "unkempt."

"But then I'm not one to talk," he said, pointing to his head.

"Your hair *is* puffy."

He laughed.

"Sorry."

"Nah," he said. "So your dad says you go to Clear Creek?"

I looked over at Dad. He'd leaned his head against the window and closed his eyes. "I'm a senior."

"That's what he said," said Tommy. "What are you doing after you graduate?"

I was used to this question, but somehow when Tommy asked it, it lost some of its sting. "Thinking it through."

"I graduated from Creek."

"Yeah?" I asked. "What year?"

"Eighty-two."

"So we weren't there at the same time." I paused. So he was four years ahead of me. I wondered if it was strange I started thinking about when I was there relative to when he was there. "I guess not."

"Guess not," said Tommy. "Unless you flunked."

I laughed.

He was driving with one hand, with his other arm draped across the back of the front seat. He wasn't wearing his coat. His sleeves were rolled up. I noticed he didn't have much hair on his arms, and I wondered if he had Indian blood in him. That was what Mark had told me about himself. That he was part Cherokee, from way back, which was why he didn't have much hair on his chest.

Tommy gestured toward Dad. "He didn't last long." Dad was out, but not snoring too loudly yet.

"Dad does four things well: talking, fishing, and sleeping."

"That's three."

"Yep," I said.

Tommy laughed. "Well, what's the fourth thing?"

"He wouldn't ever tell me. And he said it wasn't *that*."

"What?"

"What you're thinking," I said.

He glanced back at me. "You're a blusher."

My hands went to my face. "Your cheeks are pink too."

He looked at himself in the mirror, laughing. "Noooo."

I smiled and looked out the window, listening to Dad snore, feeling happier and more relaxed than I had in a long time.

"So that was your boyfriend?" asked Tommy.

"Yeah. Yeah."

"He didn't like me much."

No, he didn't, I thought.

"Is he always that angry?" asked Tommy. "Hitting the door like that?"

"I've never seen him that angry," I said.

Tommy nodded. "I'm sorry I brought it up."

I shrugged. "It's all right. So you work with my dad?"

"I've worked at the plant for a year, all with your dad. He's a good guy."

I looked at Dad, wondering if I agreed.

"He talks about you all the time," said Tommy.

"Me?"

"All the time."

"What does he say?" I asked.

"Everything. He told me about a paper you wrote for class. On King Lear."

"What?"

"Yeah. How you argued Lear had an epiphany, and that even though he died right after he had the epiphany, it was important that he had the epiphany. Right?"

"Yeah," I said, feeling uncomfortable Tommy knew things about me that Dad had told him. What else had he said? "So," I said, eager to change the subject, "where did you work before the plant?"

"I was in college," he said.

"Oh, yeah? Where?"

"California. At USC."

"USC? That's cool. You didn't like it?"

"Nope."

"Why not go to another college?" I asked.

"It wasn't USC I didn't like."

"Oh," I said. "What then?"

He shrugged one shoulder. "It's complicated."

"Complicated I know."

He laughed. "Fielding lots of questions lately?"

"Yeah," I said.

"About what you're going to do with your life?"

"Yeah."

We were quiet for a moment.

"Did you know what you were going to do when you graduated?" I asked.

"No. I had an idea, but my parents . . ." His voice drifted off and he didn't say any more about it.

I figured he didn't want to talk about whatever it was and I knew how that felt. I changed the subject: "Do you like working at the plant?"

"It's fine, for now."

"And that should be okay," I said.

"What?"

I hesitated, trying to figure out what I meant. "I mean it's okay not to know. It's okay to do other things until you figure it out."

"That's what I think."

"Yeah," I said, taking a breath. "Yeah."

"Hey, you want a Coke?"

"A Coca-Colaaa?" I asked, singing the word. I paused, inwardly cringing.

I wasn't used to being so awkward. I'd always been comfortable with guys. I'd been friends with Mark for ages. When we started dating, it felt natural, even though we hadn't been best friends or anything. But we'd been friends and hung around together in the same group.

So we had bypassed awkward.

Tommy was different. Or I was different around him. Not good.

"There's some fast food up in Orange," he said.

"It's a date!" I closed my eyes. Just stop it now, Annie.

Tommy didn't seem to notice my befuddlement though. He pulled into a McDonald's just off the interstate. Dad continued to sleep and snore while we ordered Cokes for everyone, including him.

Tommy drove to the food-pickup window, and a girl who didn't look good in McDonald's colors leaned out. "Hi," she said to Tommy in a husky voice. "Interesting car." I leaned forward to see her better. She was trashy looking, I thought, as I fell back.

"I have a question for you," Tommy said to the girl, "about someone who used to live around here. In Port Arthur."

"Shoot," she said.

"You know Janis Joplin? Big rock singer. Biiiig."

"Never heard of her," the girl said.

"Sure you did!" I called out from the back. "Wasn't Janis Joplin at Woodstock, Tommy?" Dad snorted and moved around a bit, but he still slept. "Hey, she even had her own art car, remember?"

"That's right!" said Tommy. "It was that psychedelic Porsche."

"What's an art car?" the girl asked.

Tommy glanced back at me. "And Janis had to have been at Woodstock." He paused. "You do know Woodstock, right?" he asked the girl.

She giggled. "Of course I do." She leaned over the window ledge. "Is that y'all's dad sleeping?" Dad's snoring stopped, and he shifted in his seat. He then leaned his head against the glass window.

I leaned forward in the seat and pointed to Tommy, then to myself, "We," I said, "are not brother and sister."

"What are you then?" asked the girl.

I leaned back. I didn't know the answer to that.

"We're friends," said Tommy.

She handed him a drink. "Diet Coke."

"Here, Annie," he said, handing it back to me. "Have some bubbles of nothingness."

"So, how good of friends are you?" the girl asked.

"Very good friends," he said. The look he gave me made my stomach feel all flippy and nice again.

"Thanks," I said. "For the Diet Coke, I mean."

"Are you in Orange for long?" asked the girl, passing the last Coke to Tommy, but not letting it go. He held on to it too. I thought their pinkies might be touching.

"We're leaving in five seconds," he said. "Thanks for the Coke."

"You're welcome," said the girl, releasing it. "Come back anytime."

- - - - -

Neither Tommy nor I said anything else for a while. I was uncomfortable, not so much with the way the girl had acted toward Tommy as that it reminded me of my own reaction to him. I wanted to believe I wasn't anything like that girl back there. That girl would end up married to a guy in her town and stay there all her life and never do anything worthwhile.

With a sick feeling in my stomach, I thought about Mark. That was what he wanted of course. And he didn't need anything beyond what he had right now. I found I didn't want to leave *him*, but I thought I wanted to go.

"Your dad's a real sleeper," said Tommy.

"He's always falling asleep, at the movies, on the couch, in a chair at Star Furniture once. Doesn't he sleep at work?"

"Nooo. Your dad's a hard worker."

"He's asleep. You don't have to say that."

"Hey, it's true. Your dad's well thought of at work."

"I thought he quit a lot."

"Quit? He's worked at the plant for fifteen years. But you know that."

I didn't say anything.

"They want to make him a supervisor," said Tommy. "But he's resisting. Doesn't want the pressure. But he told you that, right?"

"No."

"How about that?" said Tommy.

So why was Dad telling Tommy all this stuff, and not me? He never talked about work. I hadn't even known about Tommy, but he and my dad were close. "It sounds like you know my dad better than I do."

"We're together a lot at work," said Tommy. "He doesn't talk much about your mom. How long *have* your parents been divorced?"

"What are you doing, writing a book?"

"Hey, I'm sorry."

"No, look. I'm sorry," I said. "It's okay, really. I just don't know a lot about my mom and dad." I paused, glanced at Dad. "I don't understand them really."

"What do you mean?"

"Well, first of all, I don't find them very interesting, or at least as interesting as you do."

Tommy laughed. "That's normal."

"Are you interested in your parents?"

"I tried, more than they did. Or at least more than my father did."

I thought about that, unsure about what he meant. "Hey, are you hungry?" I started going through the sack of groceries on the seat beside me. "Ah! Potato chips," I said, grabbing the bag. "Thank you, Dad! You want some, Tommy?"

"What else is in there?"

"Nothing healthy," I said.

"Jesse brought a cooler of stuff, but unfortunately it's in the trunk."

"Here's some cashews," I said, pulling out a can.

"That'll work."

While I pulled off the sealed top for him, he leaned forward and started playing with the radio. "That station's going to static."

I handed him the can, and he put it on the seat beside him and then went back to fiddling with the radio. I ripped open the bag of chips gleefully. "By the way, do girls always act that way around you?"

Tommy glanced back at me quickly. "Who? That girl back there?"

"Yep. Her."

"You mean friendly."

"She was way more than friendly."

He shrugged. "I don't know. She seemed nice."

"To you."

"She wasn't nice to you?"

"She wasn't not nice to me. But she sure wasn't as nice to me as she was to you."

"Huh," he said, stopping on a station playing country music. "Do you mind country?"

I shrugged. "I'd prefer not."

So he kept searching, finally leaving it on some awful generic music station. "Nothing."

"I'll find us another cassette," I said, picking up the shoebox from the floorboard. It was Dad's. I don't know why I didn't remember to bring my own cassettes. Nothing in here was going to be after 1970, the year the music died, according to Dad.

"So why do you want to see the launch?" Tommy asked.

"Why do you?"

He laughed. "Just thought it would be a cool road trip."

Even his laugh was infectious. It just made you feel all warm inside. What was it? Because he was so good looking? It wasn't just that. Some guys were fine looking, but were missing something else. And whatever that something else was, Tommy had it. And what made it extra charming was that he didn't seem to know he had it.

"So why do you want to go?" asked Tommy.

"Well . . . ," I began, trying to figure out exactly why.

"Are you a space nerd? A big *Star Trek* fan?"

"No," I said, laughing.

"Not going to be an engineer?"

"No."

"Wanted to take a trip with your dad?"

I laughed. "No." Then I looked at my dad, hoping he hadn't heard that. But his mouth was open and he was still sound asleep.

"Okay, so I don't get it," he said. "Oh, wait. Did you just want to skip out on school?"

"I don't mind school," I said, wrapping up the chips bag and throwing it back into the grocery sack. I had to stop eating this junk.

"Huh. Well, you got me, Annie."

I smiled a little, liking the sound of that. I glanced up and saw him watching me again in the rearview mirror. I brushed off my mouth real quick to make sure there were no bits of chips hanging out.

"You gonna tell me?"

"It's not that big a deal," I said, but thinking that wasn't true. "I got to meet Christa—you know, the teacher who's flying? She's cool, and doing something really amazing. I'd like to be there when she realizes her dream."

"It's a long way to go for someone else's dream."

"Not that far," I said, watching the green WELCOME TO LOUISIANA sign go past. "It's too bad it's dark now. I'd like to see Louisiana."

"Right here, along I-10, it's flat, just like home."

We drifted into not talking.

"Hey, you want me to drive?" I asked after a while. He was rubbing his eyes.

"I'm fine."

Yes you are, I thought. "I don't mind."

"I've only been driving a few hours."

"I'd like to," I told him. "I'm wide awake."

"Okay. Sure."

He pulled over in a gas station. Dad looked up at the

sudden quiet, then stumbled out of the car into the store without saying a word. Tommy filled the tank while I went to the bathroom.

Dad still wasn't back when I settled into the driver's seat, readjusting the seat and the mirrors and trying to get a feel for the Beatmobile. Soon, we were all back in—Tommy in the front with me, and Dad sprawled out in the backseat, sleeping again.

"It's so obvious he likes to drive at night," I said sarcastically.

Tommy shrugged. "He went out last night. A friend of his was playing at a club."

I started the car.

"We're about to drive over the swamps of Louisiana," said Tommy. "It'll be a long bridge."

I got back on the interstate, sorry it was nighttime. I would have liked to see the trees growing out of the dark water. My first time out of Texas, and I couldn't see anything. Regardless, I was flipping with excitement.

Soon, I was crossing the Mississippi. Now I felt like I was going somewhere. As a kid, this famous river of song and story had always seemed like a big chasm in the middle of the country, separating my life from the bold, fascinating cities of the East like Washington DC and New York City.

It was a peaceful night, and quiet in the car. I pretended to see ghostlike steamboats floating below and to hear ghostlike blows of a jazz horn floating up from New Orleans. I'd finally leaped over the Great River.

CHAPTER 21

Hey, you doing all right?"

I looked over at Tommy. I could barely see him in the dark. A car's headlights flickered across his sleepy face.

"Yeah, I'm okay," I told him.

"I'm sorry I zonked out. How long did I sleep?"

"You were pretty quiet when we crossed the mighty Mississippi."

"Where are we?" he asked. I liked his voice. Before, I was looking at his face and not thinking about how he spoke. But now that I couldn't see him I was drawn in by his voice. It was a man's voice, but not too deep. It also had a sleepy quality to it, soft, rhythmic.

"We're in Alabama. Just."

"You're joking."

"Nope."

"You must be tired, Annie."

"We need to stop for gas."

"We need to stop for you." He looked behind him. "Your dad."

I laughed softly. "Still out. Must have been some night."

"He likes to party."

"That he does," I said. "I'm getting off here."

Dad stumbled out of the car again and toward the restroom. When he came back, he was drinking a coffee.

"That has got to be awful," I said.

"It'll keep me awake," Dad said. "Give me those keys, Annie."

I hesitated.

"Go ahead and sleep in the back, Annie," Tommy said. "I'll keep your dad awake."

"I'm okay," I said, not telling him there was no way I was going to fall asleep in front of him. What if I snored like Dad?

"We're only about four hours from the campsite. You rest."

"All right," I said, thinking I would just rest my head on the pillow, but wouldn't be able to fall asleep.

- - - - -

I woke. It was still dark.

"What was that?" I asked.

"Oh, we just ran over something," Dad said.

"What? A dead body? That was a big loud jolt, Dad."

He waved his hand. "It wasn't a dead body, Annie. I don't think."

"Where are we?" I asked.

"At the beach campsite. You okay?"

"Yeah. Yeah."

Dad left the headlights on, which lit up a clear spot. The guys got the camping gear out. Tommy set a kerosene lamp on the ground and lit it.

I helped set up the two tents. One was small, and the other was very small. I was given the very small one. I set it up pretty far away from the guys. I wanted privacy.

"Not too close to the water, Annie," said Dad.

"I'm not even close," I told him.

He peered at it, then gave a small shrug.

I threw my bag and my sleeping bag in the tent. Home, sweet home. Now it was time for food. I'd seen some sandwiches in the cooler. With Dad, no telling what they were.

"What are you doing, Dad?" I asked, picking up a sandwich that turned out to be peanut butter and banana on white bread.

"Getting wood for the fire," he said, holding a few pieces of driftwood. "Aren't you cold?"

"Did you see the sign clearly stating no fires?" I asked, glancing at Tommy.

"Sure," Dad said, shining a flashlight around. "Would you mind helping? I'm having a devil of a time finding any wood, which makes me think people haven't been paying attention to that sign you're talking about."

Tommy gave my arm a squeeze and me a small smile. "I thought I saw some when we drove up, Jesse. I'll go." He waved his flashlight at me. "Want to come, Annie?"

"Sure," I said, following him.

"A fire will be nice," Dad called out. "You'll see."

Maybe so, but it probably wasn't a good idea to yell it out.

But then again, the beach was deserted. I could see a few lights in the distance.

Tommy and I found a scattering of wood. The wind whistled in my ears as I filled my arms. It was cold. It was also three o'clock in the morning. I wasn't exactly sure why we weren't asleep. But then again, I was with Dad. I glanced over at Tommy, who was trying to pull a big chunk of driftwood out of the sand. And, yes, Tommy was here.

The fire ended up not being too big. We were close to the outer reach of the waves. I heard the sea's soft whispers as the surf gently slid over the sand. Dad was right. This was nice. I wasn't sleepy. I felt excited sitting here with Dad . . . and Tommy.

Dad had a stick and was poking at the embers under the flames. "So, Annie, if you were a boy, what would your name be?"

"Well, Dad, you are my father," I said, sipping my hot chocolate. Not the good kind made with milk, but it did have tiny marshmallows in it. "Seems like you would remember what boy names you and Mom had picked out."

"No, no. Not that. This is about you, Annie. What do you see your boy name being?"

"But I'm not a boy."

"You're no good at this," he said. "What about you, Tommy? What would your girl name be?"

"Probably still Tommy."

"No, no," said Dad.

I laughed.

"Both of you are crap at this game," said Dad.

"Well, what would your name be?" I asked him.

"Margaret."

"So why that name?" asked Tommy.

I didn't say anything.

"It's Annie's mom's name," Dad said. "It was also her great-grandmother's name. Did you know that, Annie?"

"I knew that," I said quietly.

Dad took a swig of his beer. "What was it that Ginsberg said about love in his poem 'Song,' Annie?"

"I don't know, Dad," I replied, even though I did know.

Dad was weird, just plain weird. Why did he do this? Act like he loved Mom so much, that they were two halves of a whole? If he wouldn't have run around on her, they'd probably still be married.

"The poets speak for us," Dad rambled on. "Don't they, Annie? Give us the words we don't have."

"Yep," I said.

Tommy hit my foot with his foot. "You want some more hot chocolate? I can boil more water," he said, gesturing to the Coleman stove.

"I'm all right," I said, glad he was here.

"Okay," said Dad, "if you were a city, what city would you be?" I could see him shrug in the firelight. "It could be a town."

"What city would you be, Dad?"

"I'd be my hometown of Kemah, if I could keep it from changing, that is."

"You can't fight progress," I said.

"Well, you can try," he said. "So, Tommy, what city would you be?"

"Austin, I think. Austin's cool, and it's still in Texas. I missed Texas when I left."

"Did you?" I asked. "I can see that actually. I think I'd miss it too. If I left."

"So what city would you be, Annie?" asked Dad again.

"I don't know."

"You have to answer. Tommy answered."

"Yeah, I'm trying to forgive that betrayal of his."

Tommy laughed.

"He shouldn't encourage you," I told Dad.

"Come on, what city?" asked Tommy. "Make your dad happy. He did take you on this trip, didn't he?"

"Now I do feel betrayed!"

"What would it be, Annie? In Texas?"

I thought about Houston, Dallas, San Antonio, Austin. None of them fit. "Not a big Texas city, no."

"What about Luckenbach, Texas?" Tommy asked, singing the song about Luckenbach a little. He had a nice singing voice, deeper than I'd thought it'd be. "With Waylon and Willie and the boys?"

"No."

"Dripping Springs?"

"No."

"Dime Box?"

"No."

"Okay, okay," Dad interrupted. "Not in Texas. Where, then? In the U.S., Annie?"

"I don't know, Dad. I've never been anywhere outside of Texas."

"Really?" asked Tommy.

"You're here," said Dad, waving his arms. "On a white sand beach in Florida."

"Well, then, maybe for tonight, I'll be a beach in Florida. And tomorrow, I'll be something else. And next year, something else. Why do I have to be one thing?"

Dad took another drink. "You don't, Annie. No, you don't."

- - - - -

I lay in my tent, on my sandy sleeping bag, listening to the ocean.

CHAPTER 22

I took a walk on the sugar-white beach. It was already after noon and we hadn't left yet. But this schedule of Dad's had its moments, like last night when we stayed up to watch the stars disappear and the orange-yellow sun peek over the horizon. Dad had looked over at me. I'd smiled back and thought of our early stargazing days—and how sharing simple moments could reach the deepest.

Now Dad wanted a freezing midday dip in the ocean. For some crazy reason, Tommy went with him. I stayed on the shore, my red-gloved hands in the pockets of my jean jacket, watching them bouncing in and out of the cold waves. I knew they wouldn't be in long.

We'd already packed up the tents and the sleeping bags, and scattered the logs and the embers, so no one else would think of a fire on the beach.

I kept watching the guys having fun and finally couldn't resist. I rolled up my jeans and walked into the icy, clear green sea before me. The emerald color of this water was very different from the brown of the Galveston Gulf, muddied by river water flowing out of the Mississippi.

My feet were like ice. After a few long seconds, I splashed my way back out, rolled down my jeans, and ran back to the car. I fell into the backseat, with one door open, and shook the sand out of my shoes. I threw a blanket over me and read some of Hilda Doolittle's Imagist poems, loving the famous one about the sea, and let my cold feet dry. I didn't like the gritty feeling of sandy feet in tennis shoes.

Some of the poems I whispered as I read. I liked to hear the words out loud, especially with the sound of the surf in the background.

I was cold, so I shut myself in the backseat. I pulled out my notebook and started writing: *A wave crests / ponders the fall.*

I felt I was in that stillness, that point before movement, like the space shuttle on the pad. Was my future a fall from the crest or a rising from the earth? *Too dramatic*, I thought, and scratched out the line.

Dad and Tommy piled in the car. They were in dry clothes, and their hair was almost dry. I closed my notebook and put it away.

"Hey, start it up, son," said Dad. "Let's get ourselves to Cocoa Beach!"

Son? I stared at Dad. When had he ever called anyone son? I knew he didn't have a son, but still he had never called Mark son. He'd known Mark for years. He'd gone fishing with Mark.

"Sure," said Tommy, turning the ignition. Suddenly, a loud noise filled the car, sounding like a very, very gone-wrong engine.

"What is that?" I asked.

"Kill it, Tommy!" shouted Dad.

"What is that smell? Awful!"

We all got out, and Dad put his hands on his hips and stared at the Beatmobile. "We have a problem."

"Shouldn't you look at the engine, Dad?"

"I'm afraid I know what it is." He looked at Tommy. "I had an exhaust manifold leak, so I used J-B Weld on it as a temporary fix."

"Oh," said Tommy. "I guess it didn't hold."

Dad grinned and shrugged. "Worth a try."

"This isn't funny, Dad. Will it take long to fix?" The Beatmobile was temperamental, but I knew Dad could get any car running.

"We have plenty of time, Annie. The launch isn't until Saturday. Two days. No problem."

"Two days? What are you talking about?" I looked at Tommy, and on his face, I saw that this indeed wasn't an easy fix. I couldn't believe this. Mom had been right. Dad messed up everything. "I told you not to take this car, Dad!"

"Don't get your panties in a wad," he said.

"So what are we going to do now?"

"Well, we have to get the car to a mechanic. I can't fix it."

"You can fix anything."

"Well, thank you, honey, but no, I can't fix this."

"What's wrong with it?" I asked, not really caring. I just wanted it to work. I knew my dad, though. Things rarely went smoothly with him.

"There's a leak in the exhaust manifold."

"Get another manifold then," I said.

"No, Annie," he said patiently, like I was being hysterical, which I wasn't. "Anyway, the part I need they don't have for this car."

"Dad!"

"What are you getting so riled for?" Dad asked.

"Only that I skipped school to see this launch and now it looks like it was all for nothing." But it wasn't that. I didn't care about missing school. It was the launch. I couldn't miss it. I couldn't. "How could they not have the part?"

"Annie," he said, pointing at the car, "the Beatmobile is a 1963 AMC Rambler Ambassador, 990 Cross Country Station Wagon." I closed my eyes, knowing he was off on one of his car spiels. "It was the first year for the 327 small-block V-8."

"Mm-hmm," I said, trying to hold my temper.

"AMC doesn't make an aftermarket version of this manifold, and GM swears theirs won't work."

"Okay, Dad," I said. "What do we do then?"

He looked at the car. "I'm going to have to have it welded."

"Welded doesn't sound like a quick fix, Dad."

"Nope," he said, shaking his head. "But we'll find a mechanic. We passed a store not too far back. They'll let us make a call."

I was so angry I had to walk off. I had the blanket still pulled around me. No one followed me, which was a good thing. I had to keep moving, had to keep quiet. I walked down the beach for a bit, and then came back.

Dad was leaning against the car, waiting for me. "Annie, aren't you glad I pushed for us to leave home early?"

"Let's go find a mechanic."

I couldn't ask how long this welding stuff would take. I

didn't want to know just then. We were five hundred miles away from Kennedy Space Center. But the launch wasn't until Saturday. Like Dad said: We had two days. We were going to make it. We were.

- - - - -

About thirty minutes later, we were at the small grocery. The owner, an older no-nonsense kind of woman, recommended a mechanic. The mechanic agreed to come out and look at the car.

I glanced at the clock on the wall of the store. "This is taking too long."

"It's fine," said Dad.

The mechanic finally got out to the beach. He was a nice-enough guy, although I swear he was moving slower than Dad does. And it turned out, he and my dad had so much to talk about. Tommy stood by them, listening.

I tried very hard not to scream.

Dad finally came over. From the looks the other two guys gave me, I knew it wasn't good. "Now, Annie," said Dad, "don't go blowing a gasket."

"What?" I asked, my heart sinking.

"We'll get at it first thing in the morning. He's going to have it towed to his garage."

"Uh-huh."

"We can still make it. We're only seven, eight hours away."

The mechanic was listening to us, looking pensive. I knew that look. I'd recognized it over the years when my dad was swearing up and down something was going to happen a

certain way. And then I'd see someone in the background looking just like that mechanic looked now. It was the your-father-
is-idiotically-optimistic look. When the mechanic caught my
eye, he looked kind of guilty. "Where are y'all going?" he asked.

"To see the shuttle launch," Tommy said.

"Oh. I thought maybe you had an art-car show or something. What with your car."

"The Beatmobile," said Dad.

"Yeah," said the mechanic, looking like he had no idea
what that meant. "My neighbors have an art car."

Oh, no. No, no, no.

"Really," said Dad, running his fingers through his hair.
"What kind of art car do they have?"

The guy shrugged. "It's an old VW minibus. They call it
the Love Bus, decorated it with all sorts of couples, I guess."

"Couples?" asked Tommy.

"Yeah. You know, from books and movies. *Romeo and
Juliet. Bonnie and Clyde*, of course. Things like that."

"Can you take us over there?" Dad asked.

"Sure," he said, shrugging. "Let's go."

"The car, Dad?"

"It's not going anywhere today," he said. "Let's have some
fun."

I grabbed my book of poems so I could read them and forget how I might not be seeing the shuttle launch after all.

- - - - -

The house was small, like Mom's and mine. The yard was
filled with statues and things that twirled. The Love Bus

was parked out front. The mechanic left after introducing us to its owners, Bonnie and Clyde.

"Clyde's not his real name," Bonnie whispered to me.

"Oh," I said. These people were weird.

She glanced at Clyde, who was talking to Dad. "His real name is Millard," she said quietly.

"Oh."

"Mm-hmm," she said, nodding her head. "Now you see."

They were big people who moved slowly, but talked very quickly. Bonnie touched my arm a lot while she talked, in a motherly way. When they found out about the Beatmobile, you'd have thought they were long-lost relatives of Dad's.

A VW minibus is cool, but the art-car part was not all that creative. They'd just stuck a bunch of photos of couples from the movies on it and shellacked over them. Inside the bus, glued onto the tops of seats, the dashboard, hanging from the rearview mirror, were little wedding couples from wedding cakes. I looked up. More couples were hanging down, their feet glued to the ceiling. It was kind of creepy.

If Dad was disappointed, he didn't show it. He asked them about everything. I heard dogs barking and saw dog faces appear over the backyard fence.

We ended up settling down in Bonnie and Clyde's small den and ordering pizza, which Dad paid for. Our hosts liked to collect things—clocks, spoons, thimbles, statues, antique mirrors, baby shoes, and movie posters of couples. There was not a place to put drinks on tables because they were all crowded with knickknacks. Tommy and I ate on the floor.

"So you're stuck?" asked Bonnie.

"We'll fix it," said Dad, taking a bite of his everything-on-it pizza. "On the road tomorrow afternoon. Maybe evening. At least before midnight."

I didn't say anything. "Maybe we could leave the car here and catch a bus. So we could be sure to make it on time?"

"We don't want to waste money on a bus," Dad said.

"Make it where?" Bonnie asked.

I looked up from the Japanese fan I was holding.

"Do you like that?" she asked me.

"It's pretty," I said, folding it and unfolding it.

"You can have it," she said.

"What? Oh, no," I said.

"Sure. Where's the fun in collecting stuff if you can't give it away?" She looked back over at Dad. "Now where did you say you were going, Jesse?"

"Well," Dad said, picking up a miniature minibus and turning it over and over in his hands. "Well."

"We're going to see the shuttle launch on Saturday," Tommy explained.

"*Maybe* we are," I said.

"We'll make it," said Dad.

Right, I thought, playing with the delicate red fan. Tommy took one of my hands and squeezed it. He gave me a sympathetic smile.

"Hey, honey-baby," Clyde said, looking at Bonnie, thank goodness. "Anything going on special at the store tomorrow?"

"No." She cocked her head. "I can tell what you're thinking."

"We'd be back on Sunday," he told her.

A slow smile appeared on her face. "It'd be fun. Another experience to collect."

"I have to work Sunday night," he said.

"We can drive back bright and early on Sunday."

"Are y'all offering to drive my daughter to the launch?" asked Dad.

"You and Tommy too," said Clyde.

"I have to stay with the Beatmobile," Dad said. It wasn't a surprise he chose his car over me.

"Dad? Can I talk to you?"

"This is perfect, Annie. They can take you, and I can fix the car and drive down and join you."

I stood. "Talk for just a sec?"

"Sure," said Dad.

Once we were in the kitchen, I said, "Dad, we don't know these people. And you're going to send me off with them?"

"Not alone, Annie. Tommy'll be with you."

Tommy? Tommy will be with me.

The door swung open. It was Tommy. He closed it and came over. "You don't like this idea, Annie?"

"Well . . . we just met them," I said, realizing I'd also just met Tommy.

"If there's trouble," said Tommy, with a grin, "I think I can take them."

Oh, he had a nice smile.

"It'll be fine, Annie. Relax a little. These are art-car people."

CHAPTER 23

We stayed up late talking and ended up spending the night with our new friends. They had two spare rooms. I slept in one, Dad and Tommy in the other. All my things were in my bag in the Beatmobile. I brushed my teeth with my finger and slept in my clothes, a new experience for me.

My assigned room had a sofa bed, which Bonnie pulled out and made for me. I tried to help, but she told me to sit down and talk to her.

She didn't find out much about me, but I discovered she and Clyde had been married for ten years, after meeting at a local bar. They'd wanted kids, but she said they hadn't been blessed that way. She worked at a local grocery store. Her feet hurt because of her bunions, so she was the only cashier who got a stool. Clyde managed a McDonald's.

"How did y'all get started with the art car?" I asked her, getting up to tuck in the sheets.

"Well," she said, while fluffing the pillows, "that was me. Clyde really didn't want to at first. He thinks I get a little too obsessed with the art car and with collecting things. But then he said he liked to see me happy. So he started doing it too." She smoothed down a blanket on the bed. "Now he's the one who wants to get on the road and go to another art-car show." She looked around. "Be back in a minute." She disappeared down the hallway and came back with towels. "Yell if you need something," she said, handing them to me.

The sofa bed had a spring that poked me in the back, but I found a safe spot on the right side and was quite comfortable. I stayed awake for a while, listening to one of the dogs howl in the backyard.

- - - - -

"Thanks for letting us crash here," Dad said the next day. He was sitting in the mechanic's tow truck, his arm out the window. "Y'all are good people."

It was only seven a.m., but we were ready to go.

Dad had already been to the Beatmobile to get our bags and the launch pass. His hair was wet and he smelled like the sea, so I knew he'd taken another frigid morning dip, crazy man that he was.

"Come here, Annie," he said from the truck. He leaned out the window and gave me an awkward hug. "I'll see you on Sunday. Clyde's going to let me know where you are. It's going to be a great launch."

"I'll take lots of pictures," I said.

"I promise we'll have the Beatmobile fixed up in no time. I'll be on the road tomorrow." I saw that look on the mechanic's face again and knew it might not happen. But it didn't matter. I just wanted to see Christa fly. I glanced at Tommy and thought how I wouldn't mind if we were delayed getting back to Houston.

I waved good-bye to Dad as the tow truck left the driveway.

Tommy and I climbed in the Love Bus. We were in the way back. The seats were cracked, but covered with afghan blankets. The two German shepherds, looking like gray wolves instead of the brown and black shepherds I was used to, were in between us and their owners. The middle seats had been taken out. I was surprised to discover the dogs were brothers, not a couple. The van smelled a little like the dogs.

Finally we were on our way, surrounded by tiny wedding couples. Tommy caught my eye as I was turning my head to look at one upside-down plastic bride and groom. He grinned. I laughed, but glanced up front to make sure Bonnie hadn't seen.

Tommy leaned over and said quietly in my ear, "Are you picking out one for your cake?"

"Look at their little plastic faces. Those are not happy faces."

"I bet I can find a happy couple. How about this one?" he asked, pointing.

"They looked scared."

"All right," he said. "This one?"

"Dazed."

"What are you doing?" Bonnie yelled back to us. It was hard to hear her. The bus was loud.

"Just looking at your decorations," Tommy yelled back.

"We've been collecting them a long time. I should have showed you the 1930s one we have back home."

"Vintage wedding toppers!" I exclaimed. "Cool."

She turned back around in her seat, taking Clyde's hand. I saw him smile at her.

I felt a little giddy and pulled out my knitting to calm myself. I couldn't be more excited. The launch. Traveling with Tommy *by myself.* Well, kind of. This was cool. This was the life I'd been waiting for, but didn't know how to find. I pushed thoughts of Mark out of my mind.

"What are you knitting?" Tommy asked, playing with the red yarn.

"A scarf," I said. "So are you going to tell me why you dropped out of USC?"

"Crashed and burned."

"You flunked out?"

"I flunked the classes I didn't go to."

I laughed. "How many did you go to?"

"Philosophy and water polo."

"Ah, life skills."

"Throw me on a desert island, baby."

"I don't know. You seem pretty handy."

"I do?" he asked, with a slow smile.

That giddy feeling bubbled up in me again. That grin of his, it was wicked and kind at the same time, like he was saying, "If you come with me, you'll have fun, and I'll watch out for you, but I can't guarantee either of us will be safe."

If Mom found out about this . . . I put the thought out of my mind. She couldn't find out. She wouldn't. Dad sure wouldn't tell her.

I'd thought some of this through. Dad would be in no hurry to tell Mom about the car breaking down. I was sure he would just tell her that he saw the launch too. It was a good plan. We'd see the launch with Bonnie and Clyde. Dad would get the car fixed and drive down tomorrow. We'd drive back with him to Houston. No problem.

Tommy was looking at me expectantly, like he was waiting for an answer.

"I mean, aren't you handy?" I asked.

"I know a few things. Not like your dad. That's a guy who could survive on a desert island."

Dad? How did he get into this conversation? I was surprised at how much Tommy seemed to admire Dad. Mom thought of him as a bum.

"Did you get a scholarship to USC?" I asked. "It's expensive."

He laughed. "No scholarship. Mom and Dad's money. They both graduated from there, moved to Texas after they got married."

Must be nice to have money, I thought. But those were Mark's bitter words, not mine. "Do they live in Houston?"

"Not anymore. California."

"California?" I asked, looking up from my knitting. "Oh, you followed them out there?"

"Hell, no. When they moved, I came back to Texas. Distance, Annie. I needed a few states between me and them."

"What's wrong with them?"

He laughed. "So you're interested in my parents, but not your own?"

I was interested in everything and everyone related to Tommy.

"I do miss my little sister, though," he said.

"You have a sister? How old is she?"

"Fourteen."

"Not so little," I said.

"Not anymore." He looked at me. "So what's up with your boyfriend?"

I paused.

"I have my own reasons for asking," he said.

I knew I was staring at him, but I couldn't seem to stop. His own reasons? Well, that was nice. "What do you mean?" I asked.

He fidgeted a little. "Just wondering if you're serious with him."

My heart fluttered.

"So I guess that's a yes?" Tommy asked.

"We've been together for a while," I said.

"How long?"

"Two years." But he nodded so quickly, I wondered if he already knew.

"That's a long time. Are you going away to college together?"

I shook my head. "Mark doesn't want to go to college. He said he doesn't have the grades for it."

"What do you want to do?"

I looked out the front window of the Love Bus. Open highway. There weren't any windows in the back. Privacy. Then I noticed the rod mounted to the ceiling, with a curtain that shut off this end of the van. Bonnie and Clyde were surprising. "I want to go to Florida and see a teacher take off in the space shuttle."

"Well, we're *in* Florida."

"Yeah."

"You like this teacher."

"I really do. I can't explain it really. She's pretty inspiring. I've never wanted to see a launch before. Even after all these years of being around NASA and the people who work there, and hearing endlessly about shuttle flights at school. But with Christa, it seems more about the human experience than NASA's goals for the mission."

I knew it was partly because she was this ordinary person, a teacher. She hadn't flown in jets or gotten a PhD in physics. She wanted to teach high school kids. She did teach high school kids. And now she was going to be flying with astronauts.

"I don't know much about her," Tommy said, "but I have followed the space program. I was at Creek when the first shuttle launched. I like the idea of space exploration, seems forward thinking to look to the stars for mankind's future."

I smiled. "*Human*kind."

"Right you are," he said, yawning.

"Tired?" I asked.

"Mind if I sack out?"

He fell asleep around Gainesville.

I took out my notebook and scribbled then scratched and wrote then rewrote. I shut my notebook, frustrated. Why have words inside of you if you couldn't make them sing— and if you kept them to yourself?

I was on my way to seeing a schoolteacher fly, and *I* was mired in doubt. If she could be selected for something so extraordinary, surely I could at least try to reach for what I wanted.

I closed my eyes. Some people lived so easily, not hesitating or hiding. I knew. I'd met Christa. She was like that. So was Lea.

I was hesitating *and* hiding. I wanted to write poems, and to learn to write better poems. But most of all I wanted not to be afraid I'd reveal too much of myself if I did.

- - - - -

I jerked awake and looked out the window. We were pulling into a gas station mini-mart. I saw a woman with a big-shouldered, bright blue jacket stare at the Love Bus as she went into the store. A look of disapproval crossed her heavily made-up face. I wondered why anyone would be offended by the Love Bus. It was just an art car.

Bonnie and I got out and went to the bathroom in the back of the store. The woman with the blue jacket was in front of us in line. Her hair was high and full and bleached blond. I'd never seen shoulder pads quite that big on a jacket. No way could they be her real shoulders. I was feeling tension coming from her, like she didn't want to be standing by us. Maybe she thought art-car people were weird. Maybe she'd never seen an art car. But she kept giving us looks.

Bonnie was unique, I knew. She was wearing a bright muumuu-type dress with large red and orange flowers. I admit she was hard to ignore.

It was a one-person bathroom. There was no line to the men's room, of course. Guys went in and out through their door while we waited. A stranger went. Tommy went. Clyde went. We were still in line.

Bonnie babbled on. The shoulder-padded lady shot Bonnie looks, but Bonnie didn't seem to notice. She was talking about how she needed to add a photo of Madonna and Sean Penn to the bus.

"I haven't heard any of her songs or seen any of his movies. But I do like to keep the Love Bus up to date with what's current. And I feel sorry for that couple. All those helicopters at their wedding! They couldn't even get married in peace. They need a spot on the Love Bus."

I smiled at her as she talked. Bonnie was exactly what she seemed, a very sweet person. What did it matter if her art car was more silliness than art and if she collected tacky collectibles? She was just being herself. She either didn't know or didn't care that she might seem a little strange to others.

When the lady in the jacket came out, finally, she had to scoot by us. The hallway was narrow, and Bonnie was big, very big. The lady went by me first, and then stopped. She looked at Bonnie and back at me and sighed in irritation.

"Excuse me?" I asked her. "What's your problem?"

"She's in my way," she said belligerently. "I can't get past her."

"Oh. I'm sorry," Bonnie said, backing down the short hallway.

I was horrified. "Don't say you're sorry to her, Bonnie. She's just rude."

"You've got a mouth on you," the woman said to me as she huffed away.

"Go on, Annie," Bonnie was saying. "Your turn." She didn't look at all upset.

"Bonnie——," I said, looking off toward that woman.

"Don't mind her, honey. She's not going to spoil our good time. Now go on. Go on."

I saw the woman glaring at us when we left the store later with our potato chips and sodas. She was sitting in a blue four-door sedan that perfectly matched the color of her jacket. And she was looking down her nose at Bonnie's size?

"I can't believe that woman," I said, opening the door to the bus.

"What woman?" asked Clyde, looking up. He was checking the air in the tires.

"This woman——"

"It was nothing," Bonnie said, shaking her head at me. She whispered in my ear, "Don't tell him. He'll be upset. He doesn't like it when people aren't kind to me." She smiled a little.

Tommy had gone back to sleep, so I didn't open the chips. He'd mentioned he'd been awake most of the night with Dad's snoring.

We got back on the road, and Clyde started singing "You Light Up My Life," which is a pretty ridiculous song. But he was singing it to Bonnie in this rich tenor voice so it was kind of nice.

Tommy shifted in his seat, but didn't open his eyes. I looked at his sleeping face. He looked so vulnerable.

And then it hit me. I didn't know where we'd be spending the night. We didn't have the sleeping bags or tents with us. Would we get a hotel? With Bonnie and Clyde? I couldn't believe I hadn't thought about this.

I should've been worried about where the money was coming from, but instead all I could think about was where I would sleep and where Tommy would sleep. Would we be sleeping in the same room?

CHAPTER 24

About four o'clock, we pulled into the parking lot of a cheap motel in Cocoa Beach. We'd made good time, considering we had to stop to walk the German shepherds. Lunch was at a rest stop—baloney sandwiches and Cokes out of the cooler—where the dogs could roam a little. It'd been nice to be outside after so long in the car.

Clyde parked a ways from the entrance. We grabbed our bags. "What about the dogs?" I asked.

"I'll wait here with them," Clyde said as he scratched their necks. "Bonnie, you register the two of us."

The two of them, not the four of us. That meant Tommy and I would be together. I took a breath. Maybe we'd each have our own room. I could borrow the money from Tommy if I didn't have enough, and Dad would pay him back.

"Will they let the dogs into your room?" Tommy asked Clyde.

"We'll sneak them in," Bonnie said. "Come on, kids. Let's get registered."

Tommy held the lobby door open for me. "Do you mind if

we only get one room?" he asked, looking a little shy. "Seems a waste to spend the money on two."

"It's okay," I said, but my heart was beating really fast.

"There'll be the two beds."

"Right. Right," I said. "Two beds."

Only one person was working the desk, so Tommy gestured for Bonnie to go first. "Thanks, Tommy." She told the desk clerk she needed a double. "What time does the shuttle launch tomorrow?" she asked him.

"The launch?" he asked. "It's been pushed to Sunday morning."

"Oh no," said Bonnie.

"You didn't hear?" asked the clerk.

"We didn't see a paper," Tommy told him, "or watch any news."

"The news doesn't cover the shuttle like they used to anyway. But NASA announced the delay days ago, at a press conference. It's not launching until Sunday."

Tommy laughed. "What are you gonna do?"

The desk clerk didn't laugh. Obviously, he thought shuttle launches were serious business. "There's a storm over an emergency landing site," he said dismissively.

"Oh my," said Bonnie. "That's not good. For NASA or for Clyde and me. That changes our plans."

I looked at her. "What do you mean?"

"We have to leave early Sunday. Clyde has to work."

"You could head home after the launch and make it back by Sunday night. It'd be close, though. What time does Clyde have to go to work?"

"Let me go talk to him." I watched her walk off toward the

Love Bus. I hoped they didn't come all this way only to drive right back.

"We won't have a ride to Kennedy Space Center if they leave," said Tommy.

"And we won't have them either. I'll kind of miss them."

"Your dad will be happy to hear that."

"Don't tell him," I said.

"It'll be hard to make it out to KSC without a car," he said. "We can watch the launch from the beach, can't we?"

"I heard you can't see it lift off the pad, though," I said. "Maybe we can get a ride from someone at the motel who might be going over."

"Maybe," said Tommy.

It occurred to me Dad was rubbing off on me. I was turning into a hitchhiker and a mooch. I smiled at Tommy. "Maybe we'll run into some good art-car people."

We walked out to the Love Bus.

"This is it for us," said Clyde. "Right, honey-baby?" he asked his wife.

"Yep."

"You're just going to drive all the way back?" I asked. "You came all this way for nothing."

"Not for nothing," Bonnie said. "We're going south to see Coral Castle, this coral structure built by Edward Leedskalnin when he was jilted the day before his wedding by his sixteen-year-old fiancée, Agnes Scuffs. Not exactly the love story we like, but that man understood the power of love, to spend almost thirty years carving a sculpture garden for his Sweet Sixteen out of coral rock."

"But can't you stay tonight?"

"It's still early," said Clyde. "We'll get down there tonight and tour it tomorrow."

"I need to tell my dad where we are," I said.

"I'll call my neighbor," said Clyde. "He'll get your dad the message."

"Thanks, Clyde. Here," I said, grabbing a pen from the bus and writing down my number, remembering Christa doing this for me. "This is my number back in Houston. You need to come visit us."

Bonnie gave my arm a squeeze. "You have fun at that launch."

As we stood in the parking lot waving to the departing Love Bus, I wondered if Dad would arrive in time with the Beatmobile. Viewing the launch from the NASA causeway was supposed to be an amazing experience. It was the closest public viewing area to the launchpad.

We dumped our bags on the floor of our room. I stood awkwardly by the door, looking around. I'd never stayed in a motel before, let alone with a guy.

It was small, with hard beige carpet probably no dirtier than what was in my own bedroom. Nondescript, colorless art adorned the walls. Ugly, stiff-looking bedspreads covered the two double beds. I glanced over at Tommy and found he had looked up at me at the same time. I felt my face grow warm and turned toward a chair in the corner, wondering if I should go sit in it. I couldn't just plop down on the bed.

"Want to get something to eat?" Tommy asked.

"Yes!" I said, a little too enthusiastically.

He moved his bag to the bed farthest from the door. "Let me put on a fresh shirt."

I grabbed my purse and quickly went out our door to the balcony to wait for him. We were on the second floor with a great view of a concrete parking lot. Still, the air had that heavy sea smell, so I knew we were close to the ocean even if I couldn't see it.

I thought about the two nights ahead of me, alone with Tommy, waiting for the launch, waiting for Dad to get here. A smile twitched at my lips. I felt giddy and nervous at the same time. It felt like—*finally*—something was happening to me.

If Mark found out, he would flip. But I pushed that guilt away. I didn't want to worry about that.

I looked up when Tommy came through the door. Navy was a good color for him. It made his eyes look a darker blue.

"I guess we didn't have to leave on Wednesday after all," I said to him, as we walked to a nearby diner.

"Hey, you want to go to Disney World?" Tommy asked. "Seems like we have tomorrow free."

"It's an hour away."

"We could look into a bus," he said.

"Yeah, but Disney World's expensive."

"I have some money. It's my treat."

"I've never been to Disney World," I said, grinning.

"You've never been out of Texas," he said, opening the door for me.

We found a table by a window.

I played with the flatware, trying not to think about the upcoming night. "Thanks for paying for things, Tommy. Do you plan on working at the plant for a while?"

"Nope. I'm saving up."

The waitress, with menus under her arm, put two glasses of water on the table. "Do you know what you'd like?" The menus fell to the ground. "Sorry," she said, "I'm new."

"That's all right," said Tommy, picking one off the floor.

"Thanks," said the waitress, juggling the menus, a pen, a notepad, and some clean napkins. "I'll be back. Let me just . . ." And she was gone.

"Poor lady," said Tommy, looking after her. "Can you imagine being on your feet all day having to wait on hungry people?"

"She may not have the job much longer," I said, watching her picking up the napkins that floated out of her hands.

Tommy laughed.

The hamburger bun was stale, but the meat was thick and juicy. I didn't realize how hungry I was until I bit into the burger.

We got to talking about hobbies. Mine—knitting, reading, watching Mom bake—didn't require a lot of energy. Tommy, on the other hand, liked to skydive. He'd just done his one-hundredth jump.

"It is a rush, Annie. Nothing like it. You're up there, in the sky, so high up, and you can see so much. It's like you're flying."

"Scary, but fun, I guess."

"Nothing like it," he said again. "You should come with me sometime."

"Maybe," I said, pleased.

"You might?"

"I might."

I mentally slapped myself on the head. What was I thinking? Mark. Mark. Mark. I had a boyfriend.

"Do you think you've torn up that napkin enough?" asked Tommy.

I looked down at the white hill of napkin pieces. I fidgeted when I was nervous and I was really nervous the faster we were getting to the end of this meal. "It's a nice little hill."

Tommy pulled another napkin out of the silver holder on the table and handed it to me. "Here's another to play with."

Laughing, I took it. "Thank you, kind sir."

CHAPTER 25

When we got back to the room, the silence was deafening. Even Tommy seemed nervous.

I got my pajamas, which were gray sweatpants and an old shirt, from my suitcase. I would have picked something else to wear at night if I'd known my dad was bringing Tommy along. Nothing frilly or sexy or anything provocative like that, but at least not so drab.

Shutting the bathroom door, I sat on the side of the tub. This was ridiculous. There were two beds. Nothing was wrong. Things would be fine.

I brushed my teeth and changed. Taking a breath, I opened the door. Tommy was reading a book, lying against some pillows propped up against the headboard. Mark never read.

I put my stuff away and lay down on the other bed, on the side farthest from Tommy's. I felt stiff and uncomfortable. Even my breaths felt forced and unnatural.

I looked over at him, around the lamp on the table between us. "What are you reading?" I asked, trying to make things seem more normal than they were. God, I felt awkward.

Tommy sat up on the side of his bed. *"The Republic."*

I moved closer, looking at the cover. "Plato?"

"Have you read it?" he asked, holding it out for me.

I sat up on my bed, across from him, and took it. "Is he the one who drank poison?"

"That was Socrates," he said.

"And why did Socrates commit suicide?" I asked, flipping through the pages. "I've forgotten."

"It was mandated by the state, his punishment for corrupting the minds of the youth."

I laughed. "Even the old Greeks thought we were so impressionable we couldn't think for ourselves."

He laughed too. I liked his laugh. I liked the way he looked when he laughed.

"So you're interested in the ancient Greeks, then?" I asked, giving him the book back.

"Particularly classical Greece," he said, looking like he was thinking about my question. Mark never paid much attention to my questions. "So much rich history there. Mesopotamia. Persia. All fascinating."

"Have you been to any of those places?"

"I'm part Greek," he said. "My mom's grandparents. She and my sister and I took a trip over." Something flitted across his eyes, some hesitation or sadness, but then it was gone, and I wondered if I imagined it. "When I was in high school."

"I bet it was cool."

"Beautiful," he said. "We saw Athens, the Acropolis, but mostly we island hopped."

"I want to travel," I said.

"Isn't that what we're doing?" He grinned.

I smiled, but felt a little self-conscious in the quiet that followed. "Have you been anyplace else? Outside of the U.S.?"

"No, but one day . . . ," he said.

"Mark only wants to travel where he can surf."

"Where do *you* want to go?" he asked.

"Everywhere." I thought I could do that, using Texas as a home base. I'd love to go on trips to visit and explore, and then return home. I wanted both lives.

"Could you narrow it down?"

I picked up the Japanese fan I'd left on the bed. "Tokyo." I opened it and leaned over to fan him.

He laughed, grabbed it. "Where else?"

"Hong Kong before the Brits hand it over to the Chinese."

"I don't think it's closing down like a bar."

"You know what I mean. I'd also like to go on one of those grand tours of Europe, like young people used to do in the nineteenth century."

"You mean the wealthy," Tommy said.

"Wealthy young *men*, at that."

"So when are you going to get started?"

"As you said, I'm traveling now!"

"That you are," he agreed. "So you might bum around Europe for a while?"

I laughed. "Yeah, that would be my grand tour: hostels and Kit Kat bars."

"What do you want to see most? The Eiffel Tower? The ruins of Rome?"

"I want to see Van Gogh's paintings." I leaned forward.

"I heard a woman say that seeing *Starry Night* was nothing like seeing the print of it, that she found herself crying in the museum because she was so moved by it. Isn't that amazing? That Van Gogh painted something so beautiful, so powerful, that it made a woman cry one hundred years later."

"Look at you," he said, reaching over to run his hand up and down my arm. "You've got goose bumps." His touch was warm and nice, and thrilled me a little too. I missed him when he drew back.

"And I want to see where he lived," I said, "where he painted."

"You like Van Gogh."

"I don't know anything about art," I said. "I just know how it makes me feel when I look at it. And I like the feeling." I paused. "I like color. Van Gogh's colors are so amazing. You look at the colors and you feel like he's painting feelings, and that those feelings are the key to everything."

But thinking of the envelope I was carrying around like a priest's hair shirt made me realize I couldn't even express what I felt about Van Gogh's paintings.

"Hey." Tommy tapped my knee with the fan. "What's wrong?"

"Oh," I said. "Nothing. I just thought of something." I shook my head, trying to dismiss it.

"It is something. What's going on?"

I looked at him.

"Come on, Annie. What's wrong?"

He was looking right at me, like he really wanted to know. "I . . . oh hell, let me show you."

I grabbed my bag off the floor and pulled it onto the bed. I tried not to let my undies spill out while I searched through it. I found the unopened envelope and gave it to him.

"What's this?" he asked. "It's addressed to you. And, hey, it's from you. You're writing yourself these days?"

"It's a rejection letter for a poem I wrote," I explained. "Literary journals gift you with rejections in the envelopes you send in with your submissions—so you'll grow to hate your own handwriting."

"You write poetry?"

I nodded once.

"Your dad said the two of you talked poetry. He didn't tell me you wrote it."

"He doesn't know."

Tommy looked at me quizzically and was quiet for a moment. "You haven't opened the envelope."

"You get acceptances back in *their* envelopes, not your own. Or so I've heard. I've never gotten an acceptance."

"So you're upset you got a rejection?" he asked. "It's one rejection."

"No," I said. "That poem has been rejected twenty-six times. There's no other place to send it to. The poem's crap. I write crap."

He raised the envelope. "Can I open it?"

I gestured for him to.

Why was I letting him do this? Maybe it was because being in this motel room in Florida with someone I just met two days ago didn't seem like any part of my real life. But it was something more than that too. I *wanted* to show him. Telling

Christa about my desire to write poetry had opened up something in me, something that wanted to reach out and talk to someone about my poems.

Dad would want to hear about it, but I resisted that, had always resisted telling him about my poetry. I kept Dad at a little bit of a distance, knowing he wanted more from me, but not trusting him completely. I knew how he could hurt people.

Maybe I should tell Mark, but he wouldn't understand, and that would make me feel more alone.

Tommy was here and so easy to talk to.

I watched him rip open my busted future and pull out the contents. Two pieces of paper. It would be the rejection and my own poem returned to me.

"It's a rejection," he said quietly.

"Yeah."

"Can I read the poem?" he asked, holding it up.

"Ye-es," I said carefully, wondering if I meant it.

"Are you sure?"

"As long as you remember it's been rejected twenty-six times. Sorry, twenty-seven."

To my horror, he read it out loud, but it was in his warm, sensual voice. And he read it so well, getting the rhythm, the inflections, hitting the pauses, almost just like I wanted, like it sounded in my head.

I Swim in a Sea of Yellow

I struggle
in seas of amber

suns melted below
streams of blackening
blue stalks
of wheat sting
my face wild
wind distorts
crows' wings rushes
into my soul all I see—
is color

He looked at the paper. "I like it, Annie."

"It's Van Gogh. One of his paintings. How I see it, at least."
I gestured to the poem. "I look at things and words pop into
my head. And I feel restless until I can describe whatever I'm
looking at or what I'm feeling when I'm looking at it."

I'd never said any of that to anyone. Not to Mark, not to
Lea, not my mom, Mr. Williams. It was a relief.

Writing poetry felt silly, not practical. It was poetry. I
wasn't exploring space here. But it felt necessary to me.

"Then you should keep doing it," he said. "You will,
right?"

"I keep trying to quit. When I got that rejection, I promised to quit again. But it's like the words won't leave me
alone." I shrugged. "I can't quit."

"Can I keep the poem, Annie?"

I smiled, feeling uncertain. "Sure."

"I'd like to see more if you ever want to show me."

"Okay. Sure."

He looked down at the poem again. The room was quiet

except for the hum of the heater cutting on and off. Someone besides anonymous editors in remote business offices was reading my poetry.

I felt lighter.

"If we're going to Disney," said Tommy, "we'll need to get up early. You still want to go?"

"I must see Mickey."

Tommy took a small bag from his backpack and went into the bathroom. I tried to adjust the heater so that the fan was blowing even though the heater was off because I liked white noise. But that wasn't an option. I left it off and crawled under the cool sheets, after folding the bedspread so that I was only half covered by it.

Tommy came out of the bathroom. "Annie?" he asked quietly.

I raised my head. "Yeah?"

"Mind if I turn out the lights?"

"No," I said. "Go ahead."

I put my head back down, and the room went dark. It was so quiet I could hear every little noise. I found I was holding my breath; I let it go. Relax, Annie. I heard Tommy get into his bed. His breathing slowly turned to sleep breathing.

I kept seeing Van Gogh's painting and thinking of my poem. I'd always thought I could write poetry from anywhere; I could stay in Clear Lake and write. But I wondered if I would have written the poem differently if I'd seen an actual painting and not just a print. If seeing a painting had moved that woman to tears, what would it do for my poetry?

CHAPTER 26

W hat do you think the temperature is today?" I asked, looking out across the water. We were in a good spot. I wanted to pretend I really was in England and not at a fake Epcot pub.

I should be exhausted after the ungodly hour we had to get up and the bumpy bus ride over from the Cape. But I wasn't. I felt awake and ready for anything.

"Sixty? Sixty-five?"

"It's so nice out."

He gestured to me. "You're making love to your coat over there."

"I'm a Texan. I need my coat." The weather was nice, so there were lots of people here. "I think I'd like to drink in every country."

"I'm not going to let you drink," Tommy said.

"You're not going to *let* me? Back up, buddy."

"Your dad would kill me."

"Honestly, I don't think he would care," I said.

"Annie."

"You're not my babysitter," I said, offended.

"You'll get carded."

"I could pass for nineteen. Isn't that the drinking age here?"

Tommy smiled a little, shaking his head. "You'll get carded."

Now I really was offended.

"What would you like?" asked the waitress in a broad English accent.

"Are you really from England?" I asked.

"Liverpool."

"You've got to be kidding me! That is cool." I couldn't believe I was meeting someone from the same town as the Beatles. "Did you ever go to the Cavern Club?"

The waitress laughed. "I'm twenty. Not even born then. But," she added, with a grin, "my aunt was into the Beatles like mad."

"No. Get out!" I said, not believing her for a minute. "And I appreciate your use of the word 'mad.' It helps with the whole Epcot-British-suspension-of-belief or suspension-of-disbelief, whatever it is, thing."

"Sorry?" the waitress asked.

"What's your name?" asked Tommy.

The waitress lit up. "Jane."

"Jane Austen?" asked Tommy, laughing. I stared at him, thoroughly disappointed. Not only was he flirting with this girl in front of me, he used that too-easy Jane Austen reference.

But Jane's smile back to him was equally flirtatious. "Sure."

"Well, Jane Austen, what kind of beer do you have on tap?"

I didn't like this at all. "Yeah, I'd like a beer."

"We have Bass, Guinness—"

"I'll take whatever brown ale you recommend that's on tap," I said, trying to say it confidently. The waitress barely looked at me enough to know I wasn't nineteen.

Tommy raised two fingers at Jane, the British barmaid, who I thought was annoying. At least I'd get a beer.

"Nothing to eat for you?" asked Jane, only looking at Tommy.

"Nope," said Tommy. "Not for me."

"Not for me either," I said, knowing the girl wasn't listening.

"Be back to you soon," said Jane, scooping up the menus and leaving.

"Hey, what's wrong?" asked Tommy.

"Nothing."

"You're getting your beer."

I looked at him. He thought of me as some high school kid. Here I'd been thinking all sorts of things about *him*, and I realized he thought of me as someone he had to watch over.

"You like Jane?" I asked him.

He looked confused. "Yeah, she's nice."

"You were flirting with her."

A slow grin spread across his face. "Just having fun." He looked at me carefully, dropping the smile. "What's wrong, Annie? I'm not going to go off and leave you, you know."

That thought hadn't occurred to me. My confusion must have shown on my face.

"Annie, what's going on?"

I felt my cheeks warm, feeling so young. I wasn't acting like me. "Nothing."

We fell into silence, looking out over the water at the birds playing.

"Hey, have you thought about how we're going to get to the launch tomorrow?" Tommy asked. "You didn't meet any art-car people at the motel, did you?"

"I called the desk when you were in the shower. Our favorite desk clerk said we could walk to a fairly good spot." I shrugged. "I'd really like to see it from the causeway on-site, but if we can't, we can't."

"Don't give up. Maybe we can find someone tonight to go with."

"Maybe," I said, knowing it was doubtful. I was, in fact, very disappointed. But there wasn't much we could do. And I was definitely going to see the launch, just maybe not from the causeway.

"Here you are," said Jane, setting the pints of beer in front of us.

I sipped mine as I watched Jane watch Tommy. My eyes, through no will of my own, flickered over to Tommy. I found him staring right at me, not at Jane. Startled, my grip on the beer wavered just a smidge and beer splashed up.

"You okay?" asked Tommy.

I wiped my mouth with a napkin, slightly embarrassed.

"Thanks," Tommy said, dismissing the waitress before turning his attention back to me.

"Sure," Jane said, disappointment in her voice. I knew she'd been expecting something different. The waitress left, her stiff upper lip set in a firm line.

"You didn't have to be rude to her," I said, happy.

"Rude?" Tommy laughed. "I can't seem to win here. I'm either too friendly or not friendly enough."

I smiled at him, a little smile. I liked the way he made me feel. All light and easy, while something scary and sweet floated inside. But I also didn't like it. The feeling was nice, but it pulled me off balance. I never felt that way with Mark.

I took another sip of my beer, not really liking it. I'd never had a dark beer before. It was full and thick and bitter. And it was cold, so it was making me feel colder. I pulled my jean jacket tighter around me.

I sipped my beer again, trying to focus on liking it.

Tommy laughed. "You hate that."

I laughed with him. He seemed to relax. He leaned back in his chair. "So, Annie, I'm confused about something. For a girl who is so interested in seeing all the countries in Epcot, why are you even thinking about staying in Clear Lake?"

"How did you know I was thinking about staying?" I asked, trying to remember if I told him that.

He smiled sheepishly. "Your dad."

They did talk a lot about me. This made me more fidgety. What else did Dad tell him?

"So?" Tommy asked. "Why would you stay?"

It was a good question. But I wasn't sure I could explain it. My family had lived in the Gulf Coast region of Texas for generations. And they were proud of that. Despite the hurricanes and the flooding, the mosquitoes that never stopped biting, the flatness of the land, they were drawn to the place. But I didn't think I could make someone who didn't feel that understand it. Maybe a poet could, though.

"Well, you know," I began, "all my grandparents were born in Galveston County. The Porters and the Graces have roots firmly in the soil around here, or there."

"So you want to stay because everyone else has?"

Roots, place, rooted to this water-logged place. "I like feeling I belong somewhere."

"You feel you belong in Clear Lake?"

"You know Clear Lake is a new town. It sprang up in the late fifties and early sixties with NASA. But the other small towns in the area, League City, Webster, Kemah, Seabrook, have been there a long time."

"I'm from there too, you know, Annie," he said, with a grin.

"Oh, right." I smiled. "Sorry."

"So you feel you belong there?"

"In a way. And also, not," I admitted. "It's funny. All my friends, the kids at school, they're all so sure about what they want to do, whether it's stay, or whether it's go off to college because they want to be this or be that. I want to do both. I want to stay. I want to go. I wish I knew."

I'd surprised myself, talking to a stranger this much about my feelings about *after*—after graduation. I looked at Tommy, who was listening intently. Listening like he didn't already have in mind what he wanted me to do.

When Mark listened, he was all set to influence me to stay.

When Mom or my teachers or Lea listened, I could see their opinions about my life perched on their tongues ready to spill out.

Their expectations were so loud in my head I couldn't hear my own wishes.

But with Tommy, as he sat here, just listening, not expecting, that chorus of voices was finally, blissfully, hushed.

I looked at him, grateful. I leaned forward. "I don't know what I want to do." I sat on my hands to warm them. They were chilled from clutching the cold beer.

He nodded. "I know that feeling."

"Really? Is that why you left USC?"

"Not exactly."

I studied him. His mind was someplace else. "Why, then?"

He swirled his beer. "I know what you're feeling because I've been there. I *am* there. Early on, my mom and especially my dad had their own ideas about what they wanted me to do." He shrugged. "When I told them what I wanted . . ." He shook his head. "They didn't like it."

"So," I said quietly, "what did you want to do?" I was very curious. It must be something cool and adventurous. I could see Tommy hiking in the Amazon looking for wild plant life.

"I want to be a teacher. A high school history teacher."

My surprise must have showed on my face.

He laughed. "Not what you thought I'd say?"

"No," I acknowledged. What was with hot guys wanting to be high school teachers? It was usually crones with rulers. Okay, maybe not. But it definitely wasn't guys like Tommy and Mr. Williams. This was a coup for teenage girls.

"Yeah," said Tommy. "So that's it."

"And your parents don't want you to?"

"A loser job, according to my father. I wouldn't be able to support myself, a family, on and on."

"They'd rather you work in the plant?"

"Well, no." He took a drink of his beer. "Nothing wrong with the plant, you know."

"No, I know."

"Your dad's a good worker, Annie. You seem to think he's, I don't know, in a dead-end job or something. He's good at his job. Really good. And he likes it."

I was quiet.

"I'm sorry," Tommy said. "If I said too much."

"I'm just thinking about what you said."

He nodded. "So all you want to do is drink in every country in Epcot." He laughed and pointed at my beer. "At this rate, it will take us a long time!"

I looked at his empty glass and smiled. "I didn't say I wanted to finish a glass, just that I wanted to drink in every country."

"Well, then, you ready to go to France?"

"I think Canada is closer."

"Who cares what's closer? We've got time."

He stood and threw some cash on the table for Jane Austen. We were off to France.

CHAPTER 27

I couldn't remember when I'd had such a good time. I felt guilty all the time with Mark, like I wasn't doing enough for him. I didn't know when things had become that way between us. We'd been good friends first, with easy laughs and sweet—and passionate—kisses. But senior year had changed us.

"Ready for Magic Kingdom?" Tommy asked. "Space Mountain? Big Thunder Mountain Railroad? More food?"

He reminded me of a kid wound up on candy.

He grinned. "What?"

We'd been wandering the countries of Epcot for hours. Drinking in every country had become tasting in every country, whether it was a pastry in France or a Coke in the good old USA. We were now eating enchiladas in Mexico, or trying to. I was stuffed. "I'll be sick if I eat one more thing."

"Right. No more eating. But you still gotta see Mickey Mouse." He hopped up like a spring released. Man, the guy had energy. Mark moved slower. I knew I should stop comparing them. Mark was my boyfriend. Tommy was a friend, my dad's friend really. And Mom hadn't been particularly pleased about that.

Oh no.

I hadn't thought of Mom since I'd been here. I hadn't *talked* to Mom. I was supposed to call her when I got to Cocoa Beach. That was last night, a lifetime ago.

I jumped up. "I need a phone."

Tommy scrunched his eyes.

"I need to call my mom!"

"Hold on there, little missy."

"You don't understand. I need to call my mom."

"Okay, let's find a phone," he said, grabbing my hand and heading back toward the park entrance.

His hand was in mine. My hand was in his. In the midst of the panic about Mom being freaked out and worried, I thought about the feel of Tommy's hand, strong and warm. I liked it. I liked the way a girl we passed looked at Tommy, then glanced back at me, surprising me with the open curiosity on her face.

"There's a phone in the information office," said Tommy, weaving us through the crowds. "They'll let us use it."

Huh? What were we doing?

Oh, yeah, Mom. I had to call my mom. I'd walk faster, but Tommy was already pulling me along at a good clip. Again, I thought about how I sauntered around with Mark, always going at his speed, which was easy and slow. He would never go faster. He would just pull me back, slowing me down, getting irritated if I walked at my own pace.

There was a line in the information center. Of course there was a line. This was Disney World. But everyone at the desk ahead had a Disney smile on his or her Disney face. They were always so happy. It was a little creepy, but I liked it.

It was warmer in the office. And Tommy was still holding my hand. I had a boyfriend. I couldn't be holding some other guy's hand, even if that guy was the finest guy I'd ever met in my life.

No.

I let go.

"So you were supposed to call your mom when you got here," Tommy said, looking at me.

"She's going to kill me."

Tommy looked thoughtful. "What are you going to tell her?"

"That I'm in Florida, that I made it here safely. I'm sure she's freaking out. What time is it in Houston?"

Tommy glanced at his watch. "Three."

"She's gonna be mad."

"She'll be worried. But when she finds out you're okay, she'll be okay."

I didn't think so.

"So," Tommy asked, "are you going to tell her you're here with me and not your dad? And that we're sharing a motel room together?" I bit my lip. Our eyes locked.

"Nothing happened," I said. Tommy was looking at me, with raised eyebrows. Nothing happened? I couldn't believe I actually said that. Nothing happened?

Tommy flashed that wide smile of his. The older woman in front of us gave us a quick, amused look.

"Am I blushing?" I said softly. "I'm blushing, aren't I?"

"From here," said Tommy, touching my forehead with one finger, "to here," he ended, moving to my chin.

He was looking right into my eyes. There was a beat of stillness as I stared back. It was one of those sweet moments that could turn into a long, deep kiss, if we weren't standing in a crowded room. And if I didn't already have a boyfriend.

I looked at my tennis shoes. That seemed a safe place to look. When I glanced back up, the moment was gone.

"What's wrong?" I asked him. He was going through his pockets.

"Did I give you the motel key?"

I shook my head. Again, I looked at my shoes.

"We can get another one when we go back." Tommy craned his neck, looking at the people working the desk. "What's taking so long?"

When I finally did get to a phone, my hands were shaking. "Hello."

Mom *sounded* calm. "Mom?"

"Hi, Annie!" she said, in a very happy voice. Something was wrong. Why wasn't she mad? "It's so good to hear your voice, Annie. Are you having fun?"

"Yeah." I heard someone talking in the background. "Is Donald there?" So Donald's there and Mom completely forgets about her own daughter?

"She's having fun, Donald," said Mom.

I couldn't believe this. I'd been so worried Mom was in a panic, and here she was almost giddy. It was because she was with her boyfriend. She was becoming one of those kind of mothers. But I should be glad. I was off the hook.

"Your dad called and said y'all were having a good time down there. But it's still good to hear your voice. Because, well . . ." Mom didn't finish, but said something else to Donald. She must be covering the phone. Her voice was muffled.

Tommy was looking at me. I rolled my eyes at him.

So Dad had called. I wondered what he'd said. Obviously, he hadn't told Mom what was really going on, which made me feel very relieved and very anxious. I hadn't had a chance to think about what I was going to tell Mom. I was sure I would have ended up telling her the truth because I'd never been a very good liar. At this moment, it was very disappointing Dad hadn't passed along that gene.

But now—

"So what are y'all doing?" I asked.

Mom laughed. "You're the one on vacation in Florida. So they're going to launch tomorrow, is that right?"

"Yeah," I said. "We're at Disney right now."

"That's great! Have you visited that new park?"

"Epcot? Mom, it's been open for four years."

"Oh, that's right."

"I have to go," I said. Mom sounded so happy. I thought she'd be a little worried. She'd been so worried when we left. Worried about Dad. And it turned out Mom had been right about that.

"Okay, Annie," said Mom. "You'll call tomorrow? I mean, it's good your dad called, but I want to hear from you."

"I'll call after the launch."

"You're leaving right after?"

"Yep. Back on the road tomorrow afternoon."

"Okay," said Mom. "Talk to you then."

I hung up.

"What?" Tommy asked.

"Huh? Nothing." I looked at him, shaking my head. "Ready to go to Magic Kingdom?"

CHAPTER 28

Crowds, dark, fear, stars, alone, Tommy touching my hair—

Then we were off. Our space shuttle whirled to the right. We entered a long tunnel with flashing blue lights. I laughed.

"You okay up there?" asked Tommy, patting my head from his seat behind me in our space shuttle.

"Yeah," I told him.

His hands were on my shoulders. "This is going to be fun, Annie."

A sweet rush of excitement flipped my stomach over. I thought of the astronauts and the giddy anticipation they must feel twenty-four hours before launching into space. A girl in front of me screamed, and I laughed. The ride hadn't really started—

"Whooooooa," I shouted as our rocket flew down the track, pushing and pulling us through turns, and dropping, dropping. I could see little—the person in front of me, other space rockets in the distance, the dark sky filled with stars and comets. I was flying.

"Oh man!" yelled Tommy in a voice filled with amazement. "So coooool!"

It was cool, so cool, and I wanted it to go on and on, just riding this rocket, alone, but not, in the dark, but not, with this sweet feeling soaring through me. I was happy, so happy.

And then I was screaming along with the girl in front of me as our space shuttle barreled down the last steep incline. I could feel the smile on my face as we went down and down, and the wind rushed by my cheeks.

When we reached the red wormhole at the end of the ride, I was so let down that it was coming to an end.

"Liked that, did you?" asked Tommy, throwing an arm around my shoulder when we got off the ride.

"Oh *yeah*."

He laughed. "*Oh yeah* is right."

"Wanna go again?" I asked.

He grinned and grabbed my hand, pulling me past the people taking their time on the way out.

"The line will be long," I called out as we jogged.

He just grinned again, and I grinned back. That smile stayed on my face for two more long waits in line and flights through the dark.

It was late when we got back to the motel.

I plopped into an uncomfortable chair in the lobby while Tommy stood in line to pick up a new key. Next to me, a couple of men with beers in their hands were talking. When I heard one of them mention the shuttle, my ears perked up.

"They think it's going to be too cold," one of the men said.

"Isn't this the fourth delay?"

"More than that. We're never getting this one off the ground."

"Excuse me?" I asked.

The men looked at me expectantly.

"Are you talking about the shuttle launch? Has it been rescheduled again?"

The first man nodded while the other took a sip of his drink. "Slipped until Monday."

"Thanks," I said, feeling enormously let down. And I remembered the lines from May Swenson's poem "August 19, Pad 19":

All my system's go, but oh,
an anger of the air won't let me go.
On the screen the blip is MISSION SCRUBBED . . .

Tommy was also disappointed. "Aw, man. You got me really excited about this."

"I thought you wanted to come all along," I said, on the way back to the room.

"I did. But your talking about Christa and the flight all the way here has gotten me jazzed."

I wondered how this was going to affect my plans. I wasn't going home. A day ago, I would've thought Mom would have forced me to come home, would have driven over here to get me. But after talking to her today, I didn't think Mom would care that I wasn't coming home tomorrow. Of course, she didn't know about my being here alone with Tommy.

But it was a relief too, wasn't it? In a way, it was. But something else nagged at me.

Oh, forget it, I thought, sitting in the chair in a corner.

I picked up my knitting, studying my work. I was so close to being done. I got back to it.

Tommy flipped through the channels on the television, settling on *Magnum, P.I.* I realized, with a start, that this was the first time I'd felt really relaxed with Tommy since I'd met him.

He lay back against the headboard with the pillows propping him up, grinning with that impossibly infectious grin. And in a second, I went from relaxed to anxious. I shouldn't be looking at him all the time.

I'd only known him for three days, but it seemed like so much longer.

He glanced at me. "You want to go to the beach tomorrow?"

I grinned. "It's too cold for a launch, but we can still go."

"We'll bundle up."

"Let's get up early again, Tommy. I'd really like to see the sunrise over the Atlantic. I bet it's beautiful."

"You have the best ideas," he said.

"Not really."

"Are you kidding me? This whole trip was your idea."

"I guess it was," I said. Somehow I'd gotten myself off my couch. I knew if I hadn't met Christa, I wouldn't be here, in Florida, with Tommy. It was amazing how one person could make you see things differently and change what you did. But it wasn't Christa making the changes: it was me. She'd just been the inspiration.

Maybe I *would* see the world, starting with France. I could follow the footsteps of Van Gogh's life.

"Done," I said, jumping up.

"With your scarf?" Tommy asked.

"No, silly," I said, reaching over and wrapping it around his neck. "With *your* scarf."

He looked so touched it made me smile.

"I *was* making it for me," I said. "But you looked so cold when we were camping on the beach, I decided you needed one." I pulled at the bottom of it. "There, I made it longer."

He took my hand, startling me, and pulled me down beside him. He grabbed both my hands. "Thank you, Annie."

I felt shy. "You're welcome."

But he kept looking at me. And suddenly, I remembered how very alone we were in this room. He kept looking. I could see in his eyes he wanted to kiss me. That scared me. What scared me more was how much I wanted him to kiss me. And that he saw it.

He drew closer, but I looked off.

I stood quickly. "You're welcome," I said. "You're welcome." I had to keep saying it, so I didn't sit back down with him.

He didn't say anything, but looked thoughtful. "Thanks for the scarf, Annie."

I curled under the covers in my bed, feeling excited, hopeful, sad, and frightened out of my damn mind.

CHAPTER 29

The pink sunrise leisurely stretched along the horizon. We were drinking hot coffee and sitting on a concrete table on the beach, quietly watching.

"I can't believe they didn't launch," Tommy said, opening the sack of doughnuts. "It's a beautiful morning."

"Beautiful."

And the rich colors in the sky, the soothing rush of the waves, the fine sand, was only part of it. Tommy was the other part. I swung my feet back and forth and munched on doughnuts. I watched a crab crawl by and remembered how Mark and I used to capture them and try to keep them in castles of sand.

I hadn't called Mark yet. I knew he was probably mad about it. In the last two years, I'd never gone three days without talking to him. I rarely left Clear Lake, but Mark did, to go surfing or to see his mother's family in west Texas. And he'd call me every day.

Tommy and I sat on the table, just enjoying the morning

as it warmed up. Like Tommy, I couldn't believe they didn't launch. It was so nice out. Christa must be anxious, ready to go, tired of the emotional roller coaster of delays.

Some tourists walked by wearing Teacher-in-Space T-shirts.

"Hey, I want one of those!" I said, knowing I didn't have the money.

"Really?"

"Too dorky?" I asked.

"Not if you want it," he said, jiggling my arm.

I lost my words. If every time he touched me I forgot how to talk, it was going to get really weird between us.

More people were out now, moms and dads, kids and teenagers, young couples and older people. Some dared to venture out into the waves, but most were walking, throwing Frisbees, enjoying the day—waiting for the launch. Christa flying was like one of us flying. The newspaper said the renewed interest in NASA and the space program was all because of her.

The seagulls squawked overhead, taking dives to snatch up something from the water or the junk food on the shore. I laughed when one swooped down to steal a cinnamon roll from a nearby table. The owner of the breakfast threw his arms up in the air, but was laughing in disbelief.

Seagulls, hunger, desire, white wings, blue sky, soar, Christa, soar.

"That guy looks like my dad," Tommy said, pointing to the man who'd been ripped off by a seagull, "except for the part where he's laughing."

"Your dad never laughs?"

"He doesn't stay still long enough. No vacations. No hobbies. No interests but business. Not like your dad. My dad works all the time. He didn't go on one summer trip or spring vacation with my mom and sister and me. Can you imagine that? Not wanting to go anywhere."

"Maybe he likes where he is," I said.

"All he cares about is work. Not a surprise he thinks I'm a total washout."

"Tommy," I said, "he can't think that."

"Oh yes, he does. We have the traditional father-son relationship, where the son disappoints the father for not living up to his potential. It's an old story."

"He thinks that because you want to be a teacher?" I asked.

"Yes, among other things." He looked at me. "You look so concerned." He tweaked my hand. "Don't worry. I'm used to it."

"But you're not really, are you?" I asked. "It bothers you."

"Not enough to get a business degree like he wants me to," he said. "The thing is, I admire my dad. I wouldn't want his life, but he's very smart, motivated. He thinks for himself. I like that about him."

"You want him," I said softly, "to see something in you that he admires."

"Yeah, I do." He was gazing at me. "You are such a surprise, Annie."

"Why do you say that?" I asked, thinking of jumping off the bench to throw my trash away.

He reached over and tucked my flying hair behind my ear.

It was his touch that stopped me. He quickly dropped his hand, but was still looking at me. "It's going to be hard to go back to my life in Texas after meeting you. It'll feel empty without you there."

I didn't move. I couldn't seem to move.

He leaned in, his face close to mine, his eyes looking into mine. I still didn't move away. And then I closed my eyes, not wanting to worry or to think, and I let his lips touch mine, and his kiss was sweet and tentative, which I didn't expect. So I kissed him back.

We drew apart, looking at one another, and I was surprised to find my hands were touching his face. I dropped them and pulled away.

He reached for me, taking my hand. "Annie."

"I can't do this."

"I'm sorry. I shouldn't have." And now our only touch was his hand holding on to my fingers.

But I let go and slid off the table.

We started walking along the water's edge.

"I have a boyfriend, Tommy," I said, not able to look at him, my eyes burning. "And not just a casual boyfriend. A guy I've been with a long time."

"Do you love him?"

"Do I love him?" I asked.

"Yeah, that guy who punches at doors."

"He doesn't normally do that."

"Just sometimes?"

"I've never seen him do that before," I said. "Only when some hot guy . . ." I glanced at him, embarrassed.

He laughed like he couldn't stop. "You should see your face."

I touched my cheeks. "Am I hot?"

He laughed even harder.

"Not that funny," I said, knowing my face was bright red. And the more I thought about it, the hotter my face became. But then I started laughing too. And we couldn't stop for a while. I held on to his arm and covered my mouth trying— and failing—to stop the guffaws from coming out. Which made him laugh even more.

"Enough," I said. "Enough."

"I'm sorry," he said, stopping, but still grinning. I hit his arm playfully, and started walking again, with him beside me. I was still embarrassed, but I felt closer to him suddenly, with the kiss and shared laughter.

"So do you, Annie?" he asked again. "Do you love him?"

I thought of Mark, the way he would place his hand lightly on the small of my back when we walked through the halls at school. How he'd stroll through cemeteries and read old gravestones with me. How he'd taught me to shoot a rubber band when we were in fifth grade. And how I hit him in the nose accidentally with one as I practiced. I could still see his little fifth-grade face with the red mark on his little fifth-grade nose.

Did I love him? I just didn't know anymore.

CHAPTER 30

We'd only been away from home for four days, but it felt like a whole season had passed, like Tommy was the only person I knew now, the only person in my life.

That was why it was such a shock to see Dad at the motel when we got back from the beach. We ran into the lobby, away from the rain. The weather front that had delayed the launch had finally arrived here.

"Hey there, Annie," Dad said, giving me a quick hug.

"You look terrible, Dad," I said, pinching my nose. He smelled and felt like rotting sandy refuse on a beach.

"I've been sleeping out under the stars."

"You made it!" said Tommy. "How's the car?"

Dad laughed. "She's running, after I emptied out my bank account."

"Running's good."

"That it is, Tommy. Thanks, son, for taking care of my girl." Dad squinted at me. "What's wrong? Your eyes are puffy." He glanced at Tommy, either with a look of suspicion or just confusion; it was hard to tell.

"Sand in the eyes, Dad," I said quickly. "Come on up to our room. The room." I wasn't sure how he was going to take the news that Tommy and I had been staying in a room together. I didn't think he'd mind. He was always so laid-back about stuff.

"The motel isn't that nice, but it's cheap," I said, on the way.

"And it's got a good location," Dad said. "Not too far from the beach."

"Nothing's far from the ocean here."

"Where are Bonnie and Clyde?" he asked.

"They had to go back," I explained. "Ready to get wet? The stairs aren't covered."

"Bonnie and Clyde left?" he asked, then got quiet.

Tommy was quiet too.

"Let's go," I said, going out into the rain and up the concrete steps. I didn't want to look at Dad. I was thinking about the kiss with Tommy and was afraid my face would give it away. Then Dad would think something worse than just Tommy and I sleeping in the same room together.

Dad was close behind me when we went in the room. I grabbed some towels out of the bathroom and gave one to each of them.

Dad looked relieved to see the beds unmade, both of them. But his lips were still pressed together in an irritated grimace as he dried his neck and face.

"The maid service isn't the best here," I said.

Dad looked at Tommy. "I don't like this. You staying here alone with my daughter? For God's sake, Tommy, you're twenty-two years old."

"Dad—"

"I'm talking to Tommy."

"You're right, Jesse," said Tommy, looking very guilty. "I'm sorry."

"I don't like it, Tommy. Not at all."

"Dad, stop talking to him about this. I'm eighteen," I said. "I'm an adult. You talk to me about it. I make my own decisions."

"All right, then. What were you thinking, Annie?"

"I was thinking I didn't have much money, and Tommy offered to pay for the room. You know, Dad, you sent me off with these people you didn't even know—"

"I thought you were safe with him." He shot Tommy a look.

"And I was safe. Nothing happened, Dad." There was no way I was going to tell him about the kiss. "It was fine."

He pulled one of his hand-rolled cigarettes out of his pocket. "I gotta go for a smoke." He left, slamming the door.

Tommy and I looked at one another.

"It's my fault, Annie. I'm sorry. I just don't think of you as someone in high school. You seem older than that to me."

That made me smile. "Don't tell my dad that, okay?"

"No," he said, shaking his head. "No way."

Eventually Dad came back, smelling like smoke, quiet. At least he wasn't so mad anymore. He didn't bring up the subject again, but I worried he might tell Mom. But then I dismissed that fear: he wouldn't tell her because she'd blame him for it.

"So they launch tomorrow?" he asked me. He still wouldn't look at Tommy.

"At 9:36 a.m.," I said. "We need to leave early, though. About 7 a.m."

"It can't take more than thirty minutes to get out there," Dad said. "And it's not going to lift off any earlier."

"Lea's mom said we needed to be at the gate two hours before launch because there's going to be a lot of people."

"But to leave at seven? I'm still on Central time."

"Dad."

"Fine," he said. "Early it is."

He didn't mention that the launch delays would also delay my getting back to school or his getting back to work. Of course, it wouldn't be in Dad's nature to worry about that anyway.

It was good he was here, that there was a dad to keep Tommy and me apart. I had things to think about.

I wondered if you could be in love with one person and want to kiss and be with another. I hadn't been thinking about what Mark had been doing these last few days. I hadn't called him. I should be thinking about my boyfriend. Maybe it was because I just met Tommy and everything was new and different.

This trip was supposed to be about fun, an escape, a break from thinking about big decisions. It was a chance to watch someone who was brave and sure of herself reach for something beyond her ordinary life.

I wasn't anything like Christa. I was the opposite of her. But I'd been thinking that if a teacher living a simple life in Concord just one year ago could now be launching on the space shuttle, then maybe my life could be an adventure too.

Everyone around me knew what to do next. They were making choices about their lives like it was the easiest thing in the world to slide into college or to send in an application to NASA to go into space. Even Mark was sure what he wanted, which was to marry me and live in Clear Lake for the rest of our lives.

Mark knew me so well. He knew my mom, my grandma, my cousins, my friends. He understood that part of me that loved to cross the Kemah Bridge over and over again.

But there was Tommy . . . he was older than I was. He was cooler. He was prettier. He listened to me. I'd even told him about my poetry. I'd never shared that with Mark.

Yes, it was good Dad was here.

Dad and Tommy settled in to watch the Super Bowl. I read, and listened to the rain outside. I hoped it would stop soon. To come all this way and not see a launch would be so disappointing. Not to mention the frustration poor Christa would feel at being delayed again. Surely it would happen tomorrow.

I also sneaked peeks at Tommy. I liked watching him watch the game and talk to my dad.

The Bears beat the Patriots by a whole bunch.

We got a cot, and Tommy insisted on sleeping on it. It was a little weird settling down to sleep in a room with not just Tommy, but Dad too. I hadn't slept in the same room with Dad since I was a little girl. And to have another guy there. Weird.

Dad stepped out to smoke another cigarette on the balcony, which made things a little easier. I curled up in my bed and pretended to sleep. But I couldn't stop thinking.

I needed to talk to Mark, to tell him how I was feeling, how confused I was about us. It would break his heart. But it wasn't fair to keep this from him. It would have to wait until we got back.

I would stay away from Tommy in the meantime. I would.

Golly Moses, as Lea would say, I needed to buck up here. Here I was lying awake worried about talking to Mark, and right down the road the astronauts were probably all sound asleep, even though they were about to go for a high ride.

CHAPTER 31

The next morning was cold for Florida. The news said it was forty degrees.

"This is Florida," Dad said. "It's supposed to be warm all year."

"The news guy said it's usually not like this."

"They should have launched yesterday morning," said Tommy. "Geez."

I grabbed a sleeping bag and some blankets. "I wish I'd brought something thicker than my jean jacket." Tommy helped me gather things up.

We drove out to the space center with our car pass in the windshield. We weren't in any VIP area or anything like that, but we did have a great view of the pad across the swampy water of the Banana River. We parked alongside other cars on a small strip of land and carried our sleeping bags and cooler out to a grassy area to find a spot.

Excitement was in the air. I dodged a couple of laughing kids who ran in front of me, one of them stepping on my toes.

"Well, ow," I said.

"Sorry!" the boy yelled over his shoulder as he chased the other one.

We spread out the sleeping bags. I wrapped myself in a blanket. Almost every bit of grass was taken up by a blanket or a folding chair. People were everywhere with cameras and grins and coats. It was cold.

At the river's edge, photographers had set up tripods. A few people had telescopes. I itched to take a look at the pad through one.

"How far away is that?" asked Tommy, looking toward the pad.

"Six or seven miles," I told him. I sipped the hot coffee Dad had gotten for us at the diner. He'd bought a thermos full. "Will you hold my coffee? I want to take a picture."

"Sure," Tommy said, taking my coffee. "The shuttle is going to look very small in your photo, though."

As I looked through the viewfinder, I knew he was right. "Still, I want a photo." I snapped a couple of shots, then turned around and took one of Tommy while he grinned at me. That was one photo Mark wouldn't see. But I'd show it to Lea. I had to have something left of Tommy after this trip.

Announcements were made over a loudspeaker. It sounded like some public-affairs guy at NASA. We could also hear some technical chatter going on between the launch-control center and the astronauts, who were already onboard and strapped into their seats, according to the very informative young boy standing next to me.

"They're lying on their backs in the crew cabin," he

told me, gesturing with his hands, "and their feet are up in the air."

Christa was a long way from her classroom in Concord. There she was, way over there, across the water, in the shuttle, on the launchpad.

"That can't be comfortable," Tommy said.

"No, it's not," the boy said very seriously.

Tommy started asking the boy questions because he did appear to be our expert here, even though he couldn't have been more than ten or eleven.

I looked over at my father. "Dad?"

"Yep?" he asked, looking through binoculars at the pad.

"What did you tell Mom?" I asked, jumping up and down to get warm.

The question startled him a little. "You want the binoculars?"

"No, Dad." I pulled them down from his eyes. "Stop changing the subject. What did you tell her?"

"Honey, why do you want to be worrying your mother for? Everything's fine. I knew she'd freak if I told her the car had broken down and you'd gone on without me. She doesn't know Tommy like I do," he said. "She wouldn't have understood."

"Dad—"

"Everything was fine, right?"

"Yes, Dad—"

"And Tommy took care of you, right?"

"Dad—"

"And was a perfect gentleman, right?"

"Dad!" I called out.

I glanced at Tommy, who was obviously pretending not to be listening. I was sure Dad wouldn't be one to think a kiss was ungentlemanly, but Tommy looked worried. Yesterday Dad had been plenty mad about the motel room.

Dad laughed. "Annie, everything's fine. What your mom doesn't know won't hurt her."

"Okay."

"And anyway," he continued, "she seemed distracted."

"What does that mean?" I asked, but I had thought the same thing.

Dad shrugged. "I don't know," he said, looking through the binoculars again. I knew I wasn't going to get anything else out of him.

I looked over at Tommy and he winked at me. My heart fluttered. Or was it my stomach? Something fluttered. One wink and I was feeling off balance: I was in trouble.

Then I heard the crowd groan. "What?" I asked, looking at NASA Boy. "What happened? I wasn't listening."

"They're holding the countdown."

"But," Tommy asked, "didn't you say they've got *planned* holds in the countdown?"

"What do you mean by planned holds?" I asked.

"T minus twenty minutes doesn't mean the launch is twenty minutes away," Tommy explained. "Because NASA counts the clock down to certain times and then holds there."

"But they should be starting the clock again," said the boy. "There's a problem with the hatch."

Dad laughed. "Seriously? They can't close the door?"

"They closed it, but they're not sure it's locked."

"How do you know all this, kid?" Dad asked.

The boy pointed to the loudspeakers.

I laughed. "I guess he listens, and we don't."

"My daughter knows the teacher," Dad told the boy's father.

"Really?" asked the dad, taking off his sunglasses. "Is she your teacher?"

"No," I said. "I just met her twice."

"She ate dinner with her," Dad said.

NASA Boy was suddenly very interested in me. From the way he was looking at me, I thought he might be falling in love. "How many people were there?"

"At dinner?" I asked him.

"Yeah, were there like a hundred?" he asked, waving his arms. "Was it a big dinner with lots of people there?"

"No. There were about twelve. It was at someone's house."

"You are so lucky!"

"What's Christa McAuliffe like?" his father asked.

"She's friendly, really nice," I said, feeling a little special.

Both the boy and his dad were nodding. The dad looked back at the shuttle. "Well, I bet she's tired of waiting."

The boy's freckles were small and perfect dots sprinkled across his nose and cheeks. "Did you know there were nine shuttle flights last year? And thirteen more scheduled for this year?"

"Nope."

"Did you know that they want to launch twenty-four a year?"

"Really. Wow."

"I want to be an astronaut," said the boy. "Do you?"

"No," I said.

"Why not?"

"I don't like small spaces."

"But you'd be going into space! And you could look out the window and see the Earth. That'd make you forget about the small spaces!"

"You're probably right."

He rubbed his chin like an old person, looking at the shuttle in the distance. "I'd really like to go into space one day."

Finally, NASA was satisfied the hatch was locked. But when the technicians closed it again, a pesky four-inch bolt kept them from removing the door handle.

"These things happen," NASA Boy told me. His father gave me a quick smile over the boy's head.

"Hey, anyone want to play cards?" I asked. "I brought some."

"Sure!" said the kid, who just might've been my new boyfriend.

The five of us settled down to play Gin and War for a while, but the wind had picked up. We had to put cards under our legs to keep them from blowing away.

NASA eventually got rid of the handle—with a hacksaw and a drill, which cracked Dad up—but by that time, the winds were so high there was a possibility the shuttle wouldn't be able to do an RTLS—Return to Launch Site abort—in the event of an emergency.

So there was one more delay while we waited for the winds to die down. The boy and his father pulled sandwiches out of their cooler. I was too nervous to be hungry.

I lay back on the sleeping bag and covered myself with the blanket. It had warmed up a little—now in the fifties—but the wind was very strong, gusting up to thirty miles per hour and keeping us cold. Tommy lay down beside me. I looked over at him and he grinned. He was so good looking it was ridiculous.

I turned over to my side and looked at him. He touched my nose. "You look like Rudolph." Then he took his new red scarf and wrapped it around both of us. "It's good you made it so long. It warms both our necks."

"It's not really long enough for both of us."

"But isn't this nice?" he whispered.

"Annie, you won't believe this." I looked up at Dad, who was pointing toward the pad. "Did you hear the announcement?" He glanced back at me quickly.

"No," I said, jumping up, a bit worried that I'd been staring into Tommy's eyes. I couldn't stay away from this guy. "What's going on, Dad?" I looked at my watch. It was just after noon.

Dad hesitated for a moment, looking at Tommy getting up, and then back at me. "I don't think it's going to happen, Annie."

"What, the launch? Don't say that."

Even NASA Boy looked worried.

"Man, I wish they'd launch this bird," Dad said.

The boy was shaking his head. "The astronauts have been lying on their backs for four hours."

His father looked our way. "I don't think they're ever going to get this shuttle off the ground."

Tommy and I started to listen to the public-affairs guy

talking over the speaker system. The wind was really gusting. I'd drunk so much coffee, I was sick to my stomach.

And then came this:

"WE HAVE JUST HAD AN ANNOUNCEMENT FROM
THE LAUNCH DIRECTOR TO THE CREW AND THE
LAUNCH TEAM THAT WE ARE GOING TO SCRUB
TODAY."

The crowd groaned.

"Aw, man!" the boy yelled out.

"I can't believe that!" said his father, pouring out his
coffee. "That's it for us."

"What do you mean, Dad?"

"We've got to get back to Georgia. I've got work."

"Daaad," the boy complained, his shoulders slumped.
Poor kid.

We said our good-byes, and they walked off—NASA Boy
dragging his feet.

"*We're* staying," I told Dad.

"This has been one interesting trip, Annie," Dad said. "At
least we're not at the plant, right, Tommy?"

"True," said Tommy. "And the trip's had its good points."
He began helping me fold up the blankets and sleeping bags.

CHAPTER 32

We'd already checked out of the motel, as we were going to drive back to Houston after the launch. We had to see if we could get our room back, which turned out not to be a problem.

"A lot of people are going home," said the desk clerk, shrugging. "They can't stay for another attempt."

I asked Dad and Tommy if they'd bring me back a burger from the diner. It'd been a long day. The traffic had been heavy and slow coming out of the space center. And after the scrub, people were not in good driving moods. It was nice to be by myself for a little bit.

I settled down to watch the news, welcoming the warmth of the room after being out in the cold wind all day. The anchor began the newscast by saying, "Yet another costly, red-faces-all-around space-shuttle-launch delay. This time a bad bolt on a hatch and a bad-weather bolt from the blue are being blamed. What's more, a rescheduled launch for tomorrow doesn't look good either." He called it a "high-tech low comedy."

The news showed footage of the weary astronauts leaving the Astrovan for their crew quarters. They looked disappointed and frustrated.

Enough television. I turned it off.

We were not going to leave for home until we launched. I was determined to argue with both Mom and Dad if they refused me. I had to see this liftoff. The more we delayed, the more I wanted to be there when Christa left for space.

I was lying on the bed trying to read *The Letters of Vincent Van Gogh* when Tommy came in with a foam container. I sat up, sitting cross-legged, laying down Vincent's words about how the sun shone more brightly when you were in love.

"Your burger," he said, handing it to me. "And fries."

"Thanks." I put it on the bedside table. "Where's my dad?"

"Talking to the waitress. You doing okay?"

"Sure," I said.

"I don't think you are."

"I just have a lot on my mind, a lot to think about."

"Mark?" he asked.

I smiled ruefully. "I thought this would be a road trip of pure fun. I didn't expect to be faced with more confusing decisions. It was supposed to be a break from all that."

Tommy sat down beside me on the bed. "Annie, have you thought you might be with Mark just out of habit, because you've known him so long?"

"Well, I'm glad you've figured it out," I said.

"I came up with the answer I like best." He smiled.

"Yes, you did," I said, fingering the red heart on my locket.

"Tell me, Annie," he said. "Is there hope for me here? With you?"

"There's . . . hope."

"Okay. And if there is, shouldn't we have a chance to see what's there? What's going on with us?"

"Not now. Mark doesn't know . . . any of this yet."

Tommy was quiet for a moment. "You could call him."

"Call him?" I asked incredulously. "Call him?"

Tommy took my hand. "I like you, Annie." My stomach flipped. "More than I've liked anyone in a long time."

"You don't even know me," I said, thinking of Mark and how long we'd been going together and how long we'd been friends before that.

"I feel like I do. From your dad. But also you're just . . . something else," he said, shaking his head. "I can talk to you. You're kind. You're a thinker. You're funny."

Little tremors of nervous happiness went through me. I couldn't remember ever feeling quite this way. "I don't think I'm funny."

"Annie," he said, squeezing my hand. "I want to be with you. I want this vacation to go on and on. I don't want to go home, because I don't know if you'll agree to see me when we go home. And Mark, I'm so jealous of that guy. So, yeah, it's selfish of me."

He was too close, and I couldn't think. I tried to pull my hand away.

"Annie, don't pull away. Please give us a chance," he said softly. He leaned forward, touching my cheek with his hand.

I shook my head, pulled back. "I can't."

I left my hand in his.

"Just tell me if you feel the same way," he said.

I couldn't help the smile that flitted across my lips. "I like you," I said, which I knew was a drastic understatement to the way I felt, the way my heart was pounding.

He grinned. "That's good."

"I can't do anything until I talk to Mark."

What was I saying? Being here with Tommy made me think I should be with him. But was that just because Mark wasn't here? Maybe it was natural to have these feelings. It could be physical attraction and nothing else. I pulled my hand away.

"Okay, but . . ." Tommy was quiet for a moment. "We don't have to wait—"

"Yes, we do," I said. "Mark has been my boyfriend for two years. I've known him almost all my life."

"When you talk to him, will you tell him about me?"

"Of course I will." *If* I decide to tell him. What was I getting myself into? I couldn't think.

Tommy shrugged. "It'll just piss him off."

"Yeah. And hurt him. A lot." I felt very sad when I thought of Mark. "But I have to. He's not just my boyfriend. He's always been my friend," I said, my voice breaking.

"And see," said Tommy, "your caring about him like that, it makes me like you even more."

I smiled.

"Which makes me want to kiss you again. It's been very difficult to sit here and not kiss you."

That sweet feeling folded into me, layered with the sad feelings. I tried not to look at him. How I wanted to kiss him too. I stood up. "I gotta go . . . somewhere. Outside for just a minute."

"Okay," he said, surprised. "But it's dark, and it's cold."

"I'll just stand right outside the door," I said, my hand on the knob. Cold would be good right now.

"But you don't have your coat." He grabbed it off the chair and handed it to me.

"Thank you."

He grinned. My knees weakened. I couldn't think around him.

"I'll just be outside," I said.

CHAPTER 33

Hey, little girl, what'cha doing out here?"

I stomped my feet to get warm. It was freezing outside. "I'm hardly little, Dad." I pulled my gloves out of my pocket and put them on.

He leaned up against the railing, the wind blowing his hair around. "Mind if I smoke another?"

I gave him a look.

"Fine," he said, slipping a cigarette back in his coat pocket. He studied me for a moment, which I tried to ignore. Why couldn't he go inside?

"What's going on with you, Annie?"

I shrugged.

"Don't shrug a shrugger. Something's eating at you."

"Nothing, Dad."

"It's Tommy, isn't it?"

"Nooo."

"I've seen the two of you look at each other, Annie."

"Dad, really, nothing happened."

"I probably shouldn't have let you go off with him," he said. "It's good I'm here to chaperone you two."

"Dad." *Please go insiiiide*, I thought.

"Are you going to tell Mark?"

"There's nothing to tell," I said.

"Right. Well, I wouldn't tell him. What he doesn't know won't hurt him," he said. "Oh, don't give me that look, Annie. It's your mother's look." He took out one of his hand-rolled cigarettes. "Honesty's overrated."

I opened the motel-room door. "Just have a smoke, Dad."

"Stop fretting so much," he yelled after me as I went inside.

Tommy was reading. He sat up, put the book on the bedside table. I kept my coat on, still cold from outside.

"Vicious cold out there," he said. "Can't believe they're going to be able to launch tomorrow."

I nodded, threw myself on the bed, stomach first.

He laughed. "Annie, Annie. It's not that bad."

"Yeah," I said.

We were quiet for a moment.

"I heard what your dad said," Tommy said finally.

I looked up. I flipped over and lay on my side.

"Y'all were talking," he said, shrugging, "kind of loud."

"The wind," I said.

"You know, Annie, I was wrong. Your dad is wrong. You're right. You should tell Mark."

"I know." I took a deep breath. "Of course I will." I looked over at Tommy. "You know, Mark's really a good guy." My cheeks hurt. "Really the best."

"You don't want to hurt him."

It was more than that, wasn't it? "No. I don't."

"Yeah."

I nodded.

"Well," he said, "let's not think about it right now. We're here for the launch, which you really want to see. Let's just have fun. We'll put us on hold."

Us, I thought. Was there an us?

"I'll pull back," Tommy went on, "I promise. No more pressure from me. You just have fun. Okay?"

"That'd be nice."

"It's good to see you smile again."

"Mind if I turn on the TV? I can't think to read."

"Sure. Sure."

We turned off the lights, got in our beds, and watched show after show. TV was comforting. Those nagging voices inside my head were drowned out by funny bits, canned laughter, and cheesy melodrama. It was great.

The late news came on, and there was Christa in an old interview. I got closer to the TV, still sitting on the bed. She was saying, with that bright smile on her face, "I touch the future. I teach. And I really appreciate that sentiment. And that's going to go with me."

"You are so cute," said Tommy.

I looked back, laughing, a little embarrassed. I pointed toward the TV. "She's just so . . ." I shrugged.

"I can see, actually."

"See what?"

"Why meeting her would inspire you to come all this way. She's got something special. I can see why NASA selected her."

"I know, right?"

"How many teachers did they say applied?"

"There were eleven thousand." I shook my head and then kind of squealed. "And she's going to launch into outer space tomorrow. We hope."

"Man, I'd do that."

"You would?" I asked.

"Oh, in a minute. Sign me up now."

I clapped my hands, not able to contain my excitement. "They'd better launch tomorrow. I have to see this."

He was giving me such a look.

"What?" I asked, smiling.

He had that smile. "Nothing."

I looked away, pleased, but not wanting to think about anything confusing. I didn't want to let go of my happiness. I turned off the TV and lay in my bed, my bad mood replaced with excitement. Tommy picked up a book to read, but I just tried not to squeal in happiness again.

CHAPTER 34

The next morning, I woke to the smell of day-old cigarette smoke. I lay in bed looking at the thin curtains bathed in light. I shot up. What time was it?

"Seven thirty!" I screamed to the two sleeping forms. "Seven thirty." I yanked open the curtains.

"Whoa. Whoa," said Dad, looking up from the cot.

"Dad! Launch is at 9:38!" I grabbed my jeans. "We're supposed to be there two hours before. And it's already 7:30!"

He squinted at me. "You're sure liftoff's not 9:39?"

"Oh," said Tommy, sitting up in bed, his hair tousled around his head. I didn't understand why boys looked so good in the morning.

"Get up!" I yelled, as I disappeared into the bathroom to throw on my clothes. "I'm not missing this!" I yelled through the door.

Dad was gone when I came back out. Before I could scream, Tommy told me he was off to get coffee and would meet us at the car. We got out of there in twenty minutes, which was doubly surprising considering the layers of clothes we had to put on. It was freezing.

Dad was scraping the ice off the windows when we came down the stairs. "The waitress at the diner said it was twenty-five degrees." We started helping him. "She said it was record-breaking temperatures."

"No way are they going to launch today," said Tommy.

I stopped scraping, my driver's license in midair. "They have to."

I hadn't come all this way for nothing. But looking at Tommy and thinking of our time together riding in the Love Bus, roaming Disney World, watching the sunrise, talking about our lives, I knew it hadn't been for nothing. Still, I *had* to see this.

"They'll launch," said Dad, as we piled in the car. "The world is watching."

I breathed a sigh of relief when the car started up. Go, Beatmobile, go.

"We'll never make it," I said.

"We'll be there in thirty," said Dad.

And we were. The traffic wasn't nearly as crowded as the day before. So many people had gone home after yesterday's aborted launch.

I slapped my forehead when we were parking. "We forgot to check out of the motel."

Dad shrugged. "We'll be back in time." He was always so optimistic—and often wrong.

Fewer people were here today. But there were still tripod photographers, excited kids, and many, many blankets. Everyone looked a little weary. It was very cold, much colder than the day before. Even with gloves on, my hands were freezing. I pushed them into my pockets. "This is crazy weather."

Dad glanced around. "Only the diehard fans are left. But NASA's going to do it today, Annie. I just know it."

"What are we going to do without NASA Boy?" I asked.

Tommy laughed. "That kid? He was great."

"I think he's going to be an astronaut one day."

"He'll probably head up NASA."

Because there were fewer people, it was easier for me to make my way down to the amateur photographers lined up at the edge of the water. I asked one of them if I could look through the lens.

When I peeked through, I could see the shuttle so much better. It looked beautiful and proud on the pad, the gleaming white orbiter, two booster rockets, and the rust orange tank on the orbiter's belly.

"Why are we delayed?" I asked two photographers talking about it.

"There's ice all over the pad, thick stalactites hanging down. If the icicles break during liftoff, they could hit the spacecraft and damage it."

"Do you think we won't go?" Surely we wouldn't scrub again today. And then I realized I'd said "we" instead of "they." I was becoming a part of this.

"NASA's hoping it'll melt; hence the delay."

More delay.

"This is stressful," I told Tommy. "How are the astronauts able to have the patience for this?"

"They must *really* want to go," he said, with a grin.

The original liftoff time came and went. I climbed into one of our cold sleeping bags and looked up at the deep blue winter sky. Dad was still talking to some of the photographers. Tommy sat down on a blanket beside me. "Your teeth are chattering."

I nodded.

"If you keep moving, you won't be so cold."

"No," I said, shaking my head. "Not getting up." I had stopped listening to the chatter on the loudspeaker. "I just want to hear the words 'ten, nine, eight, et cetera, et cetera.'" I closed my eyes. "Wake me then."

"It could be a while. You'll turn into an icicle."

"Is she an icicle?" asked a voice.

I looked up into the eyes of a little girl wearing a thick pink coat and carrying a Cabbage Patch doll under one arm and a book under the other.

"She will be," said Tommy, "unless she listens to me."

"Oh-ho!" I exclaimed. "Why should I listen to you?"

He brushed my hair out of my eyes, smiling at me, not saying anything.

"Your fingers are cold," I told him. "I should have knitted you gloves too."

"Is she your wife?" asked the girl.

I laughed.

"Yes, she is," said Tommy. "Isn't she pretty?"

The girl looked at me silently with large brown eyes. Then she held out her book to Tommy. "Will you read this to me?" He took it, and she sat down on one of our sleeping bags on the other side of me.

He smiled at her, charming her as much as he did the older girls, I was sure. "Where are your mom and dad?"

"Right there," the girl said, pointing behind us. I took her word for it because I was too lazy to sit up and look. But Tommy waved at someone.

The girl reached over me and tapped the book. "It's called *The Stars.*"

"I haven't read this one," said Tommy, opening it to the first page. "But it looks like one I'd like."

"You can't have it." The girl reached over me and took the book back from him.

"No, I didn't mean—," Tommy began.

"It's about the stars and the planets," she said in a sing-songy voice, "and the sky." She flipped a few pages and showed us a picture of a constellation. "See." She put the book down and looked at me. "Why are you in that sleeping bag?"

"To keep warm."

"My coat is really warm. Really, really warm." She picked up her book—"Bye"—and ran off.

I looked at him. "You were good with her."

"I used to read to my sister. About rocks."

"Rocks?" I asked. "Rocks?"

"She's always loved rocks." He grinned. "You can't help what you love."

Finally, the countdown picked up again. The new launch time was 11:38. People cheered.

"Yeah, right," I said. "They've fooled me too many times. I'm not getting up."

Tommy lay down.

"You'll get cold too," I told him.

He hugged me and my sleeping bag, and I let him, glad Dad was still down by the water. "Have some of my body heat," Tommy said.

I closed my eyes, feeling toasty warm in the sleeping bag with Tommy's arm around me. My exposed nose and cheeks were still cold, but it was a good cold feeling, not a bad one.

Tommy was quiet then. I listened to all the voices around us: two sisters laughing about a Christmas long ago, the squeals and shouts of kids running around, a couple sharing binoculars and talking about other launches they'd seen. I drifted in and out, snatches of words tangled up with dreams.

Tommy woke me.

I sat up quickly. "What? What?"

"They're picking up the count!"

"Get up there, Annie," said Dad.

"No fooling, right?" The crowd was clapping. I jumped out of the sleeping bag, blinking awake. "Are we going to do it?"

Tommy side-hugged me. "They're going to launch, Annie."

Excitement squeezed my stomach. "They're going to launch," I repeated, gazing across the water at the shuttle that appeared so small and vulnerable. "I wonder what Christa is thinking."

"NASA could still stop the clock," Dad teased.

"Not a chance," I said, hitting his arm. "We're going! *Eeee*."

The crowd was buzzing with excitement. We all had launch fever. After all the delays, it was going to happen.

"T MINUS SEVEN MINUTES THIRTY SECONDS, AND
THE GROUND LAUNCH SEQUENCER HAS STARTED
RETRACTING THE ORBITER CREW ACCESS ARM.
THIS IS THE WALKWAY USED BY ASTRONAUTS TO
CLIMB INTO THE VEHICLE."

Someone in launch control said, "Let's go for orbiter APU
start," and one of the crew responded with, ". . . performed
APU start."

"All right!" yelled out someone in the crowd.

"APU start must be good," I said to Tommy.

He smiled. "Thank you, Annie."

"Thank you? I had nothing to do with APU start," I
teased.

"That means auxiliary power unit," the woman beside me
said excitedly. "The APUs provide hydraulic power for all
sorts of things, like the elevons, the main engine gimballing,
the landing gear." She pulled her hat tighter down on her head.

"Oh, thanks," I said, looking back at the shuttle.

"I mean thanks for this trip," Tommy said, as if the woman
hadn't spoken. He was looking into my eyes so intensely I
forgot the shuttle for a second. "It was just what I needed."

"It was?"

He nodded.

"You'll need to thank Christa McAuliffe," I said, smiling,
so giddy.

"THE SOLID ROCKET BOOSTER AND EXTERNAL
SAFE AND ARM DEVICES HAVE BEEN ARMED . . .
T MINUS FOUR MINUTES AND COUNTING. THE

FLIGHT CREW HAS BEEN REMINDED TO CLOSE
THEIR AIRTIGHT VISORS ON THEIR LAUNCH AND
ENTRY HELMETS."

"You want the binoculars?" Dad asked.

"Yes!" I exclaimed, taking them. I looked through them,
adjusting the eyepieces, thinking how great this was. The
shuttle looked a bit bigger. It wasn't like looking through
the telescope, but it did make me feel like the pad was closer.

I was ecstatic, so proud of my little coward self that I got
myself here to see the launch.

"T MINUS THIRTY SECONDS AND WE'VE HAD A
GO FOR AUTO-SEQUENCE START."

"A go!" shouted a kid, her ponytail bobbing as she jumped
up and down.

Yells of excitement burst here and there from the crowd.
Many started counting down with the clock:

"T MINUS TEN . . . NINE . . . EIGHT . . . SEVEN . . .
SIX . . . WE HAVE MAIN ENGINE START . . ."

A white cloud of smoke puffed up from the pad. Dad
threw an arm around my neck.

". . . FOUR . . . THREE . . . TWO . . . ONE . . . AND
LIFTOFF. LIFTOFF OF THE TWENTY-FIFTH SPACE
SHUTTLE MISSION, AND IT HAS CLEARED THE
TOWER."

Out of a white cloud, out of hope, a dream rises . . . , I thought.

The crowd erupted in cheers, whistles, and applause.

"Ya-hoooooo!" a kid screamed.

I lowered the binoculars, wanting to see this with the naked eye.

"Look at her go," said Tommy. "Wow. Wow." I felt him grab my arm, but I couldn't look away from the shuttle climbing in the sky.

"What a sight!" Dad yelled.

"Man, man, man!" came a cry from behind me.

I felt goose bumps crawl up and down my arms as the shuttle rose into the rich blue sky, a column of brilliant fire pushing it along, leaving a white tube of smoke trailing. A delayed rumble like a contained but crackling bonfire flew across the water to us. The sound was powerful, exciting. I could feel it in my chest, like it was tearing through me.

It was unbelievable. There were people in that shuttle, pulling away from Earth, blasting toward space. And what a complex, amazing achievement of metal, wires, computers, engines . . . all of it put together to create this vehicle that could fly like that. Like that.

I laughed out loud, wiping tears from my eyes. She was doing it. The teacher was flying. Look. At. Her. Go. *Oh, Christa.*

"*CHALLENGER*, GO AT THROTTLE UP."

"Roger, go at throttle up," replied another voice.

"That's Dick Scobee, the commander," said a woman

to her daughter, standing behind her with her arms around her neck.

It had only been a minute since liftoff and already the shuttle was so high up. I could only see the white column of smoke the shuttle was leaving behind as it rose over the Atlantic, higher and higher, and pulled farther away from us.

"Hey, what was that?" said a man behind me, pointing at the sky, at the same time a woman let out a high-pitched scream. But others were clapping and cheering. A man yelled out, "No, no, no!" All I could see was a big billowing cloud of white smoke.

"What is that, Dad?" I asked, grabbing his coat.

"Maybe booster separation," he said. "But something doesn't look right."

I whipped my head around to look at him. "What?"

He was looking up, silently shaking his head.

I looked over at Tommy. He met my eyes. He looked as confused as I felt.

The public-affairs officer announced the shuttle's position:

"ONE MINUTE, FIFTEEN SECONDS, VELOCITY TWENTY-NINE HUNDRED FEET PER SECOND. ALTITUDE NINE NAUTICAL MILES. DOWNRANGE DISTANCE SEVEN NAUTICAL MILES."

"That's not right," said the man.

"Where's the shuttle?" someone asked.

"I think that's it! There!"

"But there are two . . ."

The little girl with the book of stars pointed. "What are those, Momma?"

"I think . . . those are the booster rockets, sweetie."

And then it was quiet, no one was talking, the sky was silent.

"FLIGHT CONTROLLERS HERE LOOKING VERY CAREFULLY AT THE SITUATION. OBVIOUSLY A MAJOR MALFUNCTION."

The voice was so calm, as if this were commonplace and there was nothing to worry about. A chill crept through me, heavy and bleak.

"WE HAVE NO DOWNLINK."

"It's gone," said the man in front of me. "It's gone," he said again as if to convince himself.

I looked at the sky once more. My eyes hurt.

Christa.

For the first time, I understood. *Shock.* The faces around me were frozen, no sadness pulling at the eyes, no anger tightening the mouth . . . just shock.

Then hands were over eyes, on cheeks, at throats, on arms close by as people stared into the sky. A woman beside me fell to the ground, still looking up. I heard crying, then realized it was me.

"WE HAVE A REPORT FROM THE FLIGHT DYNAM-ICS OFFICER THAT THE VEHICLE HAS EXPLODED.

THE FLIGHT DIRECTOR CONFIRMS THAT. WE ARE LOOKING AT CHECKING WITH THE RECOVERY FORCES TO SEE WHAT CAN BE DONE AT THIS POINT."

I looked at Tommy. "Annie," he said, wiping my tears away. "I'm sorry. I'm sorry."

Dad was looking up, his face weary.

I grabbed his arm. "Daddy?"

He threw his arm around me and pulled me close. I looked back up at the cold blue sky that couldn't be more beautiful, and the debris falling, leaving white sad strands in their wake, like a twisted fireworks display.

A sick sense of dread hit me, settling deep, but at its darkest place was fear.

"Daddy's here, baby."

CHAPTER 35

I stayed huddled into my dad. I couldn't stop crying. Another announcement came on:

"WE WILL REPORT MORE AS WE HAVE INFORMATION AVAILABLE. AGAIN, TO REPEAT, WE HAVE A REPORT RELAYED THROUGH THE FLIGHT DYNAMICS OFFICER THAT THE VEHICLE HAS EXPLODED. WE ARE NOW LOOKING AT ALL THE CONTINGENCY OPERATIONS AND AWAITING WORD FROM ANY RECOVERY FORCES IN THE DOWNRANGE FIELD."

People were standing around, like they were still trying to figure it out. Some faces were blank; sadness contorted others. Many were crying. I didn't like looking at their faces. I wanted to leave, but I still hoped.

"Do you think they can save them, Dad?" I asked.

He shook his head. "I don't know, but I don't think so, Annie."

"But isn't there a chance they survived the explosion?" I bit my lip. I couldn't stop the tears running down my face. "They could be in the water."

"Annie, even if they survived that," he said, waving at the sky, "they would have . . . died when the . . . shuttle hit the ocean."

"But then why are they even talking about recovery teams? If there's no hope?"

"Annie." He put his hand on my cheek. "I'm so sorry, baby."

"Because they didn't say 'rescue,' they said 'recovery'? Is that why you think that?" I wanted answers, needed them.

I heard the loudspeaker crackle and turned to it:

"THIS IS MISSION CONTROL, HOUSTON. WE HAVE NO ADDITIONAL WORD AT THIS TIME."

"Oh, come on," a man yelled out, throwing up his hands. But the announcements then continued:

"REPORTS FROM THE FLIGHT DYNAMICS OFFI-CER INDICATE THAT THE VEHICLE APPARENTLY EXPLODED AND THAT IMPACT IN THE WATER WAS AT A POINT APPROXIMATELY 28.64 DEGREES NORTH, 80.28 DEGREES WEST."

Tommy looked at his watch. "Five minutes. It's only been five minutes since they launched." His face looked stunned.

I couldn't stop crying. I pressed my fingers to my eyes, but the tears kept flowing. "I have to get out of here." I wanted to go home. I wanted to be in my house. I wanted to see my mom's face. I even wanted to see Mark.

I walked toward the car. *Christa, Christa, Christa.*

"Annie!" Dad yelled.

"I want to go home!" I yelled back.

I wanted to wash away that horrible image of the shuttle becoming white smoke in a rich blue sky. The sky should not be so blue for a moment like this. I would always remember the color of that sky that ate dreams.

I lay down in the backseat with my face turned to the vinyl. I heard voices, the trunk open, the doors open. Neither my dad nor Tommy said anything when they got in the car. My chest hurt. My throat hurt. I couldn't talk. I didn't want anyone to talk.

The car began moving.

I kept seeing Christa's smile. I shut my eyes. I didn't want to see anything but dark. I didn't want to hear anything but the sound of the tires on the road. That sound was the only thing soothing me right now. It reminded me of Mark, of our sunrise trips to Galveston to fish or to surf, with me half asleep listening to the road in the quiet of the morning. Peaceful times, safe, certain, knowable. Not like this.

Finally, we made it to the hotel.

"Annie, here's a blanket," said my dad, as he covered me up. "Just stay here, baby girl. We have to get the bags."

"We'll be right back," I heard Tommy say.

I lay still and thought about all the families of the astronauts. The kids, the wives, the husbands, the moms, the dads, had all come out on this brilliant blue day. It was families, excitement, fun, ocean, Disney World.

But now it was this, a rapid plummet to a darker side of dreams.

Dad and Tommy were gone for a while. Finally, the car doors opened again.

"Do you want me to drive, Jesse?" I heard Tommy ask.

"I will," Dad answered.

The car was moving.

My head was pounding. I was going home.

CHAPTER 36

Dad sprang for a room at the Holiday Inn. I'd heard him talking to Tommy about whether they should drive straight through. Dad quietly said he wanted to get me out of the car for a little bit.

"Come on, baby," Dad said, opening the door.

"Where are we?" I asked.

"We're outside of Tallahassee."

"What time is it, Dad?"

"After ten," he said, helping me out of the car.

"I'll get the bags," Tommy said.

I crawled into the bed after swallowing some Tylenol. I tried not to move my head because it would pound harder if I shifted on the pillow. It hurt so much that my stomach hurt too. Nausea and pain enveloped me.

The room was quiet and dark, and the sheets felt good against my skin. But I was so cold. It was an ice cold that crept through me, like I would never be warm or happy or trusting again. I buried my head in my pillow so no one would hear me cry.

CHAPTER 37

We got up with the sun. When the guys went to load up the car, I called Lea. I knew she'd still be asleep because it was only six a.m. or so in Houston. I was glad she was the one who answered the phone. I didn't want to talk to her parents.

"Annie? Where are you?" asked Lea.

"Not so loud, Lea," I said quietly. "My head hurts a little."

"I'm sorry."

"It's better today," I said. "We're still in Florida. But we're on our way back. Dad says we'll be home in eleven or twelve hours."

"It's terrible. So terrible. Did you see it?"

"Yeah. The shuttle just wasn't there anymore, Lea. It was just smoke." I bit tears back.

"My mom's so upset. Her eyes were red and swollen this morning. I heard her crying last night."

I wanted to be home. "Lea, I have to go, okay?" I wanted to be with my own mom.

"When will you get home?"

"It'll be really late."

"Are you going to school tomorrow?"

"I don't know. What day is it, Lea? I'm so mixed up."

"It's Wednesday."

"Okay, well, I'll get in too late for school tomorrow. I'll be too tired." But I found I wanted to go, to be back in my normal routine. I wanted to see Mark. I had to see him.

"Mom said they're going to have a memorial service."

"Where?" I asked.

"Here. I mean, at the space center. President Reagan is coming."

"Lea, can I go?"

"I don't know, Annie. I don't think they'll let others in. It's just for the families and the employees. Mom and Dad are going, but—"

"I really want to go, Lea. No, I mean I *have* to go."

"Okay, I'll ask Mom. Call me tomorrow, okay? First thing?"

"First thing."

I called Mom next.

"Annie! Are you okay?"

"Yeah."

"You don't sound okay. Where are you?"

Hearing my mom's calm voice made my throat feel tight. "Mom." It was good to hear her voice. "We're still in Florida. Outside of Tallahassee or Pensacola. I really don't know. We're leaving now."

"Good, good. Grandma called. She's so worried about you. Are you all right?"

"Yeah," I said. "No, Mom. I'm not."

"I'm so sorry, sweetheart. I know how much this meant to you."

"I want to be home, Momma."

"I want you home," she said, with a sad sigh. "Put your dad on, honey. I need to talk to him."

"I can't, Mom. He's paying for the room."

"Okay. When will you be here?"

"Late."

"I'll wait up," she said.

"No, Mom. It'll be late. I'll come wake you up. Make sure you're there, okay?"

"Of course I'll be here, Annie."

"I have to go. See you tonight."

I stared at the phone. I picked up the receiver and dialed again.

"Mark?"

"Thank God, Annie! You haven't called. And then this happened. I've been so worried."

"I know. I'm sorry. We're on our way back."

"Are you okay, Annie?" Mark asked.

"I'm all right."

"Why didn't you call?" he asked.

"I just— We've been busy, Mark."

"I wish you would have called. I called your mom and she said that you were fine and at Disney World."

"Don't be mad at me right now, Mark."

"I'm sorry. I've just been worried. Are you okay?" he asked.

I took a ragged sigh. "Not really. I just want to be home."

"When will you be here? I'll come over."

"It'll be late, Mark. I don't even know when. I'll call tomorrow."

"You need to call, Annie. You need to call me when you get here."

"I will. I have to go."

"I love you. Bye."

"Bye, Mark."

I sat by the phone for a long time. I was afraid to turn on the TV. It usually brought me comfort, but today it didn't seem to offer any. Part of me just didn't want to hear what the newspeople had to say, especially about Christa. But I also wanted to hear something about her, to have some connection to her, even if it was through the news.

I sat down on the floor and turned on the TV. And then I couldn't stop watching.

All the stations were showing liftoff and the shuttle disappearing into fire and smoke over and over. I hadn't been able to see the explosion from the ground. But the cameras caught a closer view.

So much of the news was centered on Christa. They showed clips of old interviews. How could she be talking right there, looking so alive, with so much energy and spirit, and not be here anymore?

To cover the launch, reporters had been at Concord High School in New Hampshire, where Christa taught. The camera showed students in an auditorium watching before liftoff, wearing party hats. When the shuttle rose from the pad, they blew horns and threw confetti. But then their faces fell.

"She was a part of us," said one girl. "She was part of a family." I reached out and touched the screen, the girl's face. "She'll be remembered," she said. Another said, very calmly, "It was a hell. Just a hell."

I wished I was there with them, to be around people who cared about her, who were inspired by her. I knew I wasn't her student. But wasn't she the nation's teacher now? Wasn't that what it was supposed to be about? I turned off the TV.

I wondered where Tommy and Dad were. Looking out the window, I saw them huddled over the engine of the car.

"No," I said out loud to no one. "No."

I ran outside, slamming the door, not caring who I woke.

"What's wrong with the car, Dad?"

He looked over at me with a worried face. "It's an easy fix, baby. I promise."

"Don't 'baby' me. I thought you got it fixed!" Tommy gave me a look. I must be really yelling, but I didn't care.

"This is a different problem. I just need to get the auto parts—"

"Not again!"

"You need to calm down." He wouldn't look at me. He ducked his head back under the hood.

"Look at me, Dad!"

He wouldn't. "I'm going to fix the car, Annie."

"You can't fix it. You can't fix anything. Everything is always broken around you." I stomped off around the side of the hotel, having no idea where I was going. I couldn't believe I was going to miss the memorial service. Even if Lea's parents did everything they could to get me in, my *stupid* father would mess it all up.

I heard footsteps running toward me from behind. I didn't turn around.

"Annie," Tommy said. "Annie." He grabbed my arm, trying to slow me down.

"Tommy, don't. I need to be alone."

"Talk to me for a minute. Just a minute. Then you can go off, okay?"

He was so calm, it calmed me a little. And the fact that he didn't tell me to calm down made me feel better.

"Okay?" he asked. "Just for a minute?"

I gave him a quick nod.

"Okay," he said. "Let's sit here." He pointed toward the pool area. We sat in cold metal chairs. I pulled my gloves out of my pocket and put them on. I noticed Tommy was wearing the red scarf I made him. I stared at the unused swimming pool.

We sat for a few minutes, neither one saying anything.

Slowing down was making me less angry, but more sad. I didn't like the feeling. I'd rather be angry. It felt like I had some control when I was angry, even if I really didn't. Being sad was just hopeless.

Tommy took my hand. "I'm sorry, Annie. I'm so sorry."

I felt my lip trembling, and I couldn't stop it. "I'm sorry I got so mad." I looked up at Tommy. "I just can't believe it. I just can't."

"It's like a bad dream," he said.

"Yeah. That sight, Tommy, of the shuttle. It was so horrible. It is so horrible to think Christa, the others—"

"Annie." He moved his chair close to mine and pulled me to him. I put my head on his shoulder, and he put his head on mine. It was comforting, but it also felt wrong.

I pulled away and sat up, wiping my eyes. "Thank you." I looked down at his hands. "Are your hands cold?" I grabbed his in my gloved ones. I rubbed them to try to get them warm.

"Are you better now?" he asked.

"Better."

CHAPTER 38

Dad hitched a ride on a motorcycle to go to the nearest auto-parts store. We were told to get out of the room by noon, or we'd have to pay for another night. Dad said once he bought a new set of points, it'd be an easy fix and we'd be out of here.

I settled in a booth with plastic seats at a coffee shop down the street from the hotel. The waitress was getting tired of refilling my cup of coffee, but it was so cold outside. Drinking hot coffee comforted me, made me feel like I was home in my mom's kitchen.

Tommy slid into the seat across from me.

"Hi," I said, watching the cars go down the road in front of the coffee shop.

"You want to drink in every coffee shop in this town?"

"What?"

"You know, like every country in Epcot?"

I smiled. "Disney seems a long time ago."

"Yeah. It's funny, isn't it?" Then he shrugged. "Although not really."

"No, not really," I said.

Our hands were close on the table. But he didn't reach for me, and I was really glad he didn't.

"Annie, I know this is a bad time to ask you this, but have you thought more about the situation with Mark?"

"Tommy, don't," I said, shaking my head a little and looking away. "Please."

"I didn't mean to upset you," he said. "I shouldn't have asked."

"It's not that. I just don't want to think about anything else that will make me sad."

"I know. I'm sorry. I did what I said I wouldn't. It's just that you've been so distant since the . . . accident, and I already miss you. I can't believe I miss you and you're right in front of me. And I can't believe I didn't know you a few days ago, and now . . . I . . ." He looked tired and sad.

All I could do was nod. I wanted to say something to make him feel better, but I didn't know what to say. I didn't even know what I felt.

Tommy ordered some buttermilk pancakes, and I watched him eat them. They looked good, but I had no appetite.

Dad went by on the bike, behind some guy he'd never met before today. Life was strange, I thought. Life with Dad was particularly interesting.

Tommy stood up and grabbed the check. I put my hand on his arm. "Give me a minute with my dad, okay?"

Dad had already popped the hood when I got to the car. The guy on the bike was gone. Dad started talking as soon as he saw me. "Annie, it won't take me long to do this." He was talking fast and moving fast. He seemed nervous.

"Dad."

He looked at me. "I'm—"

"Dad. I know you're trying to fix the car."

"Well, yeah," he said. "I know you want to get home, Annie."

"I got upset because I want to go to the memorial service."

"What service?" he asked.

"They're having a service at JSC for the astronauts. Lea told me about it this morning. She's going to ask her parents if I can come."

"It's not today, is it?" he asked, looking slightly worried.

"Not today. I don't know when it is. Lea didn't know yet."

"We'll be back tonight, Annie."

"I'm sorry, Dad, that I got so mad."

"Aw, Annie, it's okay."

"Can I get you a Coke?"

His head came up, his eyes wide in surprise. "Sure. Sure."

"Okay." I smiled. "Or do you want a Dr Pepper? I know you drink Dr Pepper."

"Yeah," he said, "that'd be great." He ducked his head back under the hood. "Go on, then. I've got to fix a car."

PART THREE

"Follow your instincts . . . go for your dreams."
—Christa McAuliffe

CHAPTER 39

I didn't see him when we'd pulled into my driveway. I was in the front with Tommy while Dad slept in back. I'd dozed off, but woke when the car stopped. I looked over, and there Mark was, getting out of his parked car.

I felt a rush of comfort when I saw him, like I was home, like I was safe, like the world made sense again. And he was so kind to be here, to know that I would need him. When we'd last stopped for gas, I'd called him. It'd been midnight so I shouldn't have. But the world was suddenly dark and scary, and I'd wanted to hear his voice. He'd been tender on the phone.

It was dark, but would be light soon. I couldn't see Tommy's face in the dark. I sat still for a moment, as did he. I didn't know what to say. It felt wrong being here with him, especially after all that had happened with the *Challenger*. Tragedy made me want to hold on to the people I knew well. I'd felt the same way when my grandpa died.

Dad was moving around in the backseat. In the sideview

mirror, I could see Mark walking toward us. I reached over and brushed Tommy's hand with my own, quickly. He turned toward me, but I moved away and opened the car door.

I hugged Mark, not saying anything.

He held me tight, kissing the side of my forehead. I wouldn't turn my head toward him. I heard the doors of the car open, and I let him go.

"Hey, Mark," said Dad, shaking his hand. Tommy got my bag out of the trunk and handed it to me. I didn't look at him, but I reached for the bag. He held on.

I pressed my lips together and glanced up at him, pleading with my eyes for him to let it go. I could sense Mark standing behind me. Tommy released the bag.

Mark grabbed it from me and flung an arm around my shoulder. The early morning was cold and still. My street was empty and dark except for the occasional harsh lighting of a street lamp.

Dad gave me a kiss on the cheek, which startled me. "Bye, Annie."

"Dad?"

He looked at me, concern in his eyes.

"Thank you for taking me, Dad."

"I'm sorry it didn't turn out like we thought," he said.

I kissed his cheek then, startling *him*. "Bye, Dad." I walked to the door with Mark. I didn't look back, but heard the car drive away.

Mark came in and pulled me down on the couch with him. He lay down along the length of it with me against him. I leaned into him, trying not to think about anything at all.

CHAPTER 40

Mark ate Cheerios. I ate toast over the sink.

Mom was gone when we woke. I couldn't believe I'd fallen asleep in Mark's arms on the couch, that Mom had seen us together and left us there, and that we hadn't woken up until noon.

We'd said little to one another. I thought Mark must have figured out I needed quiet, but he didn't know the real reason. He thought it was *Challenger*. And it *was* the accident and losing Christa and all the astronauts, and being there when it happened, and not being able to get that image out of my head.

But it was also, I hated to admit, fear. Fear of what might happen if I followed my heart—of what I could lose—of what anybody could lose at any time. And it was guilt for liking Tommy, for kissing Tommy.

All the pressure I'd felt before we left for Florida had ramped up since the launch. I felt like *I* was going to explode.

I had thought this trip would help me figure out things,

and that maybe I'd come back and be a different person, a more together person, someone who knew what she wanted and fearlessly went for it. Like Christa. I'd wanted her outlook on things and her bravery to rub off on me. And then my path would magically appear before me, like the yellow brick road.

But now after *Challenger* . . . I was fighting the feeling that bad things happened when you reached too far. Had Christa reached too far?

"So you're going to the memorial service tomorrow?" Mark asked.

"Right. I called Lea again last night from the road. Her parents are getting us in."

"Come sit down, Annie."

The phone rang. He shrugged with a small smile.

It was Mom.

"I know I was supposed to wake you—," I began.

"I was awake when you got home."

"What?" I asked, confused. "I didn't see you."

"I know. I saw Mark waiting out front in his car. I wanted to give you some time with him."

"Oh," I said. "Thanks."

"Anything you want special for dinner?" she asked.

"No," I said, not caring at all.

"Okay," said Mom. "I'm sorry about Christa. It's awful. Just terrible. I know how much she meant to you, Annie."

Meant to you: past tense. It seemed more real when my mom said it.

"I'll be home early today," she was saying. "We'll talk then."

"Okay. Bye."

I sat at the table and took Mark's hand.

"Let's go for a drive," he said. "Anywhere. You name it."

"Galveston."

We got in the car, and I put my feet up on the dashboard. I rolled down the window and leaned way back in the seat. Mark cranked up the radio. An old Bob Seger song from the seventies was playing, which was just fine with me.

I watched him as he drove. He looked at me with his kind eyes and squeezed my hand. I thought of the summer before our junior year, when we went from good friends to more.

All we wanted that summer was each other. We got jobs at the original Clear Lake movie theater and asked for the same schedule. On slow days, we shared long kisses in the ticket booth. When we weren't working, we hung out at my house, sometimes with Dad, sometimes completely alone. We took long drives, like this one. It had been a sweet summer that extended into junior year.

I was so comfortable with Mark—being with him felt right, like it was where I belonged. I felt safe. I needed safe right now.

CHAPTER 41

The memorial service for the crew of *Challenger* was the next day, a Friday.

I looked at the many faces around me, a true sea of faces. Most were NASA engineers and other employees. I was glad to be here around people who really cared about the astronauts and the space program.

Standing here with them made me feel like I was part of their NASA family too. I watched their faces, so many of their eyes hidden by sunglasses, and wondered if they all felt like they had failed in some way, that they were each to blame.

Thousands stood around the three ponds in the middle of the white 1960s buildings of the space center, the mood somber. A speaker's platform had been built for the ceremony. It was surrounded by folding chairs in a roped-off area. We were outside the ropes. An Air Force band played heavy, solemn music.

Lea's father had gotten us a good spot under a pine tree on a little hill right behind one of the ponds. It was a pretty day, clouds drifting in the sky. It felt like March, not the last day in January. Despite all the formality and the size of the crowd, it had the same feeling as my grandpa's small funeral.

Mrs. Taylor said that many famous people were there, including U.S. senators and President John Kennedy's children, Caroline and John. The families of the astronauts came in last with President Reagan and his wife. They sat in the front row of the folding chairs in front of the platform.

I could barely see President Reagan, but I could hear him through the loudspeakers. He talked about each member of the crew. My eyes stung when he spoke of Christa. His words described my own experience with her:

"We remember Christa McAuliffe, who captured the imagination of the entire nation, inspiring us with her pluck, her restless spirit of discovery; a teacher, not just to her students, but to an entire people, instilling us all with the excitement of this journey we ride into the future."

I pressed one finger to my lips trying not to cry, remembering that very gesture was what Christa had done when she'd been announced by Vice President Bush as the Teacher in Space. I closed my eyes and said silent words of my own to her, thanking her for her kindness and for making me feel like I mattered.

The hardest part for me was when Reagan said: "Dick, Mike, Judy, El, Ron, Greg, and Christa—your families and your country mourn your passing." A woman beside me began to cry then. To these people at the space center, standing around me, this wasn't a public event with a president and a dead president's children there. It was the loss of family.

I let my tears flow then, not trying to be strong anymore. Lea put her arm around my shoulder, and I leaned into her.

I thought of Christa's students, those I had seen interviewed on TV, who had been watching when she died. One girl's face still haunted me. Her words had been so quiet, so lost, so without the hope that had seemed to flow out of Christa effortlessly.

I was sorry that girl couldn't be here. Christa's students should be here. I wasn't one of them either. But I felt like I was, and that was because Christa had made me feel that way. She had a gift for talking to people, especially those who were my age.

I would have liked to be in Concord at the mass they were holding for her on Monday at her church, impossible as that was for me. But I wanted to be with people who'd known Christa as their teacher and had a connection to her that I wished I'd had.

Four jets flew in formation overhead. All eyes went to the sky. A lone plane pulled up and away, bringing to my mind W. H. Auden's grieving lines:

Let aeroplanes circle moaning overhead
Scribbling on the sky the message He Is Dead

This was not how it was supposed to end.

CHAPTER 42

I woke thinking of *Challenger*, with odd images and colors from my dreams floating through my head: Christa and Tommy riding in the Love Bus together, NASA Boy with his freckles telling me he wanted to fly, bits of the shuttle in an ugly red sky. I pressed my face deeper into my pillow and let myself fall back asleep.

The ringing phone woke me, but I ignored it.

My door opened. "Annie, are you awake?" Mom asked.

"No," I said into my pillow.

"It's ten o'clock, Annie. And Mark's on the phone. He's called several times."

"I'm not awake."

There was no shutting of the door. I opened the eye not on my pillow. Mom was still there, looking at me.

"Fine," I said, dragging myself out of bed and into the kitchen. I picked up the receiver lying on the counter. "Mark?"

"Hey! Your mom said you were still asleep," he said. "Aren't you working today?"

I put my hand to my throat, convincing myself it felt sore. "I think I'm sick."

"What's wrong?"

"I think I'm getting a cold."

"Go back to bed, Annie. I'll call in for you."

"Thanks, Mark."

"You want me to come by later? After work?"

"Sure," I said.

I crawled into bed, but couldn't go back to sleep. I felt guilty. Guilty for calling in sick when I (probably) wasn't. Guilty about Tommy.

I pulled out my Vincent van Gogh book, studying his eyes on the cover: so tormented, as if he too had seen a friend die right before his eyes. I read another of his letters. Vincent was distressed. His mentor had become irritated when Vincent had told him: "I am an artist." He thought his mentor was upset because claiming you're an artist suggested you were "always seeking without absolutely finding."

I too was seeking—and absolutely *not* finding.

Christa had seemed to be a seeking person, but also a finding one, a person satisfied with what she achieved. If she'd arrived safely back home, I believed she would have been filled up by her week-long experience of living among the stars, filled up by sharing that experience with her students.

I was a stargazer and a dreamer. But I had wanted the road trip to help me find peace and answers—instead I felt restless and unsure.

Was it Van Gogh's constant seeking that created his body of art? If he'd been finally satisfied, finally contented, he might not have accomplished what he did. I thought perhaps if he'd found a way to capture all the colors in his head, all the stars in his heart, we wouldn't have his paintings. Was he sacrificed for his art? Was Christa sacrificed for her desire to see and share the stars?

My head hurt. I put the book down.

Mark came by later with Blue Bell Homemade Vanilla ice cream. I gave him a kiss and brought two bowls to the den and sat by him while we ate.

He put his hand on my knee and watched television, stealing kisses with cold ice-cream lips when Mom walked out of the room.

"You might get sick," I told him, teasing.

"You look good for a sick girl."

Mom came back in, a book in one hand.

"It's Saturday night, Mom," I said. "You and Donald don't have a date?"

"Not tonight," she said, looking at me and then going back out.

"Is something wrong?" Mark asked. "She looks worried."

"She is worried. About me, since we got back from Florida."

"I'm worried about you too."

"No one needs to worry about me. I'm fine." I put my hand on my throat, saying with a fake scratchy voice: "Except for this sore throat."

He held my hand, playing with my charm bracelet. "How was the trip to Florida, by the way? I mean, before the accident."

"It was fine," I said, feeling nervous, suddenly wanting my hand back.

"What did y'all do? I know you went to Disney."

My stomach clenched. "Yeah, we went to Epcot and Magic Kingdom, hung out on the beach a little." I frantically tried to think of something to change the subject. "Dad was taking freezing dips into the ocean. You know how crazy he is. What did you do while I was gone? Any surfing?"

I knew he was looking at me, but I lowered my eyes. I grabbed my knitting from the basket by the couch just wanting to feel the yarn in my hands, to hear the click of the needles.

He didn't say anything else. I knitted, knowing I was lying to him.

CHAPTER 43

Hi, it's Tommy."

I couldn't help the excited, sweet feeling that shot through me. "Hi, Tommy." I switched the phone to my other ear.

"Is it okay to call?" he asked.

"Yeah, yeah." *Probably not*, I thought.

"I know it's only been a few days, but I've missed you."

I hesitated. "I've missed you too." It felt good saying it. It felt like the truth after days of lies.

"How are things? Are you okay?"

"It's been weird," I said.

"How so?"

"The trip and everything that happened," I said. "And then coming back home feels like nothing's changed."

"Has anything changed with you and Mark?" he asked quietly.

No, I thought. *It's exactly the same.*

Although Mark hadn't asked about Tommy directly, I knew that he wanted to, that he was waiting. I could feel it. My stomach was torn up with confusion.

"Annie?" Tommy asked.

"I'm sorry. I just . . ." Suddenly, I felt like crying. I was so much on edge, with all these intense feelings fraying my nerves. I didn't know what to do with them. They were complicating everything.

Tommy was quiet. "It's all right, Annie," he said finally.

"I just can't think right now," I said. "I'm sorry, Tommy."

"You don't have anything to be sorry for. Not at all."

I took a deep breath. "Thanks." But he was wrong. I may not owe him an apology, but I owed one to Mark.

"Have you been writing poetry?" he asked.

"Yeah," I said, relieved he'd changed the subject. "I've been trying to work on poems about Christa, but it's too fresh." My eyes stung. "It hurts." I didn't like to talk about her to anyone, although many people had asked at school today, including teachers. My grief felt private. But Tommy had been with me when it happened. He understood.

"Write about other things until you can write about her."

"Yeah," I said. "I have this idea, actually, for a collection of poems. I've been thinking about that, writing a little."

"That's cool. What's it about?"

I paused. "I don't want to talk about it yet."

"Sure," he said. "Annie, I'd like to take you somewhere."

"I don't know, Tommy—"

"Not on a date," he said quickly. "We can go in broad daylight."

"I don't think it would be right," I said, conflicted.

"I want to show you something."

I knew Mark wouldn't like it. But I wanted to go so

badly. Tommy made things seem light and fun. I needed fun right now.

"When?" I asked.

"This Saturday. About ten? I'll pick you up."

"Okay," I said quickly, before I could change my mind.

When I hung up, I realized I was smiling for the first time in days.

———

CHAPTER 44

I'd fallen asleep last night on the couch with the TV on. Mom had woken me up, and I'd climbed into my bed and burrowed under the warm, soft covers. Now it was five a.m. and I was wide awake. I lay there, thinking of Christa, trying to push her out of my head. Finally, I gave up.

I grabbed a can of Diet Coke from the fridge and got the newspaper from the driveway. While drinking the Coke, I started the coffee going for Mom. I liked the smell of coffee. It made me think of my grandma.

There was a photo in the *Houston Chronicle* showing Christa's husband, Steven, and their nine-year-old son, Scott, leaving her funeral in Concord. The caption said that their six-year-old daughter, Caroline, had also attended. I remembered Christa talking about her wedding, where she wore daisies in her hair and danced until dusk.

I hoped I wouldn't always feel such sadness when I thought of her. People who lost others couldn't live with this heavy emptiness every day; it *had* to get better. I still missed my grandpa, but the ache had lessened as the days went by.

It wasn't just me Christa had affected. She'd pulled an entire nation into her heart. Probably because she was so fearless, but also because she didn't just reach out for what she wanted; she called on each of us, wanting us to do the same.

"Coffeeee," said Mom, coming in. "Thank you, Annie!" She poured a cup and sat beside me. "You're up early."

"How can you drink that black?"

Mom took a sip of the steaming cup. "Mmm. Perfect." She grabbed some of the paper while she leaned over to see what I was reading. "Who's that a picture of?"

I hesitated. "Christa's husband and son."

Mom frowned. "Don't look at that, Annie. It'll just make you more sad." She pulled out the Lifestyle section.

I wondered at my mother's ability to shut out the world and only deal with the pleasant things. Sure, Dad irritated the crap out of her, and she complained about it. But she didn't let it affect her life, not really. This was partly how she did it: ignore the headlines, ignore the sad things.

And then I saw it. I couldn't believe I hadn't noticed before.

"What?" Mom asked, staring at me.

I looked down at the ring.

Her left hand immediately closed.

"Were you going to tell me?" I asked.

"I was waiting until the time was right."

"And you didn't think I would notice the ring?"

"I hoped you'd be happy for me, Annie."

"Oh, I so am," I said sarcastically. "When's the wedding? Am I invited?"

"I know you don't like Donald now—"

"I don't *dislike* him, Mom. I just don't care. And you want me to embrace him like he's my long-lost papa."

"Annie," she began, "do you remember when I told you there were two reasons why I wanted you to let Donald pay for your college?"

"Yeah, maybe."

"I didn't tell you the second reason. I . . . I just want you to feel like you're part of a family. That you have people who will take care of you."

"I already have a *family*, Mom. I have more family than most of my friends with you and Dad and all my aunts and cousins living right here in town. I don't have a problem there."

"But you don't have a responsible dad—"

"I do have a dad, and it's not Donald."

A look of irritation crossed Mom's face.

"Now, see, what's that face about, Mom? Just because *you* hate my father—"

"Annie, I don't hate—"

"—doesn't mean I do. Sure, he's irresponsible and thoughtless and just a mess, at least to you, but he's my dad. And I like being with him. I mean, even though the car kept breaking down, he kept getting it fixed and even fixed it himself when he had to—just to get me home. And he's fun. Sometimes it's exciting to be around that."

I pretended to read the paper, wishing Mom would go away. I looked up, irritated to see a smile on her face. "What's up with you?"

"I was just thinking. When your dad and I were kids, just a little older than you . . ."

I put the paper down.

". . . we drove down to Padre Island . . ."

I took a drink of my Coke. "Grandma let you?" Mom was the youngest and the only daughter, very close to her mom.

"I was a strong-minded girl."

"But Grandma is too."

"There was some clashing there. But it was 1965. And I had plans." She looked wistful for a moment, younger. "So anyway, your dad and I parked on the beach in his old beat-up Mustang. We pitched a tent and went for a long walk, picking up seashells, playing in the waves. It was . . . perfect. And your father was so . . . young, so happy all the time. Fun."

She had this dreamy look on her face. She never brought up Dad at all, except to complain about him. "Then we came back to the car." She pressed her lips together and her eyes watered.

"What, Mom?" I asked. Was she upset?

"The tide had come in." Mom's eyes were lit with glee.

"So?"

"Well," she said, "your *father* had parked the car right on the beach. And set up the tent at the edge of the water."

"Oh no."

"The tent was *gone*. Floating out to sea, along with our sleeping bags, our pillows, my little stuffed cat," she said, "that I used to sleep with and brought everywhere with me."

"Oh, Mom, you had a little stuffed cat?"

"I didn't actually see the cat float away, but I knew it was out there in the Gulf of Mexico somewhere."

"And the car?"

"We couldn't drive it out. It was flooded up to almost the top of the wheels."

"What did you do?"

"I was so freaked. I screamed, pointed at the tent. I yelled and yelled about my cat. I was so mad," she said, shaking her head. "People on the beach were laughing. One guy was taking pictures. And your dad," she said, a smile creeping up on her lips, "yelled, 'I'll find Maples!'"

"Maples?"

"My cat. And he ran into the waves and swam out. I thought he was going to drown. Well, of course, he didn't find the cat. He came back out all wet, wading through the water to the car, and he opened the trunk, and came back with two cold beers in his hand. He popped the top of one and gave it to me, and said, 'I'm sorry about Maples, babe.'"

I smiled.

Mom was watching me. "I don't hate your dad, Annie." She got up and poured another cup of coffee. Leaning against the counter, she took a sip of her coffee and looked off like she was still remembering. Then, she smiled. "But he is such," she said in a most loving way, "an idiot." She looked at me, her eyes a little teary. "I just got tired of being the only grown-up in the room."

"Yeah," I said, sad for all of us. I got up and stood by her, leaning against the counter, suddenly wanting to be near her.

She hugged me and then let me go. "It's all right, Annie. It'll be all right."

"I'll think about taking Donald's money *if* I go to college," I said. "But I'll need to talk to Dad about it first."

"Ah," she said, raising her eyebrows. "That's very brave of you. Are you sure? Because I can tell him."

"I'm sure." I smiled. "See, you're not the only grown-up in the room."

CHAPTER 45

On Saturday, when Tommy came to pick me up, Mom wasn't there. Hallelujah! I didn't want her to know about Tommy. Donald had picked her up early for a breakfast at a local café and an outing to look at possible places for the wedding reception. Mom was particularly excited about the Grand 1894 Opera House in Galveston. She'd heard they held parties on the stage.

I stood on the porch, waiting for Tommy, anxious to see him. I knew I shouldn't be so eager, but I couldn't help what I was feeling. When his car pulled up, I broke into a grin.

"Hi," I said, getting into his car. He smiled; I melted.

"Hi," he said, pulling me to him for a quick hug. He felt good. I wanted to hold on. And he smelled like fresh air. "Ready to go?"

I nodded, wanting to get out of my driveway. I was worried I'd get caught. I *had* actually thought about telling Mark. But I knew if I did, I wouldn't be going with Tommy anywhere today. I'd either be fighting with Mark about why I was going to go or fighting with Mark about breaking up.

"Was that your stomach growling?" he asked, giving me another Tommy smile that made my stomach flip. How I'd missed him.

"Sonic would be great. I'm hungry." I looked away so he wouldn't see the idiotic grin on my face.

"Sonic, it is."

At Sonic, we ordered two cheeseburgers, fries, two chocolate malts, tater tots, and two waters.

When the waitress in skates rolled out with our order, I couldn't help but notice how pretty she was and how she lit up when she saw Tommy. "Thanks for the tip," she said, giving him an extra little smile.

He just nodded at her and turned back to me.

"Thanks for not flirting with her."

"I want to be with you, not her," he said. "I've missed you."

"Dad told me that, when he was over yesterday." Dad hadn't stayed long. He'd asked a few questions about Mom, trying to get information about her and Donald, I knew.

"Really? Oh, great," Tommy said.

"He talks about you all the time now," I said, teasing him.

"I'll have to watch what I say." He grinned.

I smiled, feeling a little shy. Here we were back in Texas, back in my real life, together in his car. I looked at him. "Have you had a lot of girlfriends, Tommy?" This was something I'd been curious about since Florida, or maybe since I'd first seen him in my driveway. "I bet you have."

"I've had a few."

"Anyone serious?" I asked.

"Yeah," he said. "A girl in California."

"California? So a college girlfriend. How long did you date?"

"Until I left."

"How long was that?"

He laughed. "Well, let's see. I met her my freshman year at a friend's party. It was about midway through, I guess. Right before Christmas break."

"When did you leave college?"

"After sophomore year."

"Oh my God."

"What?" he asked.

"That's a long time to date someone," I said, feeling a little jealous of this girl from Tommy's past that had been with him for almost two years.

"As long as you and Mark have gone out, right?"

"Yeah, but those are high school years. You were with her for two college years. That's some serious dating."

He laughed. "I don't think she thought so."

"Why do you say that?"

"Um . . . when I stumbled across her making out with my roommate, I figured she wouldn't mind if I left."

"Oh no. Really?"

He nodded.

"Is that why you left college?"

"No." He thought for a moment. "Well. Kind of."

"Really?" I asked, disappointed.

"Well, no. I mean, I was staying because of her. I wanted to quit my sophomore year, but I didn't want to leave her. So I figured I'd get a degree and then figure it out. But when I found her with my roommate—and somehow it hurt more that she'd fallen for an idiot, but then, I didn't have a reason to stay anymore."

"Oh."

"What's wrong?"

"Nothing."

"Something is. What are you thinking?"

"I just didn't think you'd be the kind of guy to change what you're doing because of a girl."

"Nothing's wrong with being in love, Annie."

"No," I said. "I know."

"So is that why you want to stay in Clear Lake? For Mark?"

"I don't know. It's for me, I think. Because I don't want to give it all up. I have it pretty good, Tommy."

"With Mark?" He looked disappointed.

"I like being with Mark. I don't think he's my soul mate, if there is such a thing, but he feels like a part of me." I tossed a tater tot back in the bag. "I understand people like Lea who want to leave to find something else. Like going to college to get out of here or because they think there's a better life some-place else. But I don't think that. I think life is what you make it. And I could be happy wherever I am."

"So you might stay here?"

"I don't know what I'm going to do."

"You're biting your lip," he said, gently touching my mouth, sending a little thrill through me. "You do that a lot."

His touch felt sweet and wrong at the same time. "I wasn't aware of it."

We looked at one another, and he dropped his hand. "I

guess I'm surprised because you were so taken with what Christa McAuliffe was doing—reaching for what she wanted."

"But I don't think she did that because she was unhappy," I said, fighting the sadness that had settled inside me since the accident. "I think she thought it'd be cool to have that experience and share it with her students. But if she hadn't been selected as the Teacher in Space, I think she would have been perfectly content to stay home and be a great teacher and raise her kids."

He smiled.

"What?" I asked. "What?"

"You think a lot."

"I'm good at thinking. I just need to learn how to actually *do*." I looked at him. "Don't you think a lot? You seem to."

"About things not concerning me, maybe," he said. "But when it comes to me, I just do. React and do." He laughed. "Or maybe I just react. Here I am working at the plant, when I say I want to be a teacher."

"So what's keeping you from it?" I asked. "Your dad?"

"He'd rather me get a degree in *anything* rather than work at the plant. But then again maybe I'm waiting for him to change his mind." He shrugged. "I don't know. It might just be laziness. I stopped thinking about it as much."

"That doesn't sound good."

"No?" he asked, looking at me closely.

"No," I whispered, quieted by his gaze.

He exhaled. "You gotta stop looking at me like that." He started the car. "Ready to go on an adventure?"

CHAPTER 46

We got on the interstate pretty quickly. There wasn't much Saturday traffic. I liked being in the car, as a passenger especially so I could watch the world go by. I'd enjoyed the road part of our road trip to Florida. Being on the road was exciting, like you might be on the verge of having the best damn time of your life.

"Where are we going?" I asked.

"It's a surprise."

"Still?"

"Be patient," he said, with a smile.

We got off on an exit I'd never taken before, to a part of Houston I'd never been in before, just right off I-45, not quite to downtown. Tommy shifted into a lower gear. I liked watching him drive his standard shift. He grinned. "What?"

"I want to drive your car."

"Do you drive a stick?"

"No."

He grinned again. "Okay, I'll teach you."

Nope, Annie. Not going to happen. Get it out of your head.

"Where *are* we?" I asked. Small homes lined the street. "Tommy, who do you know here? You're not taking me to meet a crazy friend who dropped out of USC or something?"

"No, a postman."

"Huh."

"But he's dead now."

"Okay. And we're visiting his grave then?" I asked, trying to be respectful, but not knowing if he was pulling my leg.

"I can't believe you're a child of Jesse's, and you don't know about the postman."

Then we arrived and parked.

"The Orange Show," I said. "The Orange Show. Of course."

It looked like an orange and red carnival. But it wasn't. There were no rides here. It was two city blocks of folk art. I'd heard about it from my dad, how Jeff McKissack had begun collecting found pieces on his mail route and building this monument of stages and stairs, bricks and tiles, lost pieces of people's lives becoming art, all in dedication to the orange, the perfect fruit.

We paid our $1 and got our free orange juice and began to wander.

It was bright out, which was perfect. The colors of The Orange Show popped against the vivid blue of the sky. This was touchable art too. I could run my fingers along the banged-out metal of the railings and sit down on old tractor seats given a new life. This place was made of concrete, brick, and steel, but it had ponds, an oasis, and a wishing well. I thought the Romantic poets might approve.

This was chaotic harmony, pieces of junk brought together and made into art by the vision of an old country postman.

I'd seen Dad's photos of The Orange Show, but they didn't capture its magic. It had to be seen and touched and walked through in order to feel the artist's inspiration.

"You like it?" Tommy asked.

"I really do, Tommy," I said, avoiding his eyes. I didn't want to look at him because I was feeling so emotional. This place was filled with creative energy and not at all ordinary— very much the kind of thing I liked. And for Tommy to think of this for me, it made me feel like I was on the highest hill of the tallest roller coaster, looking over the edge, waiting to drop.

We sat down on tractor seats in a small amphitheater.

"It's so cool," Tommy said. "So cool that this mail carrier, in the fifties, started collecting scraps, old tires, thrown-away tractor parts, anything he could find. And putting it all together. He worked on it for decades.

"Can you imagine? He must have really believed in himself and in what he was doing to keep working at it so long."

I looked around and knew I had been wrong about art stealing the souls of its artists. Jeff McKissack hadn't given up pieces of himself for his art, or rather if he did, those pieces must have come right back to make him richer than when he began. Maybe Vincent's paintings had given him a joy he would never have known if he hadn't picked up a brush. He hadn't suffered for his art; he had *lived* for it. He had been the person he was supposed to be.

That was what Christa had told me: the thing I had to offer was me and being true to that. She would have loved the story of the postman and his Orange Show. I could see her here, reveling in someone else's dream. She didn't want to just do something amazing herself. She wanted to share it, so others would reach for what they wanted too.

But you didn't have to travel to space to inspire: you could live your life, do your job, walk across the street and still create art. Jeff McKissack had left his monument as inspiration, Vincent had left his art, and Christa had left her spirit. Such a simple idea, really, but I felt like I—finally— *got* it. I understood.

So what was holding me back?

I felt my eyes water and turned my head so Tommy wouldn't see, not wanting to share this with him or anyone else right now.

"Hey, what's wrong?" he asked, trying to pull my chin around.

"I'm fine, I'm fine."

"Stop crying," he said gently, wiping my face with his napkin. I could smell orange juice on it. "I can't be friends with a girl who cries for no reason."

"Now my eyes sting because of the orange juice."

"No more crying, though," he said.

"This is perfect, Tommy. Thank you for taking me here."

"I thought you'd like it. The art-car folks your dad hangs with told him about The Orange Show."

"The Beatmobile would fit right in." Dad had tried to get me to come here with him so many times, and I'd resisted. Over the years, I'd kept Dad at a distance in a lot of ways. But I knew I'd come here with him now.

"A couple of years ago, somebody donated a Ford station wagon to The Orange Show for an auction. A local artist created the Fruitmobile out of it."

"I think the man who created all this," I said, gesturing around me, "would have appreciated the Fruitmobile."

"He was a folk artist but he didn't even know it," Tommy said.

"And he was an artist before anyone called him one."

"I'm happy you said that." He pulled something out of his pocket. "And that's why you must read this here."

It was a piece of paper, folded up into a square. He put it in my hand. I unfolded it slowly, knowing what it was. "My poem."

He pointed to the stage.

"I can't," I said, shaking my head. "And there are other people walking around here."

He took my hand and led me to the center of the stage. Laughing, I tried to pull away, but had no luck.

"There," he said. "I'm going to sit on that tractor seat and listen."

I was nervous. I'd never read my poetry out loud to anyone before. And granted, it was just one person listening to me now—besides any wandering visitors who might peep in—but that person was Tommy.

I felt like I was at a poetry reading.

I took a breath and began: "I swim in a sea of yellow." The words felt good to say out loud. They were my words.

Chills crawled up and down my back as I read. I got into the poem, trying to make it sound like I wanted it to sound.

Fast, furious, one image pouring into the next. I looked up when I was done.

Tommy broke into applause. "Bravo! Bravo!"

"That was a blast!"

CHAPTER 47

On the way home, I was quiet, and Tommy didn't break my silence.

I was trying not to think about how much I'd miss him when he dropped me off. So instead I thought about Mark and how I'd never even told Mark about my poetry. Maybe I was afraid to find out he didn't like that side of me. So I wasn't giving him a chance.

We turned onto my street, and I began to worry. Mark was supposed to be working today, but sometimes schedules changed and he just ended up at my house. And that would be a catastrophe.

The driveway was empty. Relief.

"Thanks, Tommy," I said. "That was . . . good. I needed that."

"I want to see you again."

I felt sweet confusion in my stomach. "I can't. Right now."

He looked at me for a moment with sad eyes, then said with a quirky smile. "I didn't mean right *now*."

"Tommy, I will figure this out."

He took a breath. "Soon, I hope?"

"Soon." I hope.

We sat in quiet for a few minutes. I didn't want to get out of the car. And I knew he didn't want me to get out of the car.

I couldn't ask him in. That could be disastrous.

I had to get out of the car.

"Annie," he said, reaching over me to the glove box. He grabbed a pen and a piece of scratch paper and started writing. "This is my number." As he wrote, I thought of Christa giving me her address, connecting me a little to her life, and of me giving Bonnie and Clyde my phone number, connecting them to my life. "If you figure things out, or if you just want to talk, call me."

He offered it, and I took it.

"Bye, Tommy."

"Call anytime."

I looked at him for a moment more. And then I left.

CHAPTER 48

Mark, Lea, and I had left school right after lunch. It was crazy. I was way behind in my work after missing the week. And sneaking out of school was so not like me. I never skipped, except when boringly sanctioned and documented by parental authority.

Lea, of course, had skipped. And was always trying to tempt me to go with her. Today, it worked. Mark was going to surf. Lea and I were going to hang out at the beach. It was one of those warm Texas days we occasionally got in February, and we wanted to enjoy it.

We were at a stoplight.

"Oh, oh," Lea said, hitting my arm.

"What did you forget? Don't say your swimsuit because I'm not swimming."

"Let's do a Fire Drill."

"Do you mean a Chinese Fire Drill?" asked Mark.

"That's racist," said Lea. "What about a Writer's Fire Drill?"

"Not funny!" I exclaimed. "A Marilyn Monroe Fire Drill?"

"Get back from that. What about a Goofy Footer's Fire Drill?"

"And that makes no sense," said Mark.

"Like any of it does?" asked Lea. "We missed that light."

"I'll do it," I said. "Next light?"

"You?" asked Mark.

"Yes, her!" yelled out Lea. "Our Annie is changing."

"Not you?" I asked Mark.

"Have fun."

When we stopped again, I opened my door and raced around the car, slapping hands with a laughing Lea when I went by her. But then she pulled me back, trying to slow me down. "No, no!" I yelled, laughing. I finally yanked away. It felt so good to run. The old lady in the car behind us gave us a disgusted look. The light turned green. She laid on her horn.

"Hurry!" I heard Mark yell out the open window.

Lea was back inside. My hand was on the handle. A couple of other people blew their horns. I saw the man beside us laughing as I slipped inside. "Go!"

Mark took off, shaking his head at Lea and me. We could not stop laughing.

"It's not *that* funny," said Mark.

Lea reached from behind me and hugged my neck. "It's good to see you smiling."

"You're choking me."

"Just think, if you come to UT, we can have fun like this all the time."

I smiled back at her, but caught the frown on Mark's face.

- - - - -

"It's a beautiful day," said Lea.

Mark was surfing. Lea and I were lying on blankets. The salt air and the rush of the sea made me think of the beach in Florida. And Tommy.

"Yeah," I said, looking up at the blue, blue sky, and thinking of The Day and its blue, blue sky and wondering if I'd ever be able to see a sky like this and not think of Christa.

I looked over at Mark talking to another surfer. I watched him laugh; his head back a little, his hand sliding to his forehead, pushing back his hair. His movements and gestures were so familiar to me. He was the same, the same Mark he'd always been, consistent, loving, loyal.

When he lay down beside me, Lea went out to get her feet wet.

"You look relaxed today," he said, touching my cheek with the back of his hand. "It's good to see it."

I looked at him. "I was writing a poem."

"Writing a poem?"

"In my head."

"You could write them on paper, you know."

"I do," I said. "Lots of them."

"I figured," he said. "You're always talking about poetry. It made sense you'd write your own."

I looked at him, surprised. "Really?"

"Sure."

"That's what I want to do, Mark. I want to write poetry."

"Like right now?" he asked, picking his cap off the blanket and putting it on my head. "You look cute in that."

I pushed the bill back so I could see his eyes better. "No, I mean I want to work at getting better at writing it, trying to

develop a real skill for it, and take a little time after we graduate to see if I can do it."

"Like for a living, Annie? I don't think there's any money
in that," he said, with a laugh.

"No. I'd have to find a way to make all that work."

"You're serious? Annie, it's not practical. Poetry?"

"Yes," I said, wanting so much for him to understand. "Do
you want to hear the idea I've been thinking about?"

"Sure."

"You know Van Gogh the artist?"

"Yeah," he said.

"I want to visit the places of his life: Paris, Arles, Saint-
Rémy-de-Provence, and write poems about the paintings or
drawings he worked on at each place. And the poems, see,
would also reflect what was going on in his life at the time, so
my collection would be a biography of his life through his
paintings."

He was staring at me, not saying anything. "So if you want
to visit France, we'll go to France. Is that what you want?"

"I'm still trying to figure all that out. I just wanted to tell
you about my poetry."

"I'm glad you did," he said, pulling the cap down over
my eyes.

I pushed it back up and rolled over on my stomach. I
played with the sand, letting it run through my fingers. "Mark,
why do you love me?"

"Annie." He got closer, lying on his stomach beside me,
wrapping his arms around me, half of his body on mine. "I
just do." He felt good.

"But why?" I asked.

"I don't think people know why they love someone. They just do." He shook me playfully. "What's wrong?"

"It's just that," I began, "sometimes I think I could be anyone to you, Mark. That who you love is not really who I am."

"Annie, I know *you*. I love *you*." He kissed my cheek, his arms still around my neck.

I kept playing with the sand.

CHAPTER 49

Dad and I were washing the Beatmobile in front of my house. Lea had asked if she could help, which meant she was sitting in the grass reading a magazine while we worked. Mom and Donald were off looking at wedding cakes, so I knew it was time for me to talk to Dad and tell him about them getting married this summer.

A bucket of cold soapy water was at my feet. I was washing Allen Ginsberg's face painted on the hood of the Beatmobile. The sun was out. Dad was singing. Lea was deeply involved in her article.

"Dad?"

He stopped singing. "Yep?"

Allen Ginsberg stared at me with a challenging poetic gaze. I pushed the soapy sponge into his eyes. "Did I ever tell you"—and I knew I hadn't—"that I like to write poetry?"

"Do you? That's great."

I stopped and looked over at him, surprised he was so, well, not surprised.

"When I was younger," he continued, "I wrote too."

"Why don't you anymore?" I asked, not knowing how someone just stopped. I'd miss it too much.

"I was more interested in reading poems than writing them." He went over to the bucket. "Would you ever let me read your poetry?"

"Maybe," I said, joining him and waiting for him to wring out his sponge. "Dad, I need to talk to you about a couple of things."

"About your poetry?" he asked.

"No." Finally, I said, "It's about Mom and Donald."

He started cleaning the windshield, ignoring me.

I hated this. "They're getting married."

"Yeah," he said, glancing back at me. "I figured."

Well, if you figured, I thought, *you could have made it easier for me and just told me you figured.* But I didn't say that, because I had to get the rest of it out. And I knew the next part would be hard. I dropped my sponge in the bucket.

"Annie, I knew this was coming. It's not a big surprise."

"Well, there's more."

His eyes went wide. "She's pregnant?"

"No!" I exclaimed. Then I paused. I hadn't even considered that. Mom was over forty.

"What is it, then?" He stopped washing and leaned against the car, his arms folded. "Spit it out, Annie."

"I told Mom . . . that I would consider—and I'm not even sure I'm going, Dad—but I told her I'd think about letting Donald pay for college." I saw Lea look up from her magazine, but she didn't say anything. I knew she was probably listening.

He turned his head away from me and was quiet.

I let him be quiet. Quiet was better than him yelling. But after a few minutes went by and he still hadn't spoken, I said, "Dad. You're my dad. Donald will never be that, no matter what he is to Mom. I already have a father."

He looked at me then. "Yeah. I know, baby."

"You do? So you're okay with it?"

He kind of laughed. "No." Then he shrugged and smiled. "No."

I gave him a sad smile. "Everything's changing, I know."

"Yeah, it is." He tapped my arm with his wet sponge. "It'll be all right, Annie."

"That's what Mom said."

"Well," he said, shrugging, "she's right about that *one* thing."

I reached out for him, putting my hand on his arm. "Are you okay?"

"Yeah," he said. "Are you okay?"

I nodded. "Yeah."

"Good," he said, going back to the windshield.

I dunked the sponge a couple of times and squeezed the excess water out of it, so relieved that conversation was over. Dad went around to the other side of the car, closer to where Lea was. "I hear you and Tommy went to The Orange Show?" he called out to me.

Lea's head whipped up. "Tommy? Who's Tommy?" She *had* been listening.

I frowned. "He told you that?" I was slightly disappointed Tommy was telling Dad things about us. I could feel Lea's eyes on me.

"He didn't mean to. But he told me something you'd said . . . and then I got the rest out of him. That boy's so infatuated he's stupid with it."

Stupid with it? I felt myself blushing fiercely, but then I remembered that was what Dad had said about Mark being smitten with me.

"Who's Tommy?" Lea asked again, coming over to me.

"He was on the trip with us to Florida," I told her.

Her brow furrowed. "What? You never mentioned that."

I glanced at Lea nervously. I hadn't told her about Tommy because I felt guilty. And I felt guilty because I'd kissed him. Dad didn't know that, of course. But now he was watching me closely. And Lea was watching me closely.

"I just forgot," I snapped.

"You forgot?" she asked. "Right. And you went to some show with him?"

"The Orange Show. It's a place." I got the hose to put fresh water in the bucket, so I wouldn't have to look at Lea being mad at me. "Tommy works with Dad and wanted to see the shuttle launch."

"Annie," she said.

I stopped what I was doing. "Yeah?"

"Does Mark know?" she asked quietly. Lea said very few things quietly, so it was as jarring as if she'd yelled.

"Yes, he knows," I said. "He was there when we left."

She was very quiet now. "Why didn't you tell me?"

"I've only been back for a few weeks, Lea."

She gave me a look.

"I'm sorry. I am. I'm sorry."

"Right," she said. "I need some water." She started off toward the house. I followed her inside.

She'd been in my kitchen enough to know her way around. I sat at the table and watched her get a glass, throw some ice cubes in it, and fill it with water. She sat down and looked at me.

"Tommy is this guy," I began, "who went to Florida with Dad and me. He's twenty-two, he dropped out of USC, and he works at the plant with Dad."

She nodded.

"And I kissed him."

"What?!"

"That's why I didn't tell you about him, Lea. I've felt so bad about it."

"Gosh, Annie. You do keep secrets. How did this happen?"

So I told her about the trip. Lea hadn't asked very much about it because of the accident. She hadn't wanted to upset me, I knew, but it'd worked out: I hadn't had to tell her the details.

When I told her about the kiss, she just sat there for a minute.

"Wow," she said.

"Wow," I said, feeling sick.

She looked at me. "Do you like this guy, Annie?"

I nodded.

"Did you tell Mark?"

"No!" I exclaimed. "And you don't tell him either."

"I wouldn't, Annie."

"Well, you do talk to Mark about me, remember?"

"That was just that one time." She took a drink of her water. "Wow."

"I'm sorry I didn't tell you, Lea. I've been confused."

"It's not just this, Annie. It's other things too. You're so secretive about yourself. I tell you everything."

"I know. I'm working on that. I am."

"It's important you talk to me. We're going to be apart after this summer." Her eyes were sad. "You'll have to call me, tell me things, even boring little things going on so I can be a part of your life, wherever you are."

"I will, Lea. I will."

"All right. Now more about this Tommy, please."

CHAPTER 50

E^{rnest} Hemingway didn't go to college," I said to Lea. We were at a new café in Seabrook.

"You don't look well," she said. "Are you okay? You've got these dark circles under your eyes. It's not a good look for you."

"I'm fine," I said. "Did you know Dorothy Parker stopped school at thirteen?"

"Dorothy who?"

"Men seldom make passes at girls who wear glasses?"

"I don't think glasses matter to most guys."

"No, Lea, that's not . . . never mind. My point is, college is not a prerequisite for success."

"Well, maybe not in the olden days. It probably is today. Especially in the good old USA."

"Why do you want to go to college, Lea?"

She looked at me. "You've got your serious voice and your serious face, and I do not like it."

I munched on another salty fry. "Just answer the question."

"It's just what you do, Annie. You go to high school, you graduate, you go to college."

"Then what?"

"What do you mean?" asked Lea, stealing one of my fries.

"Hey! You should have gotten your own."

"Fries are bad for you."

"Would you answer the question?"

"Didn't I?" asked Lea, taking a bite out of my burger. I removed it from my hungry friend's hand. Lea grabbed another fry.

"So what of it?" I asked. "What are you going to do after college?"

"Get married and have kids. Ga! Don't make that face!"

"I knew you were going to say that," I said.

"I knew you were going to make that face, which is why I was stealing fries and bites of burger instead of answering you. I thought you were the one thinking of staying here to be with Mark anyway. Or has that changed now that, you know, other things have happened?"

I studied my burger really closely.

"What?" Lea asked.

"Huh?"

"Why is your burger so interesting all of a sudden?" Lea asked.

My hand on the table was suddenly covered with Lea's. I looked up. Lea's face was frozen.

"What?" I asked.

"Are you going to break up with Mark?"

"I don't know what to do, Lea. I don't think I love him," I

said, quietly. "I mean, I love him. But I'm not in love with him anymore." It hurt to say it, but it felt true. I was exhausted. I'd gotten very little sleep last night. "I don't love him, Lea."

Lea made a sad face. "I'm sorry."

I pushed my fries away.

"I'm so sorry!" exclaimed Lea. "I've made you sad."

"You didn't make me sad. All this stuff is just sad."

"Are you going to break up with him?" she asked.

"I don't know how I'm going to do it. Just thinking of it makes me sick."

"You've been together a long time. And friends for longer than we have!"

"I know."

"Do you think you're going to miss him?" asked Lea.

"Yeah, I do."

"He loves you so much. It's going to hit him hard."

"Now," I said, taking a sip of my Diet Coke, "you're depressing me."

"Oh, I'm a terrible friend!"

"So since you're feeling bad and all for making me sad, answer another question."

"Okay," said Lea, agreeing despite looking like she really wanted to keep talking about how sad Mark must be.

"Are you going to college because you're expected to or because you want to?"

"Didn't I answer this already?"

"Nope," I said.

Lea sighed. "Why do you think about this stuff?"

"Lea."

"All right." She paused, looking like she was thinking about it. "Yes, it does seem like it's expected, like it's thirteenth grade. But I'd go anyway, I think, even if my parents didn't expect it."

"Would you?" I asked. "Or are you saying that because you've been brought up to think that way, like being Methodist?"

"I like being Methodist."

I smiled. "Yes. So do you think it's like that?"

"Since that's what I've always known, how would I know? And maybe I'm glad I was brought up with that idea." She shrugged. "I'm looking forward to it. I mean, Annie," she said, leaning forward, "I think the question is, why don't you want to go?"

"I didn't say I didn't."

"But you're thinking about that, whether you really want to go."

"Maybe I should talk to Mr. Williams about it," I said.

"Any excuse to talk to Mr. Williams," she said, grinning. "Look, I don't understand what's not to like about going to college. Maybe you don't want to go because you're being rebellious, you think that's what's expected of you, so you're determined not to do it."

"That's just weird," I said. "I don't think that's it."

"Then, what is *it*?"

I hesitated. "I don't know what I want, Lea. I'm not like you or Mark or my mom or my dad or even Tommy—"

"Speaking of Tommy—"

"—all I know is I like to read." And I like to write poetry.

"Yeah. But—"

"And I like living in my house with just my mom and me with my dad coming over all the time and watching television with me. Sure, sometimes I go nuts and want my own car to get out of the house, but when I feel that way, I call Mark . . ." I stopped and looked down. "And Mark comes over and we drive and drive." I was talking quietly now. "And I like riding in the car with him. Just driving around."

"Okay," said Lea. "Okay. It's all okay, Annie. All that."

I looked into my friend's eyes, but wasn't focusing on her. "But I don't love Mark. And I can't ride around in the car with him for the rest of my life just so I won't have to stop and figure out what I need to do next."

"No, you can't," said Lea softly.

I sighed. "How can I care so much about him, but it not be right for us to be together?"

Lea shook her head. "You want different things."

"What do you mean? I don't know what I want."

"I've said all along I think you're meant for great things. And Mark just wants to be here, stay here."

"And part of me wants that too."

"Do you think, Annie," asked Lea, "that that's just the scared part of you?"

I looked at Lea for a long time before answering. "Partly. But it also feels like . . . loss. Like I'm giving something up."

"You are, Annie. But that's just what happens in life."

"Yeah," I said. "But I don't like it."

CHAPTER 51

M̲r. Williams was at my front door.

"Hi," I said. Even if it was expected, it was still very odd to see Mr. Williams in my doorway and not in front of a blackboard with a piece of chalk in his hand.

"Hi, Annie."

"I'm ready," I said, grabbing my purse.

"Is your mom here? I'd like to meet her. We only got to talk for a moment on the phone."

"She's not," I said, closing the door and locking it. I turned around. "I'm ready," I said again. I was ready for answers, and a little nervous.

On the way to Houston, I thought about how weird it was to be in a car with Mr. Williams, just the two of us. His invitation had come after I'd told him my secret. It was getting easier to talk about my desire to be a poet, especially after having my first poetry reading at The Orange Show with my audience of one.

Lea had flipped out when I told her what I was doing

today. She wanted to come, so she could stare at Mr. Williams throughout lunch. I said no.

"So, Annie?" Mr. Williams asked.

"Yes?"

He hesitated. "You haven't talked about the *Challenger* accident at all."

I still didn't want to talk about it. I only felt like I could confide in Tommy about all that.

He must have known. He let the subject drop.

We went to Vargo's, an established restaurant in Houston with a lake and a gazebo, footpaths and bridges, peacocks, and white graceful swans. It was a wonderful spot to discuss my future, and I had a feeling Mr. Williams was trying to draw me out with pressed tablecloths and rich desserts.

While we waited, I drank my iced tea and felt a bit out of place. I remembered a scene in Sylvia Plath's novel, *The Bell Jar*, when Esther mistook a small bowl with cherry blossoms for soup. She drank it up and ate the crisp flowers. I had included the scene in my own Plath poem. I read later that nearly every poet has a poem about Plath.

I wouldn't drink the finger bowl here, if there was one.

"What are you smiling at?" asked Mr. Williams.

"I didn't know I was smiling . . . ," I said, looking up at the elderly woman at Mr. Williams's side.

"Oh!" Mr. Williams said, standing. "I didn't see you there."

I'd imagined this poet friend of Mr. Williams's to have long gray hair and wear big earrings. I'd been wrong.

Introductions were made. Professor Gaines—a petite,

elegant-looking woman—sat down. She leaned forward and said to me, her head shaking a little, "I hear you are a poet."

The words sent a sweet, true feeling through me. I almost denied it, but then nodded and said, "Yes, I am a poet." Then I laughed.

"Well, it is a funny thing to be," she said.

She ordered a glass of white wine and then turned to me. "What would you like to know, Annie?"

I looked at Mr. Williams, who raised his eyebrows.

"I want to know . . . to start with, I guess, when did you know you wanted to be a poet?"

Her blue eyes matched her blue suit. She looked frail, but when she talked, her voice was strong and clear. "I was about nine years old. I wrote a poem about my mean, sour brother, comparing him to a green apple. Why do you like to write poems, Annie?"

I smiled, thinking of the why.

"Ah!" she said, pointing. "It gives you joy."

"It's putting words together, side by side, shuffling them around, finding the more perfect fit, the better word, creating the rhythm on paper that I hear in my head, like painting music with language. You're right. It does give me joy. And it helps me make sense of things, or at least get closer to the truth of things."

She glanced at Mr. Williams, and they shared a smile. I played with my forks nervously.

"But you don't want to go to college to learn more about poets and poetry?"

"My friends who want to be engineers or doctors, they're

so lucky. They'll get to do what they love and get paid for it. Those of us who want other things . . ."

"Face a more uncertain future," Mr. Williams finished for me.

"Exactly."

"There's no money in poetry," said Mr. Williams, "but then there's certainly no poetry in money and so it's all even."

"Robert Graves said that?" asked Professor Gaines.

Mr. Williams nodded.

She smiled a little mischievously. "Joseph Roux said, 'Science is for those who learn; poetry, for those who know.'"

Mr. Williams laughed.

The professor's eyes lit up with amusement. She looked at me. "You didn't answer my question, Annie. Is it very important to you to learn about poetry?"

I thought about Van Gogh only selling one painting in his lifetime. "Poetry isn't going to pay the bills."

She laughed. "You are as stubborn as I am. You still haven't answered my question."

"I feel like poetry has me, and I have it in me, and I can't silence it, but—"

She had her hand raised, so I stopped talking. "Then go to college and study poetry. That's what you should do."

I looked at Mr. Williams, and he smiled.

"What's wrong?" she asked.

"I thought we'd be discussing it more," I said, "that you'd want to know what I think."

She looked at me, her gaze so direct and honest. "I was telling you what I thought. You already know what you think."

"No, I don't think I do."

'Then you need to think some more." She picked up the menu. "Let's order first."

As we ate, Professor Gaines talked about how she too wanted to be a poet, but knew she couldn't support herself. So she went to college and worked on an English degree, and then another, and another. And she ended up teaching poetry for thirty-five years, and being surrounded by the poetry of the masters and the poetry of her students. She'd loved it.

"So you think I need to go to college?" I asked.

"College will open up your life for you, not only in what you learn, but in whom you meet and what you experience. And you'll find, I imagine, that you'll be a better poet after you study poetry. It's not always true. And it's just my opinion. Ask someone else; get another opinion. But you've asked me, and that's my opinion."

"But you haven't looked at any of my poetry," I said, thinking of the poems in my purse. "What if I don't have a gift for it? Can I learn to be a poet?"

"No one knows the answer to those questions, Annie."

But I needed answers, was desperate for them.

"Professor Gaines," I said, reluctant to bring up this topic but pushing myself on, "a poet has to reveal so much of herself in her poetry. Even when the subject isn't personal, the poem feels very personal to me. If what I write isn't any good, I'll have put myself right out there for nothing."

"Do you think so? Do you think it will be for nothing?"

"I don't know," I said. "If a writer or an artist is gifted, then even if she's not able to make a living at it while she's alive, she'll leave something behind for people to enjoy. But what if you're not gifted—not even a smidgen of talent—what if your poems or books or paintings are never enjoyed by anyone but you." I shrugged. "Is it worth it to pursue it? How do I know if studying poetry is the right choice for me?"

"It might not be. But finding that out is learning something too."

I nodded.

"You look disappointed," she said.

"No," I said, "just thinking."

"Annie, I know you want answers, but have you considered that the journey to finding out these things is part of the point?"

I smiled at her. "I thought you'd be enigmatic, you know, giving me subtle messages that I had to decipher."

She laughed. "Because I'm a poet?"

"Yes," I said.

She peered at me. "You thought I would be like a Bob Dylan song."

Mr. Williams laughed.

"You know who Bob Dylan is?" I asked.

"Pshaw. You're so young," she said. "I'm surprised *you* know who he is."

"I'm surprised both of you know who he is," said Mr. Williams.

"He's a poet," I said, then took a sip of my iced tea.

"I'll toast to that," said Mr. Williams, tipping his glass to mine.

And even Professor Gaines joined in the toast.

The times they are a-changin', I thought.

CHAPTER 52

The lunch with Professor Gaines didn't launch me into any decision making about my future. I let the days run one into the other, thinking about Mark, about graduation, but still unable to act, to do anything.

I knew Mark sensed something, especially because he didn't ask again about my trip to Florida. I thought he didn't want to know what happened on the trip or between Tommy and me.

One day, after work at the theater on a Saturday afternoon, we went to my house to hang out. I flicked on the TV. We watched show after show until finally I noticed how dark it was. The room had been lit with dusk light when we'd first sat down. Now the only light was from the TV.

The news was on. They were showing an old interview with the principal of the high school where Christa had taught.

Mark jerked. "Do you want me to turn it off?"

"No," I said, sitting up. "I want to see it." I left the couch and went to sit on the floor in front of the TV. I turned up the volume.

It was a happy interview. Christa had just been selected as the Teacher in Space. "She's sort of a risk-taker," the principal was saying. "She does the unusual. And she's not afraid of things. She lives life. She's not afraid of it."

Then the news showed a clip of a white-helmeted Christa in a T-38 waving as she went by the camera.

In another clip, she was speaking about what it was like to fly on an airplane that simulates zero gravity. "As you peak, that parabola at the top," she said, gesturing with her hand, "you have about twenty or thirty seconds of weightlessness, and all of a sudden, just like Peter Pan you just start flying up, and it was just unbelievable."

There was a laugh in her voice, and a look of wonder on her face. She had been doing exactly what she wanted to be doing and having so much fun.

What am I doing? I thought. *I'm sitting here, doing nothing.* That was what I did. Nothing.

The only thing I ever did was take a trip to Florida. And fall for a guy I hardly knew. And then I came back, sat in front of the television, and just willed life to go on—with Mark beside me.

This whole year the only thing I'd been certain and clear about was the need to see Christa fly. Seeing someone else's dream take wing, not my own.

"Annie, let's not watch this stuff. It's making you upset."

"I need a glass of water." I left for the kitchen.

I fingered the white petals of the daisies in the glass vase on the table. *I love him, I love him not.* Mark came in.

I went to the sink. Mom hadn't washed the dishes from

her dinner with Donald. Our dishwasher had been broken for a few months. Dad had offered to fix it, but Mom had said no. One sink was filled with old, cold water. And one pan. One pot. Two plates. Two glasses. Two spoons. Two knives. Two forks.

Seeing the paired dishes only made me feel really, really sad. I must be a terrible person for not wanting Mom to be happy with someone. It just made everything seem so final. And like Mom was moving on without me when I was the one who was supposed to be moving on.

Was I digging my heels into Clear Lake because of Mom? I didn't think so. But that might be a part of it.

I'd liked our life together.

I let the cold water run down the drain.

"Are you going to answer me, Annie?"

"I need to wash the dishes." I ran the water to warm it up and squirted dishwashing soap in the sink.

"I'll help," he said.

I washed and rinsed. Mark dried and tried to kiss my neck.

I scooted away, grabbing another towel. "Here, dry with this one. That one's wet."

Mark took it and was quiet while he dried a plate. I went back to washing, glad for the silence. I had to tell him. I knew.

"Annie?"

I took a breath. "Yes?"

"Is something wrong?"

I paused. This was like swimming through mud. I stared at my hands in the soapy water, feeling sad. I took a breath and wiped my hands on the towel. When I looked at him, I felt like there was a heavy weight on my chest holding the words inside. I pushed them out. "I have to talk to you."

It was like I slapped him. His face fell. He turned from me and kind of shook his head.

"Mark——," I began, reaching out for him.

"No."

"Mark, let's sit down."

"You don't love me anymore?"

I tried to say something, anything.

"Annie," he said, softly. "Annie. You're crying." He wiped my face with the towel.

"Mark," I said. "I'm sorry. I'm so sorry." I couldn't think of anything else to say.

His eyes watered, and it broke my heart.

"Mark. I'll always love you. You mean so much to me."

"But you're not . . . in love with me anymore."

I shook my head. "I'm sorry. I'm so sorry."

He pulled back, throwing his hands up in the air.

Whoosh, it was gone, the love, the caring, the sweetness . . . I really needed it right now, and he was especially good at it, but it wasn't fair to him. "Mark." I tried to reach for him. He backed up.

"Tell me the truth," he said, his eyes wet, his voice steel. "Is it Tommy?"

I hesitated.

"I knew it. I knew it. When I saw that guy, I knew I shouldn't have let you go."

I could have gotten mad. He had no right to say he shouldn't have let me go, like he owned me. But what did it matter what he said now? "Mark. You knew something was wrong before I left, that's why you got so mad when I was leaving. You sensed that I didn't feel the same way anymore."

He looked like he was going to say something, but he didn't. "I gotta go."

"Mark." I thought he was crying. "Mark, wait."

He didn't stop.

I stared out the living room window. Mark got into his car, slamming the door. When he drove away, the tires squealed. I could even hear it inside the house. I watched the cars go down the road.

———

CHAPTER 53

I looked for him at school—in the hallways, at his locker. He wasn't anywhere.

Then I went to the one class we had together and he wasn't there either.

"Where's Mark?" Lea asked in a concerned voice. She and I had spent two hours on the phone last night.

"I don't know."

I looked around. The teacher wasn't here yet, so everyone was in groups talking. No one was listening to the two of us. They all had their own stuff.

Mark walked in the room. He looked terrible. His eyes were red. His hair was not brushed, his clothes were so wrinkled it looked like he had slept in them. I silently pleaded with him to look up at me. But he avoided my eyes, walking past his normal seat beside me and sitting in the back of the room.

The whispers started. Eyes turned my way, then his. I was glad the teacher walked in right then. I opened my book and stared at the board, wishing this day would just be over so I could go home and curl up on the couch in front of the TV. Maybe Dad would come by. Life could stop, and then go on.

I waited for Mark after class. People would catch my eye as they came out, then look away like they were embarrassed for me. I was sure they were wondering what was going on. Mark and I had been a couple for ages.

I worried what he would do when he saw me. He was taking forever. I swallowed and looked down, looked back up. I didn't want to be standing here, but I had to talk to him. I was worried about him.

He was the last one out. He stopped abruptly when he saw me. "Oh," was all he said.

"Can I talk to you?"

He looked at a whispering huddle of girls in the corner. "Just leave it," he said, walking off.

I followed him. "I'm worried about you," I said, putting my hand on his arm.

He pulled away. "Don't."

I watched him walk off down the hallway.

When the last bell of the day rang, I went straight to his car. I leaned against it, waiting.

It wasn't long before I saw him walking toward me, or toward the car rather.

"What are you doing?" he asked, putting the key in the lock.

"I need a ride."

"Ride the bus."

"I've already missed the bus."

He opened the door. "What is it you want, Annie?"

"A ride home."

He sighed, looked off toward the football field. "Fine."

We didn't say anything on the way home. It was a short but painful drive. The words wouldn't seem to come to me. I didn't want to talk to him when he was driving anyway. I wanted his full attention.

"Do you want to go over the bridge?" I asked.

"I gotta get home."

We pulled up in front of my house. "Can you come in? I want to talk to you."

"I don't want to talk to you."

"I won't get out of the car until you agree."

"Fine," he said like he was disgusted with me. "Let's get this over with," he added, slamming the car door.

We went inside.

"Let's sit down," I said, gesturing to the couch.

But he wouldn't. He just stared out the window. "So you're with that Tommy guy," he said.

I wanted to tell him the truth. "Not yet. But I think I will be."

He turned around and stared at me. "He doesn't know you like I know you. How long has he known you? A month? I've known you since we were kids."

"Yes, Mark, since we were kids," I said, sitting on the couch.

He stared at me. "Why did you want me to come in here?"

My eyes were burning. "Sit down," I said. "Please."

He sat in Dad's chair.

I took a breath. "I wanted to tell you that I care about you,

Mark. And that I'm really sorry I did this to you." His sadness clutched at my heart.

He took a ragged breath. "Annie." He looked defeated. "I don't know how to be without you," he said, gazing at me with sudden desperation in his eyes. "You've been my whole life."

It tore me up to see him this way. And to know I had done it. "I wish I felt differently."

"Why him, Annie? Why him?"

"It's not just about him, Mark. He was what triggered it, yes. That, and *Challenger*, in a way. But I've felt this way for a while."

"Are you going to stay here after graduation to be with this guy?"

"If I stayed here, it wouldn't be because of him."

"I don't understand you."

"I don't understand either." I looked off, fighting tears. "But I can't make decisions about my life based on other people, on what they want me to do, or even on who they are to me."

"So you're going to go through life by yourself, Annie?" he asked. "You've got some sort of romantic idea about it, like you're this island, and you're cool because of it, because you don't want to be attached to anyone."

"We're so young, Mark. One day, I might settle down. But right now, I can only think of what I want. That's what I'm supposed to be doing, figuring out what I want, regardless of what everyone else wants for me, or even who I want to be with. I'm eighteen years old. That's it. I'm only eighteen. I get to figure out who *I* am right now. I get to figure out what my life is going to look like."

"And your life doesn't include me?" His face contorted, but he held it together, looking at me steadily.

"I wish it could," I whispered.

"We could just be friends. Still do stuff together."

"I wish we could. But, Mark, I don't think you can just be friends with me. I don't think that's going to be enough for you right now. Maybe later. But not right now."

"And so, our time together, which has been practically our whole life, is just gone. It just meant nothing."

"Oh, Mark. It meant so much."

"But it's over for you. You won't miss it? You won't miss me?"

"I already miss you. But life is about loss too," I said, trying very hard to get the words out. "You're one of my losses, and I'm one of yours."

"And this is what you wanted me to come over for?" He stood. "Great. Just great."

"I wanted to talk to you in private. Without everyone at school. I don't like seeing you in pain—"

"Too bad, Annie. I can't make that better for you. You're just going to have to see me in pain."

"I didn't mean it that way."

"Part of you did."

"You won't always feel this way. Not always."

He gave me one last look and then walked out the door.

CHAPTER 54

I stared at Tommy's phone number, wanting to call. A week had gone by since I'd broken up with Mark. But the last few nights had been very busy: studying for three tests, a night of working, and long chats with Lea about Mark and Tommy. So I still hadn't called him.

Finally, I did.

"Annie? Is that you?"

"Yes, it's me." I was nervous, but it was a good nervous.

"Hey! I can't believe you're calling."

"Is it all right?" I asked.

"I *wanted* you to call. What are you doing?"

"I'm sitting here talking to you," I said, stumbling over how to ask someone out on a date. "I was wondering what you were doing tomorrow." I didn't think that was how you did it, but that was what tumbled out.

"I'm skydiving. It's going to be a beautiful day. Want to come?"

"What? No. I don't know how to skydive."

"No, I mean, you could just come out there with me, see what it's all about."

Skydiving? I'd be watching Tommy jump out of a plane after we'd just seen *Challenger* fall apart in the sky. Probably not the best timing, but I wanted to be with him. "Sure," I told him. "Yeah."

- - - - -

He picked me up the next morning. He was wearing navy again, which was becoming my new favorite color. We grinned at each other stupidly and exchanged hellos. There was no hug like the last time I'd gotten into his car. Something felt new and different between us. I was suddenly shy, and slightly terrified by the extreme happiness pulsing through me at the sight of him.

"So, how's Mark?" he asked before we'd gotten out of my neighborhood.

"We broke up."

He glanced over at me. "Really?"

"Yeah."

"Are you okay?"

"Today I am."

He looked away from me. He glanced back, with a grin on his face. "Hell, Annie, I want to be sympathetic about it, but I'm really happy right now."

I nodded at him, knowing how he felt.

After that conversation, something shifted again, and we were less awkward and tentative with one another. We laughed a lot and teased one another about things. But there was no touching. I didn't know how he felt, but I wanted touching—I hoped he would at least reach out and take my hand. I wondered if he knew we were on a date.

"So graduation's getting close," he said.

"Yeah. Confusingly close."

He gave me a sympathetic look. "Still can't decide?"

"You know, I've been thinking about teaching."

He gave me a quick look. "Teaching?" He smiled. "Really?"

"I think at the college level, if I can hang in there long enough," I said, thinking of all the degrees I'd have to get. But the thought of going for a PhD and becoming Dr. Annie was actually kind of exciting.

"I didn't know you were thinking about teaching."

"It's been in the back of my mind. I'm not sure if it's for me. But there are things about it I would like."

"Like?"

"It'd be great to be around people who either know about poetry or want to learn about it. That'd be cool." I looked at him. "My dad and I are going to a poetry reading on Tuesday in Houston. Would you like to come too?"

He gave me a long sweet look. "I'd really like that, Annie." We were quiet for a moment. "It's cool," he said finally, "that we both might be teachers."

"You might go back to college, Tommy?"

"I'm seriously thinking about it."

It was a short drive to the tiny airport, which was in the middle of a field not far from my house. We parked next to a long, low gray building. Several jumpers—mostly guys, but some girls—were in front talking, already in their bright jumpsuits, orange, red, many shades of blue. Their excitement reminded me of being on the causeway, waiting for the shuttle to launch. I tried to push that thought away.

Tommy introduced me to a few people and left me with them while he went inside to pay and get ready. One gray-haired lady, the mother of two of the jumpers, pointed out the plane they would use—a white prop plane with red and blue stripes down the sides. "It's an Otter, on loan from Metro Airlines. They get the plane on Friday night, pull out the seats, and she's ready to go."

Tommy came out in a white jumpsuit, wearing a backpack filled with his parachutes, and a harness with straps around his legs, shoulder, and chest. He was so enthusiastic he seemed to already be up in the air.

"A natural high," he said, when I teased him about it.

"A crazy high," I said.

"All kinds of high today," he said, holding my eyes for a moment.

Whoa. What that look did to me. I was a little frightened by this charged connection between us. This was way past my comfort zone, but thrilling. The situation had changed. I didn't have a boyfriend. I was free.

I glanced over at the plane, not trusting it. "This reminds me of the *Challenger.*"

"Hey," Tommy said, grabbing my hand. "You look worried. It's fine."

His touch felt good. "How high do you go?"

"About thirteen thousand feet. We'll get about sixty seconds of free fall."

I nodded. *Challenger* had been almost four times that high when it fell apart.

"I shouldn't have asked you to come," he said, squeezing my hand. "I wasn't thinking. It's too soon after the accident."

"No, no. It's fine."

He turned toward the plane when someone called his name.

"Go, Tommy," I said. "Go. Have fun." I smiled at him.

"Okay. See you in a few," he said, jogging to the plane. He got on with the others and I gave him a little wave. I watched the plane roll away from me on the short runway.

There were other spectators. Two of the girls asked me questions about Tommy, and Tommy and me as a couple. They did it in a friendly way, making me feel part of the group. "You're the first person he's brought out here," said the girl with feathered blond hair.

"Really?" I asked, pleased.

A couple of guys pulled an ice cooler out of the back of a truck. One of them offered me something. I popped open a Diet Coke.

Someone pointed out the plane. I looked up, feeling a little rattled because it reminded me of the awful day we lost Christa. The sky had been blue, just like this. The land had been flat, just like this. And I had been looking up, just like this.

And the excitement in the air reminded me of the excitement that day.

So my heart was in my throat as I watched. But I didn't look away; I kept watching.

"Did you want to try this too?" the blonde asked me.

"Skydiving?" I asked. "I don't know."

"It's really a rush. You're flying at 120 miles per hour!"

"I think they're crazy," said a middle-aged man, "to be jumping out of a perfectly good airplane."

"There they go!" the gray-haired lady yelled.

White specks appeared in the sky as the plane flew away. The jumpers fell through the air while those around me clapped and laughed and pointed. It was all eerily similar to being on the KSC causeway with the *Challenger* crowd.

My eyes watered, but I brushed the tears away quickly. It was all right, really. I wasn't going to carry *Challenger* with me so closely anymore. I couldn't. There were too many beautiful things I'd miss if I did.

Their parachutes were popping out.

"Your boyfriend," the blonde told me, "has a dark blue chute."

I looked up, not telling her he wasn't my boyfriend. They were still too high for me to figure out who was who. "How high is he?"

"About two thousand feet or so." She grinned. "He'll be on the ground in five."

I watched them float down under colorful canopies and wondered what it must be like to be up there, looking out over Clear Lake and beyond it. They must feel a part of the sky. All these years I'd looked up to watch the stars. Maybe I'd like to look down to see my house while I floated above it.

As the skydivers got closer, I could hear them yelling out in wild whoops and hollers, like they were riding in on currents of pure joy. The gray-haired lady pointed Tommy out to me, but I'd already spied him. A couple of cameras were snapping, but I knew the skydivers would look very small in the photos.

And then Tommy's feet were on the ground and his parachute billowed out and then down behind him. I waved at him, but knew he probably couldn't pick me out from the rest of the crowd.

It wasn't long before he was running over to me, his arms out. "Hey, hey!" he said, spinning me around.

"You looked fantastic!" I exclaimed. "Was it as fun as it looked?"

"Oh, man. It was wild, a wild rush." He leaned back, a grin on his face. "You thought it looked fun. You did?"

"Yeah," I said. "Especially when your chute opened."

He laughed. "Maybe you'll come with me one day?" he asked, his hands on my shoulders. "Right?"

"Maybe," I said.

He pushed my hair out of my face. "Maybe?"

"Maybe."

"I'd like that, Annie. I'd really like to do this with you."

"You would?" I asked, leaning closer in, wanting him to kiss me.

"Yeah," he said, wrapping his arms around me.

"Your eyes are still lit up," I said. "I can see how much you like jumping out of airplanes."

"That's not the only thing that has my eyes lit up," he said softly.

"No?" I asked. *Kiss me. Kiss me. Kiss me.*

"Not even close."

I couldn't wait for him anymore. I moved in slowly, touching my lips to his, and thought of nothing else.

CHAPTER 55

The weeks began to go by quickly, rushing toward graduation.

Mom was still adjusting to my dating Tommy. She'd come off her engaged cloud long enough to register that her senior daughter was dating a twenty-two-year-old. But she was worried enough about me after the Florida trip that she'd backed off a little in regards to rules about dating older boys.

I'd gotten used to walking into school by myself.

At first, it felt a little odd. I could still almost feel Mark's hand in mine, remembering him looking at me, talking to him about any homework or tests I'd have for the day. I'd felt so safe. It had been nice to walk in with someone. More than nice.

And it was what I knew. I'd been doing it for two years.

But now, I felt free. I didn't have Mark pulling on my hand, directing me, telling me which way to go. I didn't have those thoughts about whether I was disappointing him, or not being what he wanted me to be. I suddenly felt weightless.

Over the last month, Mark had excelled at ignoring me.

He must have asked for a different schedule than I had at the movie theater because I rarely saw him there. I'd had to reduce my hours because I could only work when I could get a ride. In the one class we had together, he did everything he could to avoid passing by me or running into me.

So it was a surprise when I saw him in the hallway, and he was looking right at me. I smiled, but he didn't.

And then I saw that he was holding hands with a girl I vaguely knew. He threw his arm around her neck as they went by.

I kind of froze. I felt people passing by me, bumping me as they went by, but I just stood there.

"Hey," said a familiar voice.

I turned around to see Lea. "Hi."

"You saw them, right?" she asked, pulling me to the side. She looked down the hallway. "Mark and that girl, Amy?"

I nodded.

"It weirded you out?"

"It's okay, actually." I smiled at her.

Tommy picked me up after school. We got food from Sonic and went down to the water in Seabrook. We sat on the grass and fed the ducks and kissed and laughed and kissed some more. We'd brought tennis rackets and went to a public court and hit a few balls. It felt good to be on the court again, actually playing with a real person and not just the backboard. We stopped at a mini-mart and got Cokes on the way home.

As we got closer to my house, I saw Mark's car in front under the streetlamp. He was in the car.

Tommy parked in the driveway. "What's with that guy?"

"You have to go," I said.

He looked exasperated. "Annie, I don't trust him. How long has he been waiting here for you?"

"It's Mark. It's fine." I put my hand on his arm and leaned toward him. "It's okay. I know what I'm doing." Then I laughed, surprising myself, and laughed even more, knowing it was not the right time to be laughing.

"You're weird." But he grinned.

"Look, I know I don't have a very good track record when it comes to making decisions, but I know what I'm doing now. Go home." I kissed him. "I'll call you. Right when he leaves."

"Annie—"

I put a finger to his lips. "Shh. Right when he leaves."

I stood on the grass and waved him on until he left.

Mark got out of his car. I pulled myself up on the trunk. He sat beside me. "Hi, Annie."

"Hi, Mark."

"It's a nice night."

"Yeah," I said. "The stars are out. So bright tonight."

"Yeah," he said, looking up. "How's your mom?"

"Getting married this summer," I said.

"They're going to do it?"

"Donald the Dentist will be my daddy," I said, nodding.

He smiled. "And how are you feeling about that?" he asked.

"I'm in the wedding."

"Well, *that's* a surprise."

"Maid of honor."

He laughed.

"You'll be invited," I told him. "The whole family will be

there. They ask about you, how you are. They'd love to see you." I paused. "You should come."

"Mmm." He shook his head. "Probably not."

"Maybe one day, though," I said, hearing the hope in my voice.

We were quiet for a minute. I felt he had something to say.

He looked at his hands. "I'm sorry." Then he looked at me. "That I ignored you today."

"It's okay, Mark."

"I was trying to make you jealous."

"You made me sad," I said.

He smiled. "Well, good."

We laughed together.

I took a breath. "I'm sorry too, Mark. About everything, the way it ended between us. That I didn't tell you sooner." My eyes watered, and I looked away.

"But I knew," he said. "We both did, right?"

I nodded, but I still couldn't look at him.

"Annie, I knew but I didn't want it to be true. I hoped it was just something you were going through because of all the pressure you were getting about college. I was hoping it was that. But deep down, I knew it wasn't. I knew it was me, that you didn't love me anymore."

I slid off the car and turned away.

"Don't cry, Annie," he said, coming over to me. "Please."

"Then don't be so nice to me," I said, with a sad laugh through tears.

"Aw, Annie. Come here," he said, pulling me to him. And we hugged each other for a few moments until I stopped crying. His hand lingered in mine a minute before he let me go.

I wiped my eyes. "Mark, I know you probably don't want to hear this, but you are so very special to me."

"See, I know that, Annie. I do."

I smiled. "Good. Good."

"Hey," he asked in a lighter tone, "did you know I'm joining the Coast Guard?"

"Really? Wow. I can see you doing that, Mark. I really can." I touched his arm briefly. "I don't think they let you have surfboards, you know."

"No." He looked off for a moment. We were quiet again. When he glanced back at me, his eyes were sad and wistful.

I looked back at him.

He looked away, smiled a little, then swung his key ring around his finger. "See you, Annie."

I watched him drive away.

I lay down in the grass in the front yard, looking at the stars, feeling like a kid again. The smell of grass, the smell of flowers, the warmth of the evening . . . summer was almost here. I didn't think I'd be here next spring.

I thought about Mom and Donald, and realized that in a way, Mom was freeing me. She wasn't pushing me out the door and telling me to go. She wouldn't do that. And I felt sure Mom wanted me around even if she was getting married. But at the same time, I didn't have to worry about her when I left. She had Donald.

I felt light, floating almost.

And then it hit me. I'd thought about "when" I left, not "if." When.

I had to go to the library.

CHAPTER 56

Y̶ou know," said Lea. "Ever since you broke up with Mark, I've had to do these graveyard visits with you. I didn't realize how handy he was until he left."

"See this stone. This is the oldest grave, I think."

"You can't read the date."

"I know," I said. "That's why I think it's the oldest one." I walked over to another one. "Would you hurry? Why did you wear those shoes?" I pointed at another gravestone. "Look at how long these two were married."

"Yeah, uh-huh, nice," said Lea. "What is your grandmother doing?"

I looked toward the creek. "Fishing with her sisters."

"I wouldn't eat anything out of that water." She shrugged. "Of course your grandma and her sisters are old."

"What?" I asked.

"It wouldn't hurt them much. Thank you, by the way," she said, showing me her pink-gloved hands, "for making me these."

"I can't believe you wore that to our cemetery outing," I said, gesturing at her clothes.

"It was one of my mother's dresses in high school."

I looked at the polka-dotted, full-skirted dress. "I cannot see her in that."

"My mom has many parts to her, and one of those wears pretty dresses."

"One of the first women engineers at NASA too."

"She's a physicist," said Lea, "not an engineer."

"What's the difference?" I asked, shrugging.

"Physicists are smarter."

"You could be an engineer," I said. "I know we're not supposed to talk about your math grades and all, but it is true."

"Maybe after I finish playing, I'll be an astronaut and go to Mars."

"They won't let you wear that skirt," I said, "in space."

"Wouldn't it be fun to see it floating in zero g?"

"So you've given up on marrying the Astronaut?" I asked.

"I'm graduating. He's going into outer space. It'll never work."

"That's a relief," I said. "I do have to tell you something, Lea."

"What?" she asked.

I paused. "I'm not applying to UT."

She made a face.

"I'm sorry. But you were the only reason I was even considering it."

"I'm not a good-enough reason?" she asked.

"You're a really good reason. But UT's not for me."

She sighed. "Yeah, I figured. I'll miss you, you secret-keeping heartbreaker." She looked over at the creek. "Your grandma's lucky to have sisters."

I nudged her shoulder with mine. "You have a sister. Me."

"It'll be hard to stay close so far apart," she said, her eyes sad.

"See them," I said, nodding at the creek. "That's us in sixty years."

She gave me a little smirk. "Can I wear this dress while we fish?"

"If you can fit in it in sixty years, you can wear it."

She laughed, then looped her arm through mine. We were quiet and still, watching my grandma in the distance, fishing in the creek she'd fished in as a child. She'd never wanted to leave.

It was hard for me too, but it was time.

CHAPTER 57

"Annie," said Mr. Williams, "can I talk to you for a moment?"

"Sure," I said, while the others filed past me.

It'd been a while since I'd talked to Mr. Williams. I'd never told anyone we'd gone to lunch. They'd think he was playing favorites, which he was, or we were having a torrid affair, which we weren't. I suddenly realized he wasn't that much older than Tommy was.

The last student left the class, and Mr. Williams went over and shut the door. This worried me. What was so serious that he had to shut the door?

He sat down. "Pull up a chair, Annie."

I did. "What is it, Mr. Williams?"

"We didn't get a chance to talk about Christa McAuliffe before."

"Oh," I said, nodding.

"I know how much you liked her, Annie." He paused. "At lunch at Vargo's, you appeared to be getting closer to a decision about college. But you haven't mentioned it since. I wondered if the *Challenger* accident made you think Christa's dream of flying in space wasn't worth it."

"No," I said. "Not at all." I hesitated.

"What's on your mind, Annie?"

I found it difficult to talk about things even when I thought about them all the time. Writing was easier than speaking. "I don't know if I believe in the traditional view of heaven. But I think the spirit outlives death."

I heard the door opening. A student poked her head in. "Can I talk to you, Mr. Williams?"

"I'm busy right now, Debra," he told her.

"I really need to talk to you." She held up a paper. "About my essay. It's important."

"Come back after school."

"Fine. But I'm a senior. I have to get this done." She started to shut the door, but then poked her head back in. "I'll just wait in the hall to see if you have time." The door closed.

"Don't mind her, Annie. I want to hear what you have to say."

I liked that he was so calm, like we had all day to talk. And I knew he must be swamped with the end of school nearing. "Remember my essay about Lear? When I argued Lear's epiphany had value despite his death?"

"Your best this semester."

"Well, thank you," I said in the way I thought grown-ups might. "I think Christa's spirit, that thing in her that wanted to do this amazing thing, is still with us. And that I can tap into it and use it."

"And how are you going to do that?"

"The hard part has been figuring out *what* I want to do. The thing is, if I stayed here, I think I'd be okay, actually. But I think there's something I haven't learned yet. And I don't think I'll be able to learn it here."

I took a breath. "I think Christa might have felt that way. That she had more she needed to learn so she would have more to teach. And she loved to teach. Like you. You love to teach, right?"

"Most days," he said, glancing toward the door and laughing. "No, Annie, I do. I found what I love."

"Well, as you know, I love to write poetry. It may not build bridges or fix teeth or explore space, but there must be a reason why I have these words in me that want to get out."

I could hear the girl out in the hallway, complaining very loudly about her grade to another student.

I looked at the door, then back to Mr. Williams.

He shook his head. "Ignore that. Go on."

"And I want to study poetry with people who know poetry."

"And that means college?"

"Yes," I said.

He smiled. "Do you have the money for it? I remember you mentioning it was a problem."

"Actually," I said, "a dentist is paying for it."

"A dentist?"

"Yes."

"Annie, you've made my day."

"Really?" I asked, a little surprised he cared so much.

"It's a teacher thing." he said, standing. "Well, I've got a student, a senior in fact, to talk to, and you've got college applications to fill out. And quickly."

I reached into my folder and pulled out several forms, already filled out. "It's late, I know," I said, shrugging, "to be applying."

He took them. "Iowa, Kenyon, Hollins—"

"I probably won't get into those this year. I have others too. But maybe I can transfer in my sophomore year."

He gave the stack back to me. "Well, get to it."

"I'll need a teacher recommendation."

He grinned, looking pleased with himself. "I've already finished one for you."

"What?"

"Just tell me where to send it."

CHAPTER 58

S o," Tommy said, "there are three pedals."

"I see that," I said.

"And one of those is the brake." He touched my leg lightly. "Do you have your foot on the brake?"

I slapped his hand. "Much too close, Driving Instructor. I'll have to report you to the Texas Department of Transportation and Protection of Young Women."

"Fine. But it is hard for me to keep my hands to myself when you're wearing those shorts."

I giggled, actually giggled. Embarrassing. "So back to driving."

"Yes, driving."

"So three pedals. And this is the clutch," I said, putting my left foot on the pedal.

"Aw, a driving prodigy. Ready to move up to the clutch."

I pressed it down a few times.

"What are you doing?" Tommy asked.

"Trying to get the feel of it." I pressed it down a few more times.

"Done yet?"

"What's next?" I put my hand on the stick. "I want to switch gears."

"Okay. You know to switch gears, you—"

"—I need to have my foot on the clutch." I pushed it down and played with shifting the gears. I looked at him. "I'm ready."

He waved his hand. "Start her up."

We were at Ellington Field, which was an airport that had been here since my grandmother was a kid. Among other things, it currently housed T-38s, the astronaut training planes. It also was where Christa flew in the Vomit Comet, which was what the NASA geeks called the plane that flew parabolas to give the astronauts a few precious seconds of weightlessness, where Christa felt like Peter Pan.

Ellington was pretty much deserted on weekends. It was a good place to practice driving a stick shift for the first time. Especially since Tommy didn't want any dents in his car.

I beat on the wheel. "Excitement!" I put my foot on the clutch and the car in gear, then turned the ignition. The car started, and I looked at Tommy.

"Ready?" At my nod, he said, "Okay, let out the clutch at the same time you push down the accelerator. Got it?"

I smiled.

He laughed. "Any time."

I slowly let out the clutch and pushed my foot on the gas. The car lurched forward, then stalled. "Darn."

"Try again."

Eventually, I got the car started and we were driving along at a very slow speed.

"You can go faster," Tommy said.

"But then I have to change gears."

"Right."

"Okay," I said.

"Well?" he prompted.

"There's a lot to think about. Foot off gas. Clutch. Switch gears. Foot off clutch while foot back on gas."

"Right."

"Shh."

He was quiet this time.

I focused: Off gas. Clutch. Shift. Clutch and gas. "Yeah! I'm in second gear!"

"Yes, you are. Now, third."

When I got to third gear, it was easy. I drove the car around the narrow roads while Tommy talked to me about the fall of the Roman Empire.

"Those funny Goths," I said.

"So," he said. "Any more news about your future?"

"There is!" I said, glancing over at him. "Remember me talking about Professor Gaines, the poet I met? A student of hers now teaches at Hollins University—one of the colleges I applied to. She invited me to tour the campus this summer. There's a chance Hollins will accept me for the spring semester."

"That's great, Annie," he said, reaching over to squeeze my hand on the steering wheel. "Isn't Hollins in Virginia or North Carolina . . . someplace like that?"

"It's a women's college in southwest Virginia."

"A women's college?" He grinned. "That sounds like an excellent place for you."

I laughed. "You think so, do you?"

"Yeah. Having all those guys around would just distract you." He was still grinning, with a mischievous twinkle in his eye.

Good grief, he was gorgeous. But I was driving. I had to focus on the road. "Have you figured out what you're going to do next year?"

"I may be in college myself."

"What?" I asked, looking over at him.

He nodded.

"What? I must stop for this," I said, braking.

"The parents—"

"Just a minute," I said, putting the car in neutral. "Okay. Now, what?"

"My mom and dad agreed to pay for college even if it is for a degree in education. And more importantly," he said, smiling, "they've agreed not to complain about it."

"That's super, Tommy."

"I have tests to take. There are things to do."

"Will you go back to USC?"

"I've thought about it," he said.

I was disappointed. California was far away from Virginia. "Are you going back for that old girlfriend?" I asked in a teasing voice, although I was slightly worried.

"And lose you? I'm not stupid." He gave me a quick kiss. "No, not USC. Maybe University of Texas. Or . . ." He stopped and looked at me.

"What?"

"I don't know how you feel about this, but I'd like to be

close to where you are. If you're thinking of Virginia, I'd apply to colleges there too."

"Really?"

"How do you feel about that?" he asked.

"It would make me," I said quietly, "very happy."

"Would it? Because I don't want to scare you off—"

I put a finger to his lips to hush him up. "I'd like it. Very much."

He put his hand over mine and kissed my finger. "It'll take me a year to get my act together. So I'd be applying for fall of '87."

"Wow," I said. "Look at you."

"Look at you."

"Look at me, driving this stick. I should be rewarded. You want to go to Pe-Te's?"

"What's that?"

"Pe-Te's Cajun Barbeque House? You don't know it? It's famous!" I pointed across the highway. "You can see it. Right there."

"Cajun *and* barbeque?"

"Cajun barbeque. The pilots and the astronauts hang out at Pe-Te's. And Christa went there. Because when you fly on the Vomit Comet, you get to go to Pe-Te's. And since I successfully drove a stick, I should get to go too."

"Sure. You want to drive us over?"

"Cross Highway 3? No."

He raised his eyebrows. "Not game? I don't know if you really deserve a meal at the famous Pe-Te's if you can't drive us just right across the highway."

"Get on your side of the car," I said, pushing him back. "That's a challenge!"

"Okay. But I think *you* were on *my* side of the car."

"Here we go," I said, letting out the clutch, only to have the car die immediately. "No!" I said, hitting the steering wheel and hitting his arm. "Hey, are you laughing at me?"

"Hey, stop hitting me, woman. Back on your side. And get us," pointing at Pe-Te's, "to there."

I took a breath. "Fine." I started the car up again and glanced at Tommy.

"I didn't say anything," he said.

Slowly I let out the clutch, while accelerating. "We're going. We're going."

"We are going."

"We're going!"

"We've gone before," he said.

"Okay. Shh, shh."

I didn't let him talk again until we were at the light to pull out onto Highway 3.

"Don't be so nervous," he said.

"Because I'm making you nervous?"

"Exactly."

"The light's green," I said.

"Okay, go."

The car stalled. "It's all right," I said. "I can do this. I got it."

We missed that traffic cycle, but I got us through the next one. Driving down the highway itself wasn't hard, but it was the slowing down and stopping and starting again that worried me.

At the next light, I looked at Tommy. "What? Why do you look so scared?"

"I'm not scared. I jump out of airplanes."

"Shh," I said, as the light turned green. And I slowly let out the clutch—

—honking from behind—

—and put on the gas and jerked through the light. But we kept going and I was happy to turn into the parking lot.

I parked and collapsed.

"Now you deserve Cajun barbeque," he said.

"And a kiss?"

He leaned toward me. "We could skip the barbeque." He gave me a slow, gentle kiss, one hand in my hair. And then another.

"Wow," I whispered into his lips. We kissed again, and then I drew back. "You're good at that."

"Come here," he said.

I put a hand on his chest. "Barbeque, then kissing."

"Not sure I like the order, but okay," he said, opening his door.

"Isn't this cool?" I asked when we went through the metal doors. "It used to be a gas station." It was pretty deserted.

"Look at all those license plates on the walls, and the signs too. There are thousands."

"Every state represented, and many countries. Hey, see the dance floor?" I looked at him. "What?"

He grabbed my hands, walking backward, and started leading me to the floor.

"There's no music," I said.

He pulled me in tight, holding on to one hand, and wrapped his arm around my waist. We danced slowly. In my ear, he started singing a song I thought I knew, his breath warm and enticing.

I pulled back a little, wanting to see his eyes. "Is that Jackson Browne?"

"Yeah, 'Somebody's Baby.'" We looked at one another as we danced and he sang.

"Yours," I said softly.

He smiled and kissed me lightly, still singing between kisses.

CHAPTER 59

Tommy, Lea, and I walked around the long 1967 station wagon that was the Fruitmobile. We were at a road show of art cars, which were all parked on the narrow residential street in front of The Orange Show. Dad was late, of course.

"It is *so* hot," said Lea, fanning herself with her hands.

"It's Texas and it's June," I said. "Anyway, look at the Fruitmobile, Lea. It only cost $800 to transform it."

"Lots of plastic oranges and apples."

"And bananas and pineapples and grapes. So much bright color!"

"Everyone is here to see these cars?" she asked, looking around. "There are hundreds and hundreds of Houstonians here."

The crowd was huge, with lots of kids running around or attending one of the art-bike workshops. A television station had sent out a crew, as did National Public Radio.

"When did Dad say he was coming?" I asked Tommy. "You talked to him last night, right?"

"He will definitely be here with the Beatmobile," Tommy said, his fingers intertwined with mine. "No way he'd miss this."

I nodded, still worried. Dad had been a little down since Mom's wedding. She and Donald were on a two-week honeymoon in Hawaii.

I felt Tommy squeeze my hand. "He'll be here," he said, giving me a kiss. I smiled into his eyes.

"How are you two ever going to be apart," asked Lea, "when Annie goes to college? You're never going to make it as a couple, you know," she added in her blunt way. "Relationships don't survive distance."

"We won't be apart for long," I told her. "Tommy's applying to colleges close to the ones I'm applying to."

Lea gave us a crooked smile. "How 'bout that?"

Tommy wrapped me in a hug and kissed the top of my head.

Just then, I saw the Beatmobile coming down the street. "He made it!" I said. Heads began turning in the direction of the approaching car as the faces of Allen Ginsberg and Jack Kerouac got closer. These art cars were the rock stars of this show.

I shaded my eyes. "Is that . . . ?"

"I think it is," said Tommy.

I laughed. "I can't believe it."

"What?" Lea asked.

"The Love Bus," I said excitedly. "Do you see it? It's right behind the Beatmobile."

"The Love Bus?" asked Lea.

I looked at Tommy. "Did Dad tell you Bonnie and Clyde were coming?"

"He might have."

"You kept a secret from me?"

"I did," he said, smiling.

"Bonne and Clyde?" asked Lea.

"You'll like them, Lea," I said, smiling. "Nice, nice people."

"Not the Bonnie and Clyde I was thinking of," she said. "You know, Annie, I hate to say I told you so."

"Then don't. Come on," I said, pulling her by the sleeve toward the Beatmobile and the Love Bus, which were now parked a little ways down the street.

"Do you think they brought the dogs?" Tommy asked.

"Probably," I said, laughing. A crowd of people had already started to form around the newly arrived art cars. I couldn't see if Bonnie and Clyde had gotten out yet.

"But I have to say it, Annie," Lea continued, like she'd never stopped talking. "I told you college was the right place for you."

"It might be."

"You're going to love it."

"I'm not sure," I said, "but I can't wait to find out."

Those were Christa's words. It was what she'd told Lea that night at dinner. How could that have happened only eight months ago?

"Are you coming, Annie?" Tommy asked as he and Lea started to make their way to Dad and the Beatmobile.

"Yeah, in a minute," I said, waving him on.

If I hadn't gone that night to meet Christa, I wasn't sure I'd be here with Tommy at the Orange Show today or going off to college next year. That night I'd seen something in her that I'd wanted for myself.

It was living from your heart to your fingertips, through your soul to your toes, letting *your* spirit—no one else's—push you out and up, and through and over, and away and maybe even back again.

I didn't know why that came so easily for Christa and was such a struggle for me.

But there's poetry in the struggle.

"Reach for it . . . push yourself as far as you can."
—Christa McAuliffe

AUTHOR'S NOTE

<u>Christa McAuliffe</u>

On July 19, 1985, ten teachers stood by Vice President George H. W. Bush as he announced NASA's selection for the new Teacher in Space Project. The winner, who had been chosen from eleven thousand applicants, was Christa McAuliffe, a thirty-six-year-old social studies teacher from Concord, New Hampshire.

I was a young NASA engineer working at the Johnson Space Center in Houston when Christa was selected as the first, and only, teachernaut. Although I had the privilege to be involved in the payload training of two of the *Challenger* astronauts, Judith Resnik and Ellison Onizuka, I never met Christa. We were at the same college-campus-like space center for four months working in buildings across the pond from one another, but our paths didn't cross. Almost twenty-five years later, as I did research for this novel, I realized what an opportunity I had missed. Christa McAuliffe was one of those remarkable people whose life and spirit inspires the rest of us.

Sharon Christa Corrigan was the first child of Ed and Grace, a young couple living in Boston in 1948. She was walking at ten months and talking in complete sentences at one year old. Seeking adventure early on, she rode her tricycle down a busy street toward the city of Boston. She was discovered among the stopped cars after the family dog's barks alerted Ed and Grace to Christa's daring escapade.

The Corrigan family grew in size as Christa grew up. Over the years, she tended to her younger siblings, dreamed of flying to the moon, sung her way through high school musicals, wore the first strapless gown ever seen at a dance at her high school, and fell in love with a guy with a motorbike.

And then she married the guy with the motorbike. But not before she'd graduated from college with a Bachelor of Arts in education and history. Her wedding to Steven McAuliffe was on August 23, 1970. It poured rain that day, but the sun came out for the ceremony.

During her career, Christa mostly taught social studies and English to seventh and eighth graders. She loved being a teacher. Her mother would write later that Christa asked "but two things of her students—that they be themselves and that they do their very best." In 1982, Christa accepted a position at Concord High School to teach American history, law, and economics.

Christa was especially interested in the social history of common people and designed a course for her high school students called The American Woman. Sources for the course included diaries, travel accounts, and personal letters, because Christa felt that these firsthand accounts revealed rich history not found in the memorization of dates and places. It's not such a surprise that she wanted to fly on the space shuttle, not as an astronaut, but as a teacher who would return and share her experience with the nation's students.

Christa and her husband, Steve, were living a contented life in Concord when the Teacher in Space program was announced in August 1984. Their two children, Scott and Caroline, were born in 1976 and 1979. Steve was working as a lawyer at a prominent firm in Concord while Christa continued teaching.

One night, Christa and Steve heard President Reagan announcing on the radio that NASA intended to put a private citizen into space, and that first citizen was to be a teacher. Although Christa knew she wanted to apply, she didn't turn in her application until February 1, the very last possible day to submit one. Three months later, a list of the 114 state nominees was released to the press. Christa McAuliffe was one of the two teacher nominees from New Hampshire.

Of those 114 teachers, only ten would be selected as finalists. In one of her taped interviews as a nominee, Christa was asked her philosophy of living. She said she wanted "to get as much out of life as possible." She also told her interviewer: "I think the reason I went into teaching was because I wanted to make an impact on other people and to have that impact on myself." On June 28, Christa was told she was one of the ten finalists.

The selection process moved quickly. A little over a week later, Christa and the other finalists were at the Johnson Space Center undergoing extensive medical and psychological examinations. One test Christa was nervous about was one for claustrophobia. She was zippered into a three-foot-diameter nylon ball and not told how long she'd be left in the dark. Christa thought she'd be yelling to get out, but actually found the experience to be somewhat peaceful. Fifteen minutes later, she was released. Christa was also subjected to a treadmill test, X-rays, blood tests, dental exams, and even a ride on the KC-135, a NASA plane used to produce seconds of weightlessness. After their time in Houston, the finalists traveled to Marshall Space Flight Center in Alabama and to Washington DC for three more days of interviews.

On July 19, 1985, Christa McAuliffe was announced as the nation's Teacher in Space.

AUTHOR MEMORIES OF
INSPIRATIONAL TEACHERS

I'll never forget Mrs. Beall, my first-grade teacher. She was the first person to tell me that she thought I'd grow up to be a writer. She probably said that to everyone in my class, but when she said it to me, I was suddenly surrounded by a huge and overwhelming sense of Yes. —**Kathi Appelt**

My second-grade teacher, Mrs. Dunwoody, let my friends Heather and Naomi and me stay in at recess to write books on arithmetic paper, which we illustrated, folded, and stapled. I was charmed by the blue rinse in Mrs. Dunwoody's white hair, imagining her leaning back into the hairdresser's hands and choosing the color of the sky. —**Jeannine Atkins**

My geometry teacher's name was Dick Purdy, and he was known for being particularly T-O-U-G-H. I was known for being particularly bad at math, and, as a junior in a sophomore math class, I was dreading it! But for some reason, Mr. Purdy believed in me. He never went easy on me, but he took me under his wing, told me I should be a math teacher when I grew up, and even offered me a summer job working for him at the local swimming pool. I got my first math A ever in that class, and I worked hard for it. Turns out, he was wrong. I would have made a horrible math teacher. But it was nice to believe that maybe I could be one, even if for only one year. —**Jennifer Brown**

In class, my high school English teacher, Joann Clanton, was tough and demanding. I'm still not sure she felt I was a very good writer. But I always felt like she believed I could become one. —**Kristy Dempsey**

To Dave Christie, my high school yearbook advisor, for giving me the monumental responsibility of copy editor, knowing (even when I wasn't sure) that I would rise to the occasion. You taught me to believe in myself! —**Kimberly Derting**

Mrs. Weber was my third-grade teacher. As part of a history unit, she taught us to make soap, stitch our own samplers (mine hangs on my office wall), and spin on a wheel. But her biggest impact on me was when she sent a poem I wrote to the town paper (without telling me), and they published it—my first publication, and the first time I knew I wanted to be a writer. —**Janet Fox**

My seventh-grade English teacher, Richard Perkins, was one of the first people who made me think I might be a writer. I've tried to track him down, but without success. If I could find him, I would thank him for believing in me. —**April Henry**

The teachers that were the most inspirational to me were the ones who saw my light and believed in my ability to succeed. Their belief in me always made me try my hardest to live up to their vision.
—**Cheryl Renée Herbsman**

When you asked for a memory of an inspirational teacher, I had no trouble remembering Mrs. Stockton, my third-grade teacher at Columbia Elementary in El Monte, California. She was the one who read Mr. Popper's Penguins *to our class, taught us to square dance, and how to make candles so all of us would have Christmas presents for our moms. She was the one who always listened, who was always fair, who taught me about caring and kindness.* —**C. Lee McKenzie**

There have been many teachers who've pulled me up over the years, but one in particular stands out. She knew I was drowning on so many levels, and she spent extra time with me—often clearing an afternoon's appointments. She encouraged my writing, sought additional resources to help me find my path, and once even took photos that she said would be my author photos. She helped me gain my footing again and actually see what possibilities lay out there for me—possibilities I couldn't see myself because of all the clouds.
—**Neesha Meminger**

Most of my teachers were happy to let me fail quietly—at least I wasn't causing trouble. But my freshman/sophomore English teacher, Mrs. Redman, engaged me when I was disengaged and taught me the way I needed to be taught. She made a lover of words out of me— and I made the love of words my life. Everything I am as a writer and a reader started with her. —**Saundra Mitchell**

My calculus teacher Mrs. Byrnes took the time to encourage me and also found me a job as a math tutor at college. I was impressed that a woman, and one who seemed elderly to me, was so gifted in calculus. This was at a time when math was considered to be a strength of boys, not girls. Because of Mrs. Byrnes, I considered being a math teacher and eventually became an engineer.
—**Jenny Moss**

Mr. McMahon, my high school sociology teacher, surprised our class on the day before graduation with a beautiful send-off, complete with music, flowers, and some much-needed words of encouragement. His simple farewell gesture steadied the uncertainty in my heart and was just a small example of who he was—the teacher who cared for us as his own, who dared us to speak and live with honesty and passion, who broke the rules to help when we needed it most. I will never forget him. —**Sarah Ockler**

My most memorable teacher was my second-grade teacher, Mrs. Norma Bernsohn. She instilled me with curiosity, academic tenacity, and independence. Plus she encouraged me to write my very first one-act play—a dull little affair about Pilgrims (with authentic Pilgrim names like Julie and Marcia) landing at Plymouth Rock— and then let me perform it for the class with my friends!
—**Joy Preble**

My second-grade teacher, Ms. Schneider, believed in making each child feel special. I still have the framed picture she took of me, with these words printed on the picture frame mat: "Small caterpillar. Infinite soul of wisdom. Your wings are waiting." Teachers like her helped me to believe anything is possible. —**Lisa Schroeder**

I'm forever grateful for my hip fifth-grade teacher, Miss Storch, who not only read aloud to our class every day, but in so doing introduced me to The Phantom Tollbooth, *easily the single most influential book in my life and my writing career.* —**Joni Sensel**

BIBLIOGRAPHY

ABC News Reports: 7/19/1985; 1/23/1986; 1/28/1986.

Burgess, Colin. *Teacher in Space: Christa McAuliffe and the* Challenger *Legacy*. Lincoln: University of Nebraska Press, 2000.

Corrigan, Grace. *A Journal for Christa*. Lincoln: University of Nebraska Press, 1993.

CNN Presents. "Christa McAuliffe: Reach for the Stars." Transcript online at http://transcripts.cnn.com /TRANSCRIPTS/0601/22/cp.01.html.

Harwood, William, and Rob Navias. "*Challenger* Timeline." United Press International (UPI). Provided on http://SpaceflightNow .com/challenger/timeline.

Hohler, Robert. *I Touch the Future: The Story of Christa McAuliffe*. New York: Random House, 1986.

Houston Chronicle articles, various. January 1986.

Lewis, Richard. Challenger: *The Final Voyage*. New York: Columbia University Press, 1988.

McConnell, Malcolm. Challenger: *A Major Malfunction*. New York: Doubleday, 1987.

McDonald, Allan, and James Hansen. *Truth, Lies, and O-Rings: Inside the Space Shuttle* Challenger *Disaster*. Gainesville: University Press of Florida, 2009.

Recer, Paul. "Teacher hopes to teach 'space is for everybody.'" *Anchorage Daily News*, December 14, 1985.

Richman, Alan, and Ron Arias. "A Lesson in Uncommon Valor." *People*, February 10, 1986.

Van Blema, David H. "Christa McAuliffe Gets NASA's Nod to Conduct America's First Classroom in Space." *People*, August 5, 1985.

Wald, Matthew. "The Shuttle Inquiry; 500 Attend Mass for Space Teacher." *The New York Times*, February 4, 1986.

Wilford, John Noble. "Teacher is Picked for Shuttle Trip." *The New York Times*, July 20, 1985.

ACKNOWLEDGMENTS

Thanks so much to:

- The wonderful Nancy Gallt and Marietta Zacker of the Nancy Gallt Literary Agency.
- The brilliant Walker team: Emily Easton, Beth Eller, Katie Fee, Mary Kate Castellani, and Deb Shapiro.
- Awesome critiquers Sally Barringer, Leigh Brescia, Megan Crewe, Mary Ann Hellinghausen, Jennifer Jabaley, Morgan McKissack Lauck, Bettina Restrepo, and Christine Suffredini. And much gratitude to the Debs, who helped with title suggestions, prologue critiques, and general emotional bucking-up.
- Barbara Morgan, the backup candidate for the Teacher in Space program, who recommended Robert Hohler's book *I Touch the Future: The Story of Christa McAuliffe*, and to her assistant, Kimberly Long, for their help.
- Robert Hohler, for such a close, detailed portrayal of Christa McAuliffe. I used many quotes of Christa's from *I Touch the Future* in the hopes of providing an authentic glimpse of her enthusiasm and spirit.

- Those who filled in the gaps of my memory of Christa McAuliffe, the Johnson Space Center, the Kennedy Space Center, the Clear Lake area, and shuttle flights in the 1980s: Michelle Brekke, Mike Fawcett, Fisher Reynolds, Gene Powell, and Pete Hasbrook. Special thanks to Jerry Swain for providing descriptions of the Shuttle Mission Simulator and reading over those pages of the manuscript to check for accuracy. Thanks to Warren Greg Barringer for his help with the troubles of the Beatmobile. Any errors are mine alone.
- Ed and Grace Corrigan, for guiding to adulthood such an amazing human being.